THE CURSE OF MONSTERS

HER CURSED PROTECTORS

Shadow Shifter (prequel)
The Blood of Monsters
The Cries of Monsters
The Curse of Monsters
The Wars of Monsters

THE CURSE OF MONSTERS

HER CURSED PROTECTORS BOOK 3

MIA HARTSON

ISBN: 978-0-6457298-2-5

First printing edition 2023 in United States

Cover design by Trif Cover Design

Copyediting by Lyss Em Editing

Mia Hartson

PO BOX 1052, Golden Grove Village, SA 5125

www.miahartson.com

For the ones who need a little magic and spice in their lives.
Mia x

This story contains violence, kidnapping, torture, and mention of past child abuse. Please take care of yourself when reading. x

CHAPTER 1

~ **Raine** ~

I gasped as Darian and I exited the portal first, emerging from a ring of blue fire and entering a forest filled with colors so bright I thought we must have died and stepped into Goddess Falia's haven. Well, I would have thought that if it weren't for the three fae books still jabbing painfully into my chest, reminding me I was *very* much alive.

Darian's arms tightened around me, but I wiggled until he let me down, glad to have my feet on solid ground again. With one arm curved around the books, I bent over and focused on sucking air into my deprived lungs. *Fuck. Traveling like that's going to be hard to get used to.*

Pulling out two of his throwing stars, Darian scanned our surroundings, his alert gaze taking in the foreign trees and plants. I straightened and copied his defensive stance, watching for any signs of unusual movement. If I had to, I was ready to drop the books and draw one of my blades at the first sign of an attack. But the forest was quiet around us, save for the gentle rustling of leaves and faint buzzing of insects. Fae warriors didn't ambush us from the trees, and I relaxed my stance. No longer worried about the fae jumping out to kill us, I marveled at our vibrant surroundings.

Tall, willowy trees with flaky white bark reached high into the air, sunlight streaming through the branches laden with heart-shaped leaves and washing the forest in a rainbow of color. The shades of pink, orange, blue, and green made a spectacular display, and I lifted my free hand to let the light shine through my fingers. Smiling, I dropped my hand and stared at the thick bright-green moss that spread over tree roots and climbed up tree trunks, and the large boulders that were spread around the space, the silver rocks so smooth they resembled small, gleaming mirrors.

As Darian turned to me, his long fingers curled gently over my shoulder, and he leaned down to peer at my face. "Are you all right, lovely?"

I didn't know how to answer that. Not long ago we'd been fighting for our lives against Warrick's outliers, and now we'd just run from Zacal's wolves and had traveled to the fae realm of Zalei. *All right* wasn't exactly how I'd have described my feelings. Before I could answer him, grunts sounded behind us as the others arrived. Darian and I stepped away from the portal as Asher, Locke, and Kade appeared, their faces hard and expressions wary. Prince Azaren was still bent over Kade's shoulder, his body limp and unmoving. The moment the monsters were through, the portal closed behind them, and I sent a mental thank-you to the Goddess. If Zacal's wolves had followed us, I didn't doubt they would have attacked first and asked questions later. Battling in the forest would have been a sure way to alert the fae to our arrival in their realm.

Kade, Asher, and Locke peered around, their gazes scouring the forest before they turned their attention to Darian and me. Kade was still naked from when he'd shifted to save Prince Azaren, his sculpted body on full display, and I might have been distracted if it weren't for the fae prince's unconscious body still over one of the wolf shifter's broad shoulders. Kade lifted Prince Azaren and dropped the beaten fae, not caring when the prince's head impacted with a hard thud on the ground.

Wincing, I stared at Prince Azaren's broken face. His azure-colored hair was so thick with blood that it was plastered to his head in patches, and the eye I could see was swollen shut and a nasty shade of purple. The fae king was *not* going to be happy when he saw the state of his son.

Locke shifted his arms, readjusting his hold on the other fae books and sighed. "We need the prince alive and in one piece."

Kade ignored the vampire and kept his focus on me. "Have you been harmed?"

"I'm a little stiff but no worse for wear, thanks," Asher answered as he cracked his neck, but Kade didn't take his attention from me.

"Never been better," I replied with a determined smile. It wasn't really a lie. Sure, our situation wasn't ideal, but with these powerful monsters by my side and the magic sparking in my veins, somehow I felt as though we could handle anything.

"That's our girl," Asher said with a lopsided grin and pushed the bundle of Kade's clothing, weapons, and a leather satchel into Kade's arms. "Now, who wants to bet Zacal is already flappin' his mouth about us desertin' Katakin for the fae?" Asher commented.

My smile fell as I thought about how the monsters in Katakin likely believed we'd changed sides and had now joined the fae. Things were going to be messy when we tried to return to Katakin.

"We're lucky the portal closed before they could follow us," Darian responded thoughtfully. "It happened only after you three arrived with the prince, so I can only guess the magic somehow detected the fae had passed through and had been designed to close immediately after."

"There's no point guessing about the portal, or even worrying about what the monsters in Katakin might now believe," Locke said, pulling down the hood of his cloak and moving to the shade of a tree as Kade began dressing. "We're here to find a way to break the curse, so we should focus on that."

"And how the fuck are we goin' to find that information? We don't even know where we are. I mean, look at this place!" Asher strolled further into the forest then, examining the plant life.

Hundreds of toadstools covered the ground around us, the fungi growing together in bunches. The tallest ones reached my waist, making them look like little houses, while the smallest ones were only the size of my thumb. Asher stepped closer to a thick patch of them, his eyes twinkling with curiosity as he stared at their red caps dotted with white spots.

"Careful. We know nothing about this forest," Darian warned the demon. "We would be wise to keep our hands to ourselves."

Asher twisted his head to grin at the siren. "Since when have I ever stuck my fingers where they don't belong?"

Darian gave him a disbelieving look, and his lips formed a wicked smile. "Well, there was that one time with the phoenix shifter—" he began.

Phoenix shifter? I had no idea where the story was going, but from the devilish grin Asher sent back Darian's way, I was pretty sure I didn't *want* to know. Either way, Darian never finished his sentence. As Asher took another step forward, a faint squealing noise sounded, high and shrill.

Asher's face scrunched as a thin trail of yellow smoke curled away from his boot and toward the sky, rising into the air.

He peered back at us sheepishly and lifted his shoe. "Oops."

Moving forward, we all stared down at the tiny toadstool he'd squished into the ground.

Locke's eyes darkened, his brows furrowing with annoyance.

"For fuck's sake, Ash," Kade growled, moving closer to my side like he thought the crushed toadstool was going to attack us. Darian shifted closer to me as well.

"It's just a toadstool," I said with an incredulous look. "Sure, they might be poisonous if you eat them, but at least he only touched it with his boot." *I've seen these monsters fearlessly fight outliers that could burn them alive. Since when did they get so paranoid?*

Darian arched a long silver brow at me. "Excuse the correction, lovely, but it's a crushed toadstool in an unknown world. We have no idea of the dangers in this forest."

I was about to argue that they were being ridiculous, when yellow smoke puffed from the other toadstools around us, clouding the air and trailing upward. The air grew thick and heavy, and a sour, pungent smell burned my nostrils, making me gag. Wrinkling my nose, I brought my hand to my face as my eyes began to water. "What is that? Goddess, it smells like something died."

"We need to move," Locke ordered, stepping past Asher. "Kade, grab the fae."

But Kade never moved to the prince, and Locke didn't utter another command. I shook my head as my mind began to spin, a blur of color smudging across my vision. My body grew uncomfortably warm, and my skin prickled with sweat. *What is happening?*

Blinking, I tried to focus on the shapes of Asher and the others. The monsters swayed on their feet, and as the sheet of color cleared from my vision, I could make out their features again. But they no longer appeared like the monsters I knew. Asher's horns had lengthened on his head, reaching high into the air like twin branches, and his face contorted, his nose now large and bulbous and his lips swelling to resemble fat caterpillars. Locke's head was the size of a large boulder, while his two black eyes remained tiny and beady. Kade's body had shrunk so it was almost stick thin, while his head was short and wide, and Darian now appeared to have the features of a giant tree frog. I couldn't make sense of it, and as a feeling like warm sunlight poured into me, heating my insides, laughter burst out of me.

Asher and the others laughed as well, their strange bodies jumping in my vision as the hearty tones of their voices vibrated loudly in my ears. On and on we laughed uncontrollably, and I braced my hands on my knees as my cheeks began to ache and my chest burned from the peals of laughter that wouldn't end.

Something red and blurry flickered in the corner of my eye, but I was lost to the happiness and joy that held me hostage. Tears of laughter leaked from my eyes, and I struggled to breathe as I guffawed and spluttered.

Another flicker of red. I blinked, not really seeing it. Not really caring. Asher's strange body slapped the back of Kade's stick form, and the sight made me laugh even harder. But then I heard it. A small, barely audible giggle sounded in my ears, and I knew it hadn't come from Kade and the others. Fear pierced through my happiness, stabbing straight to my gut, though I couldn't explain why.

My brows lowered, and I opened and closed my eyes slowly, but I didn't stop laughing. Before I could make sense of the noise, my fear was soon swallowed up again by my delirium and happiness. I'd never felt so happy.

Another giggle sounded, innocent and joyful, coming from somewhere above me, and fear cut into me again. My instincts screamed a warning at me, and this time, I lifted my gaze to find the source of the noise. Thick yellow smoke clouded the air around us, reaching as high as the tallest trees, and fat crimson droplets were falling from high above our heads. *Is that...blood?* A sense of unease went through me. My body tightened, trying to lock up despite the happiness and laughter that made my muscles loosen.

I squinted, my face scrunching painfully as I tried to focus on the red droplets while also braying with laughter, but my vision was still hazed. Reaching over, I dug my nails into my other arm, forcing them in as deep as they would go and dragging against my flesh. The sudden sting of pain allowed my vision to clear enough that I was able to focus on the droplets. *No, not blood. The red dots are falling too slowly, and the shape of them...*

A shudder rippled through me as I realized what I was staring at. As I finally made sense of the white spots marring the red and the tiny faces that grinned with glee as they rose into the air before slowly drifting down toward us.

The red blobs weren't blood droplets but tiny toadstools. Thousands of the small fungi were now puffing out of the larger toadstools and were being carried by the yellow smoke to high above the tree canopy. They were then dropping slowly, their smiling mouths open wide, showing tiny white teeth, and their little black eyes shining with excitement as they fell toward us.

As one, the toadstools began singing a happy tune, and I strained my ears to make out their words above the laughter:

Yum, yum, yum, for us little ones!
Gonna put them in our tum, tum, tums!
First, we make them still, still, still!
Then we're going to kill, kill, kill!

Well, crap. The baby toadstools were going to eat us.

CHAPTER 2

I tried to focus on the danger, but it wasn't long before the happiness melting my insides made my fear feel like a delusional worry. I shook my head, determined not to forget what I'd just discovered.

Digging my nails even deeper into my arm, I forced myself to keep looking at the toadstools. They fell so slowly, their red-and-white spotted caps catching the wind as they chattered and giggled, drifting down between the trees. There were thousands of them. Too many to count.

I was more aware of the throbbing pain in my cheeks now from laughing so hard, and I tried to focus on the ache, glad it was helping to keep me lucid. My mind cleared even more, to the point I was able to stop laughing, and I struggled to swallow, my throat sore and dry. Rationally, I was now able to put together that the unnatural happiness and urge to laugh uncontrollably were likely a result of the acrid yellow smoke polluting my lungs.

Fighting against the artificial feeling of euphoria, I moved closer to where Locke was on my right. Now that my mind was clearer, his head appeared to be back to its normal size, but the vampire still laughed like a madman, his body relaxed and mouth wide. It was odd seeing him so at ease and acting like he didn't have a care in the world. A part of me liked seeing this side of him, but I reminded myself it wasn't real. "Snap out of it, Locke," I pleaded as I kept focusing on the pain in my arm and cheeks.

The vampire's only response was to grab hold of my shoulders and laugh in my face.

"Can't you sense it? We're in danger!" I told him, but Locke's eyes remained wild and unfocused.

I moved to Kade next, but like Locke, the wolf shifter didn't even acknowledge he'd heard me. His growly laughter was almost comical as it spewed out of him. *Fuck.*

The pain was helping me stay lucid, so I figured it was time to try a different approach with the monsters. My palm connected with Kade's face with a resounding smack. "The toadstools are going to kill us!" I barked. Kade's brows lowered, his laughter abruptly cutting off, and my hopes rose as I thought the slap had worked to bring him to his senses, but then he opened his mouth again, laughing heartily in my face.

I cursed internally. Peering upward, I watched as the toadstools fell, drawing closer, their little giggles and happy cries filling the air like a chorus of creepy, eager children.

A chill clawed down my spine, and the happiness inside me left me entirely. Panic went through me as I tried to scramble a plan together in my mind. *Pain didn't work, but maybe desire will.*

I pulled off my shirt then, baring my naked top half to the world. Truthfully, I hadn't thought it would work. The idea was idiotic if I was being honest with myself, but desire wasn't too far an emotion from happiness, and desperate times called for desperate measures. To my surprise, the visual aid seemed to work, and Kade and the others turned their attention to me. Their eyes remained glazed, and laughter still poured from them, but desire now swirled in their eyes as well, and I hoped it was enough.

A toadstool floated down now only a foot above Darian's head, and I launched into action. Running at the siren, I jumped into the air and flicked the fungus away with the back of my hand before it could land on his silver hair. Where the toadstool connected with my skin, tingles bloomed, and within seconds, I couldn't move my fingers.

Great, so they can paralyze us. Thankfully, I was only numb up to my wrist, but I wasn't waiting to find out what would happen if a whole bunch of the toadstools landed on me. Oblivious to the murderous toadstool, Darian laughed and kept staring at me.

Sighing, I turned my attention to Asher and put on my best seductive expression. "You want to be happy? Grab the fae and I'm yours," I purred teasingly into his ear. "But without the fae, you'll get nothing."

I almost fisted the air in triumph when Asher actually listened and lumbered toward Prince Azaren, throwing the fae over his shoulder. He moved slower than he ordinarily would have, but he was *moving*.

The fae books Locke and I had been holding were scattered on the ground, but I knew there wasn't much I could do about that. The toadstools were getting closer, much too close, and we had to get out of there.

Bending down, I snatched up the four closest books, stacking them onto my arm that had the numb hand, and I turned to Darian and the others. They were still watching me as they laughed like they couldn't tear their gazes from me. *If I can't break them free from the trance, I need to get them away from the toadstools and the yellow smoke.*

"The first one to reach me gets me all to themselves," I declared seductively. Well, I had meant to sound alluring anyway. In reality, it came out as more of a panicked order, and I had no hope it would work, but miraculously, they all nodded and followed after me.

I'd barely made it a few steps when Locke was reaching for my shoulder, but I dropped low before springing up again, avoiding his pale hand. As I moved forward, my gaze constantly flicked upward to scan above our heads for the falling fungi. The faster I moved, the faster the monsters chased me, and it wasn't long before I was running and gliding between the trees, jumping over boulders and fallen logs.

Behind us, the toadstools fell to the ground, but as I ran past more of the giant toadstools, like they could sense us, they puffed out more trails of yellow smoke and spewed new baby fungi into the air. Down, down the little toadstools fell, their tiny mouths opening as eerie, childlike laughter spilled out, and on I ran, leading Kade and the others away from the danger.

As the monsters followed me, Locke never took to the sky and Kade never shifted, and I wasn't sure whether to count that as a blessing. My lungs burned and legs ached, and I was starting to think we'd never escape the toadstools, when the sky began to clear, the toadstools thinning and the yellow smoke disappearing until all I could see was the tree line and the vibrant leaves of the trees.

Thank the Mother.

But I didn't stop. Not even when we entered a clearing with lush grass and an inviting burbling brook in the distance. As we ran, Locke and the others became frustrated when they couldn't catch me, their slower movements allowing me to stay ahead of them, and soon it wasn't the toadstools I was running from. I'd thought once we were away from the yellow smoke, they'd regain their senses, but even though they'd stopped laughing, their eyes were desperate and wild as they ran after me. The happiness that had held them prisoner seemed to become overruled by desire as if by trying to get them to feel something else, I'd manipulated the magic somehow. The further I ran, the more I started to worry about what they'd do if they caught me.

"You can stop chasing me now!" I shouted back at them. "The creepy toadstools are gone!" But the monsters continued forward, their predatory gazes focused solely on me. I ran into a thick copse of trees, and for a moment, I couldn't see the monsters. Then a hand gripped my waist, long fingers curling around my belly, and I shrieked as claws pressed against my abdomen. "Locke," I squeaked.

The vampire spun me around brutally and pushed me to the ground, sending the fae books and my shirt flying from my grasp. My back thudded onto a thick pad of grass, and the air rushed from my lungs at the impact.

Locke stared at me hungrily, and I gasped as his top lip lifted, revealing his long, sharp fangs.

"Snap out of it!" I yelled as I started shuffling backward. "You know how you like to keep yourself at a distance and be all broody and shit? Yeah, I want that Locke back."

Ignoring my plea, Locke dropped down, crawling over me with his long arms braced on the ground. There was no happiness in his expression now. The male was ruled by hunger and desire, and he looked scary as hell. Lifting my nonparalyzed hand from the grass, I fumbled for one of the knives at my hips. My frantic heartbeat pounded in my ears as Locke's clawed fingers trailed to the marks on my arm where I'd dug my nails into my skin. He raked two fingertips through my blood and brought his fingers to his lips, sucking the blood off. Before he could reach down again, I managed to pull a dagger free, and I lifted it to his throat.

"You don't want to do this," I told him, my words shaky. "That yellow smoke the toadstools gave off messed with your mind."

As he dropped his hand again, this time, his fingers brushed down the center of my pants. Swallowing, I pressed my blade harder against his throat. The sharp edge ate into his skin, and a trickle of black blood slid down his pale neck. He paused, and it was only then that I realized his eyes were clear. They were no longer hazy and unseeing but were a sharp onyx black that gave me chills.

A smile curved his perfect lips, and his gaze slid down my body. This time, I knew his actions were intentional. It was possible they had been the moment he'd grabbed me. It would explain why he'd caught up to me faster than the others. Because he'd regained his sense of self and remembered he had incredible vampire speed.

The knowledge that it was Locke who was touching me, the *real* Locke, made my body respond to him, but I didn't remove my blade.

He leaned closer to me, his body hard between my thighs as he let my blade sink in deeper, and more blood trailed down his neck.

"S-Stop," I said, wanting to take the blade away but still not willing to.

"You know what's funny," he said, his voice full of irony as his black gaze focused on my exposed neck and then fixed on my lips. "When I first realized how much you were affecting my brothers and me, I thought you were dangerous. That either you would tear us apart or we'd destroy you. But here you are with a blade to my throat after having saved us from whatever the fuck just happened back there."

I smiled weakly, some of the tension leaving me. "Well, someone has to protect you four."

His gaze lifted to my eyes, and the look was so intense that I wanted to turn away, but I couldn't. He stared at me like I was a puzzle and he was trying to decipher the invisible clues written on my skin. Seconds passed excruciatingly slowly, but a shout from close by finally drew his attention away, and I let out a long breath.

"Fuckin' Halced, what was that?" Asher asked as he emerged from a space among the surrounding trees. Prince Azaren was still bent over his shoulder, but there were twigs and leaves in the prince's hair as if Asher had barreled through the forest, not caring that there was a living being over his shoulder as he raced after me. "One second I'm starin' at a crushed fungus stuck to my boot, and the next I'm laughin' like a lunatic. *Then* all I remember is wantin' to rail Sharachi against a tree."

A grumble came from the opposite direction, and Kade appeared from behind a tree, scowling as he strode toward us. "I hate this place."

Darian stepped into view near Kade, somehow still looking pristine despite his run through the forest. His blue gaze went straight to me and the blade I had pressed to Locke's throat. "Whatever magic those toadstools gave off, it was powerful enough to make us forget ourselves. Locke, would you mind releasing our lovely Raine?" He seemed to think for a moment, then he smiled. "Or perhaps, I should be asking Raine to release *you*."

My lips quirked up at that. We both knew that a blade to Locke's throat wouldn't be of much concern to the vampire. It wasn't like I would have been able to slice his head off with my small dagger, and Locke would heal quickly from any cut I could give him. But I appreciated how powerful Darian made me sound.

Locke's gaze lingered on me a moment longer, his lips twitching as if he knew exactly why I was smiling, and then he lifted to his feet and held out a hand to me.

I stared at his long, pale fingers in surprise. Somehow, him offering me his hand felt like it was a bigger deal than him just trying to help me to my feet. I shifted uncomfortably under the watchful eyes of Darian, Kade, and Asher.

Sliding my dagger back into its sheath, I took Locke's hand and let him pull me to my feet.

CHAPTER 3

~ Locke ~

Asher and I walked at the back of the group, and I watched as Kade pulled a canteen from the small leather satchel now hanging across his chest. When we'd prepared before entering the fae portal, we'd agreed Kade and I would carry essential supplies. This included canteens of water, a few portions of dried rations, flint and steel, a roll of bandages, and some blue paste in case we needed to patch any wounds.

"Here," Kade said, opening the canteen and holding it out to Raine who strode beside him. After the incident with the toadstools, Raine had explained how one of the baby fungi had touched her and her hand had been paralyzed, but thankfully the effects had worn off within the hour. Still, Darian now held the fae books securely in his arms.

"I don't need it yet," she replied, refusing to take the canteen. She was wearing her shirt again, thank fuck, though I was sad to have lost the tempting view.

Kade kept his hand outstretched. "Drink, Mahare," he said, his words more of a plea than a command.

Raine frowned at the canteen, but she reluctantly grabbed it.

I tugged at the hood of the long black cloak draped over my body, protecting me from the bright afternoon sun of the fae realm, and thought of the satchel hanging by my own side. Like Kade's, mine had two water canteens and rations of dried meat and bread—things I didn't need, but I knew the others did. Instead of flint and steel, mine also contained vials of synthetic blood.

The stuff tasted disgusting, lacking the warmth and sweetness of fresh blood. It was enough to sustain me and keep my monster contained, but it was less satisfying than drinking from a fresh source, and I had to consume at least three vials a day to quench my hunger.

Only a few hours had passed since we'd exited the portal, and already my throat was painfully dry, the insatiable thirst starting to take over my thoughts. I could only imagine that our encounter with the fae toadstools hadn't helped, not to mention the fucking sun.

As Raine lifted the canteen to her lips and tipped some water into her mouth, I watched her throat bob as she swallowed. My focus fixed on the small veins running down her delicate neck, and the scent of her blood called to me as loudly as a siren's song. I imagined sinking my fangs into her flesh and drinking from her, and my fangs lengthened in my mouth. *Just one taste.*

"Are you sure you're all right?" Darian asked from Raine's other side. His expression of concern was enough to pull me from my dark thoughts, and I scowled, knowing just how badly I'd wanted to give in to the temptation. The sooner we broke the curse plaguing us monsters, the sooner I could be human again rather than the abomination I was. I'd do whatever I had to in order to break the magic.

Raine rolled her eyes at my siren brother, but the expression lacked her usual fire. She was shaken after our latest ordeal, and that thought...bothered me. I hadn't meant to be so rough with her. At some point when I'd been running after her, the unnatural happiness perverting my thoughts had left me, only to be replaced by a possessive desire. Then when I'd finally come completely to my senses and realized what was going on, the scent of Raine's blood had hunger overpowering my thoughts instead.

The magic that had been afflicting me had made me weaker, and the scent of Raine's exposed wound had made my thirst heighten to the point of pain. I'd pushed her to the grass and leaned into her, forcing her body to accommodate me. Cruel devils, the taste of her blood on my fingertips had been enough that I'd almost lost control entirely. A vampire's thirst for blood was linked to their sexual desire, and I'd been so close to drinking from her while I took her. Pressing her blade against my neck had been a smart move on her part, but it wouldn't have stopped me. Not if I'd decided to take her. The added scent of her arousal mixing with that of her blood was enough to all but drive me to madness, but the sting of her dagger at my neck had helped ground me. Helped me fight away the shadows of my monster.

Fucking Enzal, I cursed the devil of the damned. Darian had smeared blue paste on Raine's marks, and her arm had healed, but I couldn't get the scent of her blood out of my mind. After unclasping the satchel at my side, I began rummaging through the contents, but I pulled my hand back when something sharp pricked my fingers.

Black blood dripped from my fingertips, and I jolted to a halt. Panic made my chest tighten as I opened the satchel wider. *No. Oh fuck.* Inside the satchel was a mess of broken glass and synthetic blood. The sticky substance covered the wrapped parcels of food and coated the two canteens, making them look like dirty black lumps. Not a single vial of blood had been left intact. Not one. My nostrils flared as I tried to contain my anger. I could only guess they'd been smashed when I'd been running through the forest, chasing Raine. Unlike fresh blood, synthetic blood was nearly odorless, and I hadn't thought anything of it when

I'd detected the faint trace of the fake blood as we'd trekked through the forest.

Asher, who had been walking next to me, had stopped when I had, and he was watching me carefully. "What's wrong?"

I clenched my jaw. "They're all broken," I said, my voice devoid of emotion even though fear was already darkening my thoughts.

My demon brother didn't ask what I was referring to. He could read it on my face. Asher understood my internal struggles, possibly more than the others did. Like me, he loathed his monster form and wanted to be human again almost as badly as I did. For once, he had no jokes or lighthearted retorts. His grim expression mimicked my own, and he followed my gaze to the human who was still walking with Darian and Kade ahead of us.

• • • • • • • • • •

~ Raine ~

The fae forest was like something from a dream. Now that baby toadstools weren't falling from the sky like freaky little fungi monsters, I could appreciate my dazzling surroundings again. The gleaming white bark of the trees was contrasting against the glittering bright pink, orange, and blue leaves of the willowy trees. Bushes with long, furry leaves reached as high as my thighs, the leaves curling toward the ground, and delicate star-shaped flowers sprouted around the area, the thick petals longer than my hands.

I knew we weren't safe, but it was nice to be out of the mountain, away from the scrutiny of monsters. Well, if you didn't include the four monsters who had now taken it upon themselves to stay close to me at all times. You'd think after I'd saved their lives yet again, they'd treat me like the badass I was, but...no.

"I still believe it's a mistake leaving the other fae books," Darian commented to no one in particular, pulling me from my musings. Guilt went through me then when I thought of the fairy tales that were littering the ground back near where the portal had been.

"Maybe the toadstools are enjoying the new literature?" I joked.

"We can't go back," Kade growled from my other side.

I nodded earnestly then, eager to agree with him. "He's right. I don't know if I could handle you four losing your minds again." I said it lightheartedly, but I was deadly serious.

Asher and Locke appeared behind us again then. They'd fallen behind, and there was a tension between them that made me pause. Before I could ask whether something was wrong, Asher's face relaxed, his lips smoothing into a lopsided grin. "Oh, I don't know about that. It was nice seein' Kade laugh for a change. Even if we were about to die."

Forgetting about the tension I'd just witnessed, I grinned. "It's a sight I'll never forget."

My gaze went to Locke then as I thought about how strange it had also been to see him laugh, but the vampire was busy staring at the surrounding forest, his brow creased and his mind clearly elsewhere. I had the strange urge to fall into step beside him and ask what was troubling him, but I didn't.

No one had spoken about Warrick or the outliers since our discussion back in Katakin. It made sense that Warrick wanted to kill me, but Locke? No one had brought up the fact that Warrick had been all too ready to murder his son, and I couldn't imagine how Locke was feeling about it all. I wasn't sure if that was what he was thinking about right then, but something told me he wasn't pondering the strange toadstools we'd just faced.

To stop myself from trying to pry into Locke's mental state, I said instead, "Why do you think there weren't any fae warriors waiting for us on the other side of the portal?" Not too long ago, Locke had flown to the tree line and spotted a vast fae city in the distance, not far beyond the southern border of the forest. We'd agreed to head toward the city, but I hadn't asked the question about the portal. "I mean, I know Prince Azaren said portals to Katakin are forbidden, but I'm surprised they wouldn't have found it by now." In fact, aside from the toadstools, if you could count them, we hadn't encountered another living being in the forest. I kept expecting an ambush as we trekked among the tall, slender trees, but so far, all was quiet and peaceful.

"If the portals are forbidden, perhaps the prince traveled here in secret before creating it?" Darian suggested.

"But then how did the fae know where he'd gone?" I asked thoughtfully. Warriors had gone to Katakin looking for the prince, so they had to have found out somehow. I'd always assumed they'd simply found the portal he'd created, but now I wasn't so sure.

"We should be discussing what we plan to do when we reach the city," Kade growled. "The moment we're spotted, we'll be captured. We don't exactly blend in." He looked pointedly at Asher then, and Asher's tail flicked almost as if it had a mind of its own and it was enjoying being the center of attention. "If the fae find us with Prince Azaren like this, it won't go well," Kade added. Violence shone in his eyes, and I knew a part of him welcomed the idea of a fight. The fae had killed his mother and sister, and if I was in his position, I would have felt the same.

"So we leave the prince somewhere the guards'll find him?" Asher offered. "If it's anythin' like Katakin, there'll be soldiers stationed around the city. Maybe they'll think someone in the city beat him bloody."

Locke peered at us. His face was paler than usual, and I wondered whether it was because the sun was weakening him or if there was another reason. I thought he would chime in about our plans, but he simply stared up at the darkening sky and said, "We should rest here for a while and get some sleep."

"Sleep?" I asked incredulously. "We've only been walking for a few hours." Truthfully, a rest sounded like bliss. I was still exhausted from the episode with the toadstools, and the idea of finding somewhere to sit my ass down was appealing, but we had no idea if the fae had detected our presence in their world. I had expected Locke and the others to push us to continue until my feet felt like they would fall off. There was at least a half hour of sunlight left, going by the position of the sun, and the monsters could see in the dark either way.

"We should keep going," Kade agreed with me.

Locke's eyes hardened, and Asher gave Kade a pointed look. "Let's rest for a short while," the demon said, dragging out the word *rest* like he was talking about something else entirely.

I frowned at them, sure I was missing something, but Kade seemed to understand the hidden message, and he didn't enlighten me. His gaze briefly flicked to Locke before he nodded, and just like that the monsters set about finding a sheltered spot for us to make camp.

Knowing I wasn't going to get an explanation, I was quiet as we ate rations from Kade's satchel, and then Asher wrapped an arm around my waist and pulled me to the grass, curling me against him. "You should sleep, sweetheart. We won't be here for long."

"I still don't understand why we've stopped at all," I began, but before I could comment further, Kade dropped down on my other side, squeezing me between them, and the wolf shifter rested a large hand on my thigh. I sighed heavily. Being squished between the two large monsters was warm and suffocating but also...comfortable. We were in the middle of a strange forest in an unknown land, but right then I felt safer than when I'd been on my island. With that unsettling thought rattling around in my head, I eased against them and closed my eyes.

I must have fallen asleep quickly because I didn't remember drifting off, but it didn't last. A nightmare plagued me, the image so clear it seemed real. In the dream, Asher knelt before me. His arms were limp at his sides and his eyes were defeated as flames consumed him, the fire crackling against his skin. *No!* I gasped as my eyes flew open, my heartbeat pounding at my throat and panic tightening my chest. Blinking, I lay there as the night sky came into focus, and the scents of Asher and Kade soothed me, musk and leather mixing with sandalwood and coffee. *A dream*, I assured myself as I fought for air.

Asher's grip tightened around me as if he'd noticed my distress even while he slept, and I peered up at his relaxed face. Moonlight glinted on his violet horns and illuminated the outline of his nose, defined jaw, and full lips. *See, no fire*, I consoled myself as I stared at his handsome face, but the panic wouldn't leave me.

I knew the demon was fine. His body had been able to heal itself after I'd flooded the ballroom with magic water, but images of his burning body stayed with me. Shifting onto my left side, I turned toward Kade, hoping he might distract me, but like Asher, the wolf shifter's body was still, his eyes closed and his breathing steady as he slept.

Well, that's too bad. Moving onto my back again, I stared at the blanket of stars above me. I knew I should be sleeping. We likely wouldn't remain where we were for long, and I could use the rest, but I resisted the idea of closing my eyes again and seeing Asher's burning body. Instead, I began counting the twinkling lights above me and tried not to think about what the next days would bring.

I'd lost count of the stars and had decided to find Darian who was keeping watch when I heard a shuffling sound a short distance away. Lifting my head, I glimpsed Darian and Locke right before they slipped into the trees, disappearing from view. I frowned as I stared after them, wondering if they'd heard something and were going to investigate. The thought that the fae might have found us sharpened my senses, and I cocked my head as I listened intently. When I didn't hear any screams or sounds of battle, I let out a relieved breath. *One of them probably needed to relieve himself and the other one is there to keep watch. Nothing to worry about.*

Having successfully calmed myself, I closed my eyes only to have the image of Asher's burning form reappear in my mind. Hastily, I snapped my eyes open again. *Nope. No more sleep for me.*

Giving up on the idea of rest entirely, I slowly removed Kade's hand from my leg and wiggled downward until I was no longer squeezed between the males. I half expected Asher and Kade to jump to their feet at the movement, but they continued sleeping, and I tiptoed away from them.

Prince Azaren remained unconscious close by, his limp body splayed out on the ground where Asher had dropped him. I checked the male was still alive, then grabbed the fae books Darian had placed on the ground.

Prince Azaren wouldn't be happy when he discovered the other books had been left scattered in the forest, not after all he'd gone through to retrieve them, but I hoped he'd be able to collect them afterward. On the bright side, it hadn't rained since we'd arrived in the fae realm, so there was a good chance the books hadn't been damaged.

Dropping down, I sat cross-legged on the grass not far from Kade and Asher, and I placed the books beside me. Grabbing the fairy tale on the top of the stack, I rested it on my lap. Curiosity had been eating away at me from the moment I'd glimpsed Prince Azaren running with the pile of books in his arms, and I traced my fingertips over the buttery leather-bound cover, appreciating the golden embossed symbols of stars and clouds illuminated by the moonlight.

Carefully, I turned to the first yellowed page. The writing inked in the center of the paper was foreign and unreadable, and I guessed I was looking at the written text of the fae. The curves and strokes of the letters were artfully done, and I wished I could read it. Thankfully, beneath the fae text, a translation had been written in neat cursive handwriting.

The Diamond Princess by Sharou Zanae. I read through the translated story, delighted by the detailed hand-drawn illustrations accompanying the text on each page. The short tale spoke of a princess who was born mute but who could play music so enchanting it captivated even the attention of the gods. None of the princes from the neighboring kingdoms desired a bride who couldn't speak, but Paentoras, the God of the Night, fell in love with the princess and begged her to join him at his palace high in the stars. A place where she would become immortal and the stars would dance to her music, their lights shining brighter with every note she played. Hearing of the god's wishes, a prince from a neighboring kingdom was overcome with jealousy and kidnapped the princess with the intention of ransoming her to the god in return for his own immortality, but Paentoras rescued her and punished the prince's kingdom by shrouding the land in darkness, never to see the light again.

When I came to the final page much faster than I expected, my fingers brushed over the illustration of the princess playing a harp while a man in a long dark cloak watched enraptured. Stars twinkled around them, dancing to a tune I couldn't hear. The tale was dark but bittersweet, and I smiled as I closed the book. It was a captivating tale about love and acceptance, but I still couldn't understand why Prince Azaren had risked his life to obtain the books. I went to grab the next fairy tale when I realized Darian and Locke still hadn't returned. Lifting to my feet, I scanned the silent trees around me. They'd been gone for far too long for them to simply be relieving themselves. *What if they've been taken?*

Forgetting the book, I moved to warn Kade and Asher when a moan sounded from not too far away. It wasn't the moan of someone who was dying but a moan of pleasure. I paused, spinning back toward the darkened trees.

What the hell? Logically, I knew the moan could be coming from fae beasts who were feasting on Darian's and Locke's corpses, but my instincts told me I wasn't in danger. Still, I wasn't taking any chances. Pulling out one of my daggers, I grasped the steel hilt of the weapon and stepped slowly toward the trees.

Careful to keep my body hidden, I said a silent plea to the Goddess Falia that I wasn't about to find Locke's and Darian's mutilated bodies, or you know, even bust the males relieving themselves, because there were some things I didn't need to see. As I peeked my head around the tree trunk, my eyes flared wide, and I stilled as I took in the scene in front of me. Locke sat shrouded in darkness with his back to a tree, his long legs parted and his fangs buried deep into the soft flesh of Darian's neck. That was right; Locke was *eating* my siren.

I grasped my dagger tighter, ready to charge forward and attempt to save Darian's life, when a moan slipped from his lips. I blinked, gaping at where Darian sat slumped against Locke. Strands of Darian's silver hair had fallen loose from his ponytail and hung over his face, but I could still make out the pleasure etched into his expression. *What?*

I stayed where I was, unable to move. I knew Locke was a vampire, but I'd never seen him drink from anyone. A stupid part of me hadn't thought it was something he did. *Is this the reason we stopped for a rest? Why Locke looked so pale?* Darian moaned again, a soft sound that barely left his lips, and I knew I should leave. There was something so intimate about the moment, but a twisted part of me wondered what it would be like to have Locke's fangs buried in my own neck. I thought then of how Locke had sucked my blood from his fingers while he pressed between my thighs. Goddess, would I moan like Darian? I mentally shook myself, trying to banish the thought from my mind, but as I moved to slip away, Locke's gaze flicked upward. Predatory onyx eyes fixed on me, his dark stare freezing me in place.

Locke's nostrils flared, and I knew he was dragging my scent into his lungs. *Fuck.* Hunger swirled in the vampire's eyes, and he didn't take his gaze from me as his arms tightened around Darian's body. His fangs sank deeper into the siren, his cheeks hollowing as he sucked, and I watched, transfixed.

Darian moaned even louder, his face contorting with pleasure, and I tried to swallow, but my throat was too dry. *Ho-ly Goddess.*

As Locke drank, I started to worry about Darian's life again, but a snarl ripped from Locke's throat as he finally released the siren's neck. Black blood dripped from Locke's exposed fangs as he lifted his head, and my heart pounded hard, a steady, thumping beat in my ears.

Locke opened his mouth to speak, and I sucked in a breath, ignoring the inner voice that was telling me to run. Instead of danger, anticipation made my stomach flip, even though I knew it was wrong.

But when Locke spoke, his voice was animalistic and unkind. "Leave, Raine," he growled, and the gravel of his voice made me shiver.

I stood rooted to the spot, unable to move.

"Now!" he snarled even louder, his voice lashing out, and it was enough to spur me into action. Almost tripping over my own feet, I staggered backward before spinning around and walking briskly to where Kade and Asher remained sleeping.

Fucking vampire, I internally cursed as I settled between Kade and Asher again, but despite Locke's harsh command, and even after I'd caught him feasting on Darian, the thought of the vampire coming after me made my body prickle with anticipation rather than fear.

CHAPTER 4

~ Raine ~

The moon was still high in the sky when Asher roused me from sleep. Stretching out my limbs, I tried not to be obvious as I watched Darian and Locke from the corner of my eye. The pair of them were acting normally, but two small marks were still visible on Darian's neck. The siren's skin was pallid, and there were circles under his eyes, but I didn't comment, and neither did anyone else. Now that I'd come to my senses, I told myself I would have fought Locke off if he had tried to bite me, but I knew the only person I was fooling was myself.

Darian stopped beside Prince Azaren's limp form and stared down at the prone male. "Sweet Toros, Kade. How hard did you hit the poor fellow? If he doesn't wake soon and get some fluids into his body, I fear he won't wake at all."

"The fae should be thankful he's alive," Kade responded gruffly as he checked the sharpness of his blades. "He deserves worse than that."

I wanted to point out that the prince possibly had nothing to do with the murder of Kade's family, but I didn't. The wolf shifter was still hurting, and I couldn't fault him for that. Crouching beside the prince, I pressed two fingers to the male's slender neck, glad when I found a pulse. It was weak but still there, a slight flutter against my fingertips. *Thank the Goddess.* Standing again, I said, "We need to keep him alive. He's our only chance at stopping a war between the Katakin monsters and the fae."

"I'd wager war is unavoidable now," Asher commented as he chewed on a hunk of dried bread.

I thought then of my sister, Cara, who was still back in Katakin. I knew I was doing the right thing. Finding a cure for the curse afflicting Katakin was the only way to stop Warrick's outliers, but the idea that the fae might attack Katakin while we were in the fae realm made my stomach pinch. "What defenses are there around Katakin? How have you kept the fae away in the past?" I asked abruptly.

Kade and the others were surprised by my question, but Locke was the one to answer me. It was the first time he'd spoken since I had awoken, and having his attention on me brought back images of his fangs buried in Darian's neck as he watched me. "Katakin City is watched night and day from the sky and ground. Because the fae are able to create portals anywhere they wish, there was no point building a wall around the city."

"The alphas of the high houses are responsible for keepin' certain areas of the city safe," Asher added as he finished his bread and folded his thick arms in front of his chest.

"But what if there's a full-scale attack while we're away?" I asked, trying and failing to keep the worry out of my voice.

Having noticed my distress, Darian stepped behind me and began massaging my tight shoulders. "Katakin will lose unless the houses agree to unite and form a coordinated defense," the siren said grimly in my ear. "The council would need to bring everyone together if the monsters are to stand a chance." His fingers were like magic as they loosened the tension in my muscles, and despite what he was saying, a moan threatened to slip out of me.

"And that's about as likely to happen as Darian shittin' rainbows," Asher said with a chuckle.

The others looked at Asher, unimpressed, but the demon shrugged. "What?" he defended. "In two hundred years, the alphas and the council have hardly been in agreement over anythin'. We all know if the fae attack in large numbers, we're fucked. Well, unless Warrick's outliers annihilate the fae first. Though, from what we've seen, the outliers are as likely to destroy the Katakin monsters as they are to go on the offensive against the fae."

My muscles tightened again, and Darian shot Asher a halfhearted glare for ruining his efforts. Asher returned the glare with a grin, but as if it was his apology for being the bearer of bad news, he took hold of my left hand and began massaging my palm, running his thumbs down the insides of my fingers.

The bond that pulled me toward the siren and demon further ignited, and my head grew light as my body warmed. Closing my eyes, I tipped my head back and hummed.

"Stop that," Kade growled. "If she keeps making that face, we won't be going anywhere for some time."

Much to my approval, Asher and Darian ignored him and continued massaging me. I opened my eyes again and stared innocently at Kade. "What face?"

Darian kneaded harder into my right shoulder, and I bit my lip to stop from moaning.

Kade pointed his finger accusingly at me. "*That* face," he growled.

Asher and Darian chuckled, and I grinned stupidly back at Kade. Asher and Darian weren't touching me sexually, but need was already making my body ache, and I suddenly didn't care if we never moved from that very spot. I knew I was likely still worked up from seeing Locke with Darian hours earlier, but I didn't want to admit it to myself. Darian leaned down, his lips brushing against the side of my face before he began pressing soft kisses to my neck. I tilted my head to the side, giving him better access, and I didn't miss the way Locke's eyes became fully black as his gaze homed in on where Darian was kissing.

Kade's left eye twitched, and desire shone in his golden eyes as he watched me, his attention going from my face to the swell of my breasts, then back up as it lingered on my lips.

Goddess, the males, the *monsters*, were always too much. Warmth gathered between my thighs, and Kade's body became rigid, his nostrils flaring as he scented my arousal.

Damn wolf senses. Not that I really cared. Truthfully, if they wanted to take me right then, I would have let them. I could still remember the sweet taste of Darian on my tongue as Asher took me from behind, his huge—

"We don't have time to fuck around," Locke snapped harshly, pulling me back to the present. "We need to get the fae prince to the city before we're discovered."

The vampire's icy tone cooled some of the warmth that had been building within me, and I glimpsed the longing in Locke's eyes before he turned his back to me. The monster was so damn confusing.

Asher muttered something under his breath and released me to bend down and swing Prince Azaren over his shoulder.

Kade adjusted himself before rolling his shoulders and checking his weapons, and Darian kissed my neck softly one more time before lifting his lips to my ear. "Later, lovely," he promised.

• • • ● • ● • ● • •

~ Kade ~

I needed to get my shit together. The longer I was in the fae realm, the more my skin itched. Memories of my mother and sister haunted me, and with every step, fear gnawed on my insides. I couldn't lose anyone else. Not to the fae.

But my friends—my family—and I were in the fae realm without an exit route mapped out and with a fae prince in our grasp. If we were caught, the fae king would likely sentence us to death and declare war on all of Katakin. *Fuck.*

My gaze flicked again to the red-haired goddess walking ahead of me. It would be hard enough to lose any of my brothers, but I'd promised to protect Raine. After I'd failed my mother and sister, I'd still made her that promise, and I was a fool. My back ached from the tension in my muscles, and I cracked my neck.

Every instinct told me the forest we were in would bring only death. That this *land* was death, and I had to fight against the protective urge I had to force Raine to remain by my side at every moment. Logically, I knew my Mahare was as safe here as she was in Katakin. Now that my brothers had shown their commitment to protecting her as well, being surrounded by us four was the closest she'd get to safety. With Warrick and his outliers in Katakin, there was no haven for us. Nowhere to hide and only this path to follow.

Locke was silent behind me, his arms cradling the four fae books still in our possession. His features were as hardened as my own, and I turned toward him. "Take from me next," I said quietly enough that Raine wouldn't overhear.

My vampire brother kept focusing on the passing trees and vegetation. "Darian's blood was enough."

"We both know monster blood can only sustain you for a few hours. We all need to have our wits about us when we face the fae," I insisted, trying not to show my irritation at his resistance.

Locke's jaw clenched, and his gaze finally slid to me, but he didn't respond, and I didn't push him. I knew the male was dealing with his own issues. Locke hadn't drunk from another being for over 150 years, and from the pale shade of Darian's skin, he'd struggled to maintain control and had taken more from the siren than he should have. But I trusted him, and if he needed blood to keep up his strength, I was happy to provide it. I just wished he'd let me give it to him.

We'd walked in silence for another half hour when the faint sound of buzzing had me twisting my head to the right. Around us, the trees had grown thicker, and it was impossible to see far in any direction. I wanted to shift and scout ahead, but I wasn't letting Raine out of my sight.

Instead, I stopped walking, my ears shifting, becoming pointed and pricking upward as I listened.

Locke and the others halted and watched me intently.

"What is it?" Locke asked.

Raine shifted on the spot, and I kept her in my periphery.

"Not sure," I said, furrowing my forehead. "Sounds like...buzzing." I sniffed the air, but everything in this place smelled strange. Hints of sweet tree sap and fragrant berries mixed with the scents of moss, fungi, and foreign animal life.

After a moment, Locke placed the fae books on the ground and drew his sword, a look of concentration on his face. "I hear it now too."

Following his lead, I pulled the swords from the scabbards at my sides. Darian grabbed out two of his throwing stars, and Asher drew an ax with his free hand. Instinctively, we all circled around Raine.

"What are you doing? You're acting like it's the fae," Raine said, unimpressed. "Are you sure you're not just hearing a swarm of mosquitos?"

"Better not be," Asher said as he lifted his ax to swat at invisible mosquitos in the air. "The bloodsuckin' bastards fuckin' love me."

Raine shook her head at me, but Asher gave her a serious look.

"No, the buzzing is too loud. This is something else," I said.

"He's right. We're about to have company," Locke added, and that was when the first insect appeared above the canopy of the trees.

"Cruel seven devils," Darian cursed. "What is that thing?"

Before anyone could answer him, a dozen large, winged insects had filled the sky above the tree line. Their shiny blue bodies were as big as rabbits', four translucent wings flapped from each of their backs, and angry red stingers protruded from the ends of their thick, curved bodies. A dozen pairs of beady black eyes fixed on us, and I cursed the fucking fae and their world.

"Holy Mother, they look like giant bees," Raine said as I moved even closer to her, my protective instincts on high alert.

"They're not like any bees I've seen," Darian commented as he rolled his wrists, preparing his body for the fight to come.

"Maybe they're friendly?" Raine added hopefully, but as if they were mocking her suggestion, two of the giant flying insects changed direction, shooting toward us with the speed of poisoned arrows. Their long black antennae twitched, and aggressive red stripes appeared across their backs and heads, the distinct coloring resembling a warrior's armor.

"Or not," Raine added as she pulled two knives from the belt across her waist.

The insects drew closer, now arching lower, but before they could reach us, Darian released his stars. The weapons spun through the air, connecting with the creatures and slicing them in two. Steaming orange goo spurted from their bodies as they fell, lifeless, to the ground.

Raine sucked in a sharp breath.

We might have been in the fae realm, but I still hated the thought of wasted life. Still, as the other insects all turned toward us, I knew Darian had been right to cut them down. These weren't ordinary insects. I wondered then if the fae king had bred the creatures himself. It was possible they were his spies sent out to watch the forest for intruders. Either way, it was them or us.

Asher placed the fae prince on the ground as ten more insects sped toward us, and I braced myself. The drone of furious buzzing filled my ears as some of the insects circled around until they were approaching us from all sides, their wicked stingers gleaming in the moonlight, and then they attacked. We battled the creatures, moving fluidly as we cut them down with our weapons, and when the buzzing ceased, I relaxed my stance and peered at the mess of insect bodies and orange goo around us.

"Well, that wasn't so bad," Asher said as he wiped the goo from his ax onto a nearby tree trunk. But as I stared at the fallen insects, their bodies began to twitch and move, as if pulled by invisible strings. Slowly, the severed pieces rejoined, melding until the insects were whole again.

"You were saying?" Darian commented dryly.

A strong, sour scent permeated the air, making my nostrils burn, and then even more of the insects appeared in the sky above.

"Fucking run!" I shouted at the others before sheathing my swords. Raine had just enough time to sheathe her knives and snatch the fae books from the ground before I lifted her into my arms. Asher grabbed Prince Azaren and flung him over one shoulder, and we all surged forward as the buzzing became louder behind us.

Locke remained at the back of our group, his preternatural speed allowing him to cut down the insects with lethal precision, one after another.

Raine stretched her neck to peer over my shoulder and gasped. "Kade, there are dozens now," she warned, and the anxiety in her voice made me tighten my grip on her and run faster.

Angry buzzing sounded louder to my left, and Raine shifted in my hold, flicking her hand out to whack at the air with one of the fae books. Something thudded against the leather of the book, and the buzzing receded momentarily.

"There are too many of them," Asher said as he ran beside us. "We won't be able to outrun them. We need to try somethin' else."

"What about fire?" Raine suggested.

"We can't stop long enough to create any," I responded. I'd already thought about fire, but using the flint and steel in my satchel would take too long. We didn't have that kind of time.

"I can entrance them and lead them away," Darian said, and Raine stiffened in my arms.

Before she could protest, I spoke first. "No. We'll deal with them together." Not too long ago, Asher had almost been taken from us, and I wasn't willing to let Darian risk his life. "Can you smell that?" I asked a moment later.

Darian nodded. "The water? Yes, there must be a stream or river up ahead."

"If there's a waterfall, we could hide behind it until the insects lose interest or we come up with a better plan," I said, determined.

With that, we moved even faster, skirting past trees, ducking under branches, and dodging around fallen logs.

But as a deep valley came into view, and I took in the sprawling river and the thick sheet of water that rushed over a cliff face, I knew we wouldn't make it. The insects swarmed the air, creating a cloud of the buzzing creatures, the sour scent so strong it made my eyes water.

Raine held a book up, swatting at the insects, but there were too many. A shadow appeared to my right, and Raine's hand swung upward. Soft leather smacked against my right cheek, forcing my head to the side.

"Oops. Sorry," Raine said with an apologetic grimace, but then searing pain erupted in my left shoulder. It was as if molten lava was being poured into my body, and I didn't catch what Raine shouted next. Looking down, an angry red welt was already forming where one of the insects had stung me. Venom polluted my bloodstream, sapping the strength from my body, and Raine yelled at me to set her on her feet, but I didn't loosen my grip on her. And I didn't stop running.

Darian cut down two insects with a single swipe of his sword before one of the creatures stung him on his leg, penetrating through his pants below his knee. His steps faltered, his knee almost buckling, but he stayed upright and kept moving. With every step, the river and waterfall drew closer. If I could get her there, Raine could swim to safety.

Locke moved closer to my back, making quick work of the insects around him, but as he dispatched an insect that had been about to sting me on my hip, he grunted in pain and flicked away an insect that had stung the back of his neck.

"Asher, watch out!" Raine yelled, but it was too late. Three insects flew at his back, one of them managing to avoid his swinging arms and sting him on his ass.

He cursed as he sliced through the insect's body a second later.

My body grew sluggish, limbs shaking, but I kept moving forward. Kept stumbling toward the edge of the water. The tree line ended, and we burst out onto a stretch of grass that led down into the valley toward the river.

An insect hovered near my face, but Raine batted it away, the worn leather of the book only just missing my nose and thudding against the creature's body. "Kade, let me down!" she screeched at me, but my gaze remained fixed on the river as the insects closed in. Dozens of them curled their bodies, ready to sting us again and again.

"Oh, for fuck's sake!" Raine snapped.

I felt her magic before anything happened. Power crackled through the air, making my senses tingle, and a slight metallic taste coated my tongue. Raine's face scrunched in concentration, her hands lifting upward, and then the wind rushed past my cheeks, tugging at my clothes as it swept up the insects and carried them away from us. Sweat beaded on Raine's brow, her body taut and attention fixed on something behind me, and the buzzing receded until it grew faint.

"Stop, Raine," Locke commanded, and she listened, her body sagging against me. I didn't turn around to see what she'd done. I staggered forward a few more steps until I made it to the water's edge.

Darian took her from my arms and stepped into the water, and I fell in after them.

CHAPTER 5

~ **Asher** ~

I swam through the sheet of water, my arm tight around Prince Azaren's chest as I pulled him along behind me, and I scanned the dimly lit cavern hidden behind the waterfall. Raine, Darian, and Kade were already pulling themselves onto a wide rock shelf at the back of the space, dragging themselves away from the water and dripping all over the stone.

Locke emerged beside me, and the pair of us swam to join the others. Fucking Halced my ass ached. My right ass cheek throbbed with pain from where one of the giant buzzing pests had jabbed its stinger into my flesh.

How I hated insects. Monsters I could handle. For the most part, monsters were often predictable and usually ran their mouths more than anything else. But bugs, spiders, and other creepers...the tiny devils could crawl up your nose while you slept, and you wouldn't have a fucking clue.

I tried to forget about the pain spreading down the back of my right thigh as I reached the edge of the rock shelf and Darian helped pull the fae's soaked body onto the slab. Bracing my hands on the edge of the rock, I lifted myself out of the water and frowned as I noticed the way my muscles pulled with the effort. The movement wasn't painful or difficult, but it took more strength than usual. Whatever poison the giant insect had squirted into me, it was making me weak, and from the pins and needles that had started in my leg, I was guessing it wasn't done with me yet.

Forcing myself to stand, I moved to where the others had collapsed. Kade was busy running his fingers over Raine's body and inspecting her for wounds. His hand paused on a spot on her left ankle, and he swore.

In a few swift movements, he pulled off her boots and tore the fabric of her pants up to her shin. He glared at the two angry red welts that had formed on her lightly tanned skin. "Why didn't you tell us you were stung?"

I moved closer, falling to my knees next to them and eyeing the wound. The red swelling wrapped around her entire ankle. Lifting her leg, I stretched it out, getting a better look.

"We've all been stung," Raine responded, grimacing against the pain. "I don't see you stripping Asher's pants to get a good look at his ass."

Kade scowled. "The rest of us are monsters, but you're still human. You're more vulnerable."

"Thanks for the reminder," she quipped back.

I was glad to see she still had her fire, but it didn't stop the worry that was making my chest squeeze. Or was my racing heartbeat due to the venom polluting my system? I couldn't tell. Pushing her soaked hair away from her neck, I inspected her skin for any more marks. "You get stung anywhere else, sweetheart?"

Raine stopped to think for a moment before she shook her head. "Only twice on my ankle, I think."

Darian crouched on my other side and started his own inspection of her. Kade passed him the blue paste from his satchel, and Darian started smearing the substance over Raine's sting marks.

"You can all attend to your own wounds too, you know," she said when Darian had finished. "I'm not going to die from a bee sting."

I exchanged an uncertain look with Darian.

She sat up higher. "Wait, you don't think we're actually dying, do you?"

Honestly, I had no idea. The pain in my ass sure made it feel like I was dying, but I wasn't so sure I could rely on that assessment.

"No one's dying," Locke said calmly as he stepped beside us.

"You don't know that," Kade growled. "I can feel myself growing weaker. I can feel *Raine* growing weaker. She was stung *twice*."

"The pain in our chests is dull," Darian said as he rubbed his chin thoughtfully, the siren obviously having come to the same conclusion as Locke. "As long as the pain in our chests doesn't get worse, we'll know Raine is going to be all right. I was stung twice as well, and we'll just have to hope for the best."

"Well, thank you, strange magical bond," I said, blowing out a breath. I likely sounded sarcastic, but I truly was thankful. I was growing used to the magical bond that tied me to the spirited little female. The constant pull I had toward her, and the desperate need I had to protect her, was almost becoming comforting in a way. As long as the pain in our chests didn't worsen, I knew Raine wasn't going to die from the venom of the insects.

"It could be only a matter of time," Kade growled, shattering the calm I'd managed to find.

Groaning sounded behind us, and we all turned our attention to where Prince Azaren was starting to wake. Locke was the first to reach the fae, though my vampire brother's movements were slower than usual. Instead of him being at the fae's side almost instantly, a few seconds passed before he'd made it there.

Locke gripped the prince's throat and pulled the male into a sitting position.

"My head," Prince Azaren rasped, opening his bloodshot eyes. His body tensed as he took in the scene around him, but when his gaze settled on Raine, he visibly relaxed.

"Try to use magic and I'll rip your head off," Locke snarled in his ear, but despite Locke's threat, the fae's lips curved upward.

"It's you," Prince Azaren said, ignoring Locke as he kept staring at Raine. I shifted my massive body to block his view of her. I had no idea what magic the fae wielded, and I didn't like my Sharachi in his line of sight. Raine lifted to her feet, limping around me, and I tried to rein in my annoyance at her complete disregard for her life as I followed her closer to the fae.

"You found the books," Raine said, and the fae prince's smile softened.

"It was as easy as baking bread," he responded with a confident smile.

She raised a brow and looked up and down his beaten body. "I didn't realize baking bread was such a difficult task," she commented.

"Oh, you'd be surprised," the prince quipped back, then added, "So...I faced some hurdles but nothing I couldn't handle." I hated how he was speaking to Raine like they were fond friends. In reality, he'd only seen her once when she'd saved him from Warrick's lab.

I was close to opening my mouth to say something stupid when the fae acknowledged the rest of us. "And I see you've found your bonds," he observed.

Locke gripped the prince's throat tighter. "What did you just say?"

"What do you mean, my bonds?" Raine asked with a frown, and again the fae only responded to her.

"I'm weak, but I can still sense the magic. I told you I could sense you were bonded to others. I'm assuming you want me to break whatever magic is binding you to these four? Your attempt to free me was relatively poor, but that steel bar did the trick and you've brought me to my realm, so a deal's a deal."

"What the fuck? Did he just say, 'break the magic'?" I blurted, not sure I'd heard correctly. From the reactions of my brothers, I had.

"What the hell is he talking about, Raine?" Kade growled, his voice echoing throughout the cavern as his gaze narrowed on her.

"You didn't say anything about a deal, lovely," Darian said, a glimmer of hurt in his blue eyes.

Claws peeked from Locke's fingertips, and he pressed them against the soft skin of Prince Azaren's neck. A trickle of fear finally entered the prince's expression as Locke's claws came dangerously close to breaking his skin.

"Tell us about this deal you made with her, Prince," Locke snarled.

Raine blanched. "We're not here to break the bonds," she said quickly to the fae. "We're here to find a way to break the curse on Katakin."

Prince Azaren stared at her quizzically.

"Don't look at her," Locke spat, digging his nails in until blood dripped down the prince's neck. "Tell me about the deal."

Prince Azaren's expression became uncertain as he looked at Raine and then at me and my brothers. "I told her if she freed me, she could come with me when I returned home, and I'd remove the curse that's binding her soul to others. I–I didn't know who she was bound to then. I didn't know you want the bonds to remain."

I'd been so focused, so unexplainably angry as I glared at the prince, that I hadn't seen Raine draw a dagger until it flew through the air toward Locke. It would have missed him and sliced a line into the shoulder of his black leather cloak, but Locke caught it before it made it that far.

"I never made the deal," she seethed as she walked closer to Locke and the prince. Kade stopped her with an arm around her waist before she could get within striking distance of the vampire. Undoubtedly, it was more for her safety than Locke's. "I freed him because I thought his return would stop a war from breaking out. And if he can break the bonds, isn't that a good thing? I thought you wanted to be free of your ties to me."

I understood where Raine was coming from, but it didn't stop the hurt that twisted inside me like barbed wire, wrapping around my heart. *Did* I want my bond with the little human to be broken? I knew it'd make life simpler, but deep down I also knew it would make my life emptier as well. She was supposed to be with us. I could feel it in my bones.

Locke stayed deathly still as he stared back at her, and his eyes darkened until they were pure black. He bared his wicked fangs that were now protruding from his mouth. "You don't make any deals without talking to the rest of us first. Is this why you wanted to come to the fae realm? Why you wanted us to keep the fae alive?"

At Locke's last question, fury rocked Kade's body.

"Is this true, Sharachi?" I said, unable to keep the hurt from my gaze as I watched her.

"No!" Raine said, her eyes wide and desperate. "I'm here to find a way to break the curse over Katakin like I said. If we killed Prince Azaren, the fae would go to war with Katakin. I wasn't lying when I told you all that."

"No, but you failed to tell us about the fact the fae could also break whatever is bonding us together," Locke said, his voice devoid of emotion.

To a stranger, Locke would have seemed uncaring and disinterested, but I knew better. Raine was burrowing into his heart like she was carving out her place with the rest of us. My vampire brother was hurting.

Raine took a deep breath and rubbed her hand softly over Kade's arm which was still gripping her tightly. At her touch, his body softened.

"I didn't tell you about the fact the fae said he might be able to break our bonds because I wasn't sure if I—" She broke off then as if she was struggling to find the words, and she stared hard at Locke. A beat passed, and for a moment, I wasn't sure if she'd finish her sentence, but then she swallowed and continued, "I'm not sure if I *want* him to break the bonds, and I was afraid you'd force him to."

Silence filled the cavern again, and we all stared at her. For the first time, the feisty female looked vulnerable, a startled expression on her face as if she couldn't believe the admission that had come out of her own mouth.

In two long strides, I was at Raine's side and pulling her from Kade. I wrapped my thick arms around her small body and forced her to look up at me. "We wouldn't force you to do anythin' you didn't want to."

Tears gathered in her eyes, but she blinked them away quickly. "Right, like you didn't force me to participate in the trials?" she responded sarcastically.

Darian came up beside her and clasped his hand gently on her shoulder. "That was different, lovely. Turning into a monster would have helped you, and we hadn't known what a treasure you were back then."

She didn't look overly appeased by his answer, but it was Locke's words that seemed to penetrate to her core.

Emotion flickered in Locke's black eyes, and it was the first time I'd seen him look so uncertain. "We're here to return the fae prince to his people, and to find a way to break the curse over Katakin," he said slowly, almost as if he was telling himself more than Raine. "We can discuss the matter about our bonds later. No one will force you to do anything you don't want to."

Locke's black gaze bored into Raine, and she nodded slowly.

I crushed Raine against my chest. Despite what we'd already been through, I'd still half expected Locke to push for our bond with Raine to be broken. Not too long ago, he and Kade had been scouring the books in the ancient Katakin library, trying to find a way to do just that. I had to wonder what had changed since then, but whatever it was, I was grateful. I wasn't ready to let go of Raine. If I was bein' honest, I didn't think I ever would be.

"As touching as this all is, now that has been sorted do you think you could remove your talons from my neck?" Prince Azaren said, and we all turned our attention back to the fae.

I glared at the male as I held Raine, all too aware that it was his fucking fault we even had to think about breaking the bonds.

Locke's claws receded, though his hand remained squeezing the prince's neck. The whites returned to my vampire brother's eyes, and his fangs disappeared, leaving short, rounded teeth.

"Ah, much better," Prince Azaren said with a smile that was way too chipper for his current situation.

I was marveling at Locke's surprising show of restraint even after the fae had dropped that bit of news on us when I noticed the pain in my ass had intensified. This whole time the venom of the insect that had bitten me had still been poisoning my body, but now I inhaled sharply as tingles raced across my insides and what was left of my strength seemed to drain away. My gaze met Darian's, and from the look on his face, he was experiencing a similar sensation.

Raine started to slide down as her legs buckled, and I held her up. "Whoa, I've got you, Sharachi," I said as I held her steady, but my arms were trembling even worse than hers were, and I was starting to realize we were all worse off than we'd thought.

Locke moved his shoulders as if he was trying to rid himself of the venom. "What's happening to us?" his cold voice demanded of the fae.

"I don't pretend to know the inner workings of monsters," Prince Azaren commented. "Until quite recently, I'd never seen one of you before."

A growl left Kade's throat, and Locke looked as if he was about to strangle the prince.

"We were stung by giant insects with red-striped markings," Darian explained before someone could snap the prince's neck. "Tell us what their venom is capable of."

"Ah, I had wondered whether you'd encountered them considering we're so close to their nest. This cave is one of my favorite spots when I need to get away. An altercation with them also explains the pain in my arm and my own weakening power."

Raine frowned, her forehead wrinkling. "What nest?"

"The dazra are known to have a nest around here, and they are fiercely protective of their territory."

"The dazra?" Darian asked. "Is that what you call those insects?"

The prince nodded, his chin bobbing against Locke's hand. "Yes, they're a wild species that have nests around the forest."

"How do you kill them?" Kade growled.

"Oh, you don't kill the dazra," Prince Azaren said, looking perplexed. "Their survival is vital to the health of the forest. You avoid them by staying away from their territory. If you are unfortunate enough to find yourself in a position where you must move close to their nest, you never look them in the eye. If they cannot see your eyes, they will not attack."

I gripped Raine tighter in an effort to stop my shaking arm. *Fuck*, why couldn't I stop shaking? "Huh," I commented. "Never would have found that out."

"More importantly, how poisonous are they?" Darian asked as he stretched out his arms and shook his head as if to clear it.

The prince's expression grew somber. "The word *dazra* also has another meaning: Death to magic."

I glared at the fae. "Death?"

"Yes, the wording is rather dramatic, isn't it?" Prince Azaren said with a grin, but he clarified, "The venom from the dazra doesn't kill their victims, but it suppresses the magic in their bloodstreams. The more venom in your system, the longer it will be until your body can recover and your magic returns. Once you're stung, you begin to feel the effects almost immediately. My father often uses it on his prisoners."

"And how long does it take for the venom to leave one's system?" Locke asked.

Prince Azaren shrugged. "Well, that depends on how much venom was entered into your bloodstream. I know fae who have been stung only once and they recovered within three days."

"Three days?" I blurted. "We're not exactly swimming in time."

"Now do tell me what it is you five are hoping to accomplish here in my world? You say you're here to find a way to break the curse, but how exactly do you hope to manage such a feat? And where are the books I acquired? I've been quite forthcoming with information about the dazra. The least you can do is—"

"Drink," Locke ordered the fae harshly, and he nodded at Kade, who fished out a canteen of water, undid the lid, and handed it to the prince.

"I really don't—"

"Now," Locke snarled, and Prince Azaren blinked and lifted the canteen to his lips, taking a few long drags before Kade grabbed it off him. Kade then fished out a small bundle of bread and held it out.

This time, Locke didn't need to instruct the fae. Prince Azaren grabbed the bread and tore into it, sighing as he greedily chewed and swallowed it down. "You have no idea how good it is to finally have some food."

"So that sting on your arm," Locke began. "Because you've been stung by the dazra as well, you're also losing your power?"

Prince Azaren hesitated before saying slowly, "Indeed. So I would appreciate it if you didn't keep—"

He didn't finish. Locke's fist delivered a sharp blow to the prince's right temple, and the fae's eyes rolled to the back of his head before his eyelids fluttered closed and he slumped again in Locke's hold.

"What are you doing? If you keep knocking him out like that, you'll give him brain damage," Raine hissed.

Locke lowered the prince to the stone floor as if the royal was no one of consequence, and he stood, smoothing down the front of his cloak. "You heard what he said. I can already feel myself growing weak. It'll be too hard to guard the fae if we don't have our wits about us. He should be thankful I at least let him eat something."

Raine didn't respond to that. At first, I thought she simply understood what Locke was getting at, but then I noticed she was staring. Not at Locke or the fae prince but at *me.*

"Asher," she breathed as she stared up at me, her fingers curling into my shirt. I already knew I was shaking like a newborn calf taking its first steps, but there was something in the way she said my name that had my heart lurching in my chest. "Y-Your horns. What happened to your horns?" she asked.

Reaching up, I went to run a hand over my horns, only...they weren't there. "What the fuck?" My fingers dived into my soft, shaggy hair, gliding along my smooth scalp with no trace of bumps or any sign that my horns had once been there. I cursed under my breath, then another thought struck me. I twisted my neck as I peered behind me, but somehow, I already knew what I'd find. *Nothing.* Where my long, forked tail had once been was nothing but a hole in my pants, and mortifyingly, my damn ass crack was on display.

I let go of Raine and ran my hands down my back and over my ass, still unable to believe it wasn't there. "My tail," I mumbled, and my gaze shot to Darian and the others. "It's...gone."

Grunting came from my right, and Kade shook his head grimly, something akin to sorrow in his eyes. "I can't shift. I can't feel my wolf at all."

"I can't change either," Locke added as he stepped closer to us, claws no longer peeking from his fingers.

A soulful tune filled the air then, and I turned to see Darian singing with a look of concentration on his face.

"You're tryin' to use your magic on me, aren't you?" I said, unable to hide my grin at the look of frustration on his face.

"Why, do you feel like worshipping me?" he asked with amusement.

My grin split wider. "Fuck no."

Raine's gaze flicked among the four of us. "When Prince Azaren said we would lose our magic, I hadn't realized it meant you would become..."

"Human," Locke finished for her, and there was something in his eyes as he said it. It wasn't concern. No, it was awe.

I could understand the feeling. From the moment my mother started to lose her demon mind, I had wished to be human again. And now here I was, without the features that marked me as a creature of my kind. My arms were no longer shaking, but I didn't have my usual strength. My body felt feeble and pathetic without my monster strength, but the widest grin split my face. I peered behind me again. "Fuck, you could damn near finger my ass through that hole in my pants," I joked.

Raine snorted with laughter, and Darian pressed his lips tightly together to suppress his smile.

Kade strode over to Raine and began looking over her body. "How are you feeling?"

She shrugged. "I don't feel that different but maybe...empty somehow. It's hard to explain. The pain in my ankle has lessened though."

"The fae said the effects of the insects' venom lasts around three days for a fae who's been stung once. If we're to assume we react in the same way, that means we'll be humans for days," Darian pointed out. "And Raine and I will be without our magic for even longer than the rest of you."

Kade looked as though he was trying to shift again, and he cursed when nothing happened. "So what do we do now?"

I was glad he asked the question because I was wondering the same thing. I wasn't looking forward to trekking through a fae forest with my ass on display. I'd already been stung on one ass cheek, and that was through my pants.

Locke's face was cold again, his expression unreadable as he said, "We'll rest here for a while, then we'll head out. We can't afford to stop for long. Prince Azaren said the dazra won't attack if we don't give them eye contact. We'll have to hope they've moved away and don't spot us, but if they do, we'll avoid staring them in the eye."

CHAPTER 6

~ **Raine** ~

The five of us stood around awkwardly, still reeling from the fact that the dazra had nullified our powers and abilities, and the males around me weren't...monsters anymore. Well, for a short while, at least. It was hard to wrap my head around. Then again, the word *monster* didn't seem to have the same meaning to me as it once had.

It was odd seeing Asher standing there without horns or his long tail that usually flicked around in the air while he talked, and it was only then that I realized how comfortable I'd become with his appearance. When I'd first met the demon, his horns and tail along with his thick, muscular body and vivid violet eyes had made him appear menacing, but at some point, they'd just become parts of the kindhearted, mischievous male I'd come to enjoy spending time with.

Kade and Darian appeared mostly the same in their human forms, though the colors of their eyes were duller than usual. Locke lingered in the cave, and it was the first time I'd seen him look so unsure of himself. Instead of the confidence and arrogance I'd grown accustomed to with the vampire, there was a fragility about him that made me pause. The urge to go to him pulled at my insides, but when I took a step in his direction, he spun on his heels and disappeared through a tunnel opening at the back of the cave.

Darian moved up beside me, stopping me from going after him. "Let him have a moment to himself. This is...a lot for all of us."

I stared after the vampire. "But he doesn't even know what's in there."

"Locke might no longer be a vampire, but that doesn't mean he's defenseless. I'm sure he'll signal for us if he needs assistance," Darian reassured me. "Don't worry. He'll come back when he's ready."

Right, unless he's been eaten by a fae cave beast, I wanted to say, but I didn't. If Locke wanted space, I'd give it to him.

Kade and Asher had moved to relax at a drier spot at the back of the cave, and I followed Darian over to them, dropping down onto the stone, the four of us forming an uneven circle. No one spoke as we sat there, and my mind wandered to how the dazra's venom had affected me. Mostly, I felt the same, except I had this nagging feeling that I was missing something. Closing my eyes, I tried to focus and find the spark of energy that burned somewhere inside me, but after searching for some time without result, I snapped my eyes open. There was...nothing. Just emptiness and a feeling like there was something I'd forgotten, but I couldn't quite place what it was.

Darian had been singing for the past few minutes, and I turned to him, quickly enraptured by the soulful tune he sang. The lyrics spoke of a male who followed his lover to the afterlife, but while the words were sorrowful, the melody was lovely. When the cave was silent again, I smiled softly. "That was beautiful."

Darian lifted my hand and kissed it. "While I lament the loss of my power, it is also freeing to be without it," he said thoughtfully. "Even when I wasn't directing my magic at anyone, when I sang, traces of my power would often seep out and affect those around me. To be able to make music without restraint is...a gift."

A gift? I stared at Darian and found myself wondering what his life must have been like.

"I don't see what the fuss is 'bout these books," Asher said, shattering the moment as he slid one of the fae books in front of him and began flipping through the pages. Turning my thoughts from Darian, I leaned over to see Asher was holding another tale written by Sharou Zanae.

Who was this author, and were they still alive somewhere in the fae realm?

"Perhaps they have great sentimental value?" Darian suggested as he stifled a yawn.

Kade's jaw clenched. "I don't care to learn about the intentions of the fae."

Ignoring the question, I kept my eyes fixed on the book. A beautiful illustration of a yellow sun surrounded by wispy clouds opened up on the next page, and I shuffled closer to Asher, keen to see more. Like the other book I'd read, the story was written in a strange language, but a translation had been handwritten at the bottom of the page in a script I could understand. Annoyingly, before I could read the last word, Asher went to turn the page. As he did so, he accidentally slid his finger along the page's edge. "Fuck," he cursed under his breath, yanking his hand away.

"That's what you get for trying to turn the page before I'm done," I quipped at him.

Lifting his finger, Asher stared at the small line of black blood that had begun to well from the cut. Slowly, the droplet of blood grew larger, the wound not healing over. He stuffed his finger into his mouth, sucking away the blood, and used his other hand to turn the page.

I stared at him in disbelief. "Seriously, you were nearly burned to death, but you're worried about a paper cut?"

"It's worse than it looks," he defended. "Everythin' feels different. Like my whole body is more sensitive. I swear that cut was almost as painful as when you stabbed me in the shoulder. Besides, somethin' tells me the prince wouldn't be too impressed if I got blood on his book."

I grinned at the memory of when I'd jabbed my dagger into Asher's shoulder not too long ago. "Welcome to being human, big guy."

Kade sniffed the air then as if he was trying to detect the scent of something. He'd been doing it ever since he'd told us he couldn't shift, and a permanent look of irritation shadowed his face.

I didn't hide my concern. "Are you all right?"

Kade frowned, his dark brows pulling down. "Everything is duller now. Before I could scent the age of the algae growing on the rocks and identify the number of crabs that visit this cave when the sun goes down, but now"—he turned to me, his golden eyes tinged with sadness—"it's like an entire world has been closed off to me. Like I've been blinded. I didn't know it would feel like this."

My lips thinned, and I was silent as I tried to think of something sympathetic to say when Kade's demeanor abruptly changed, his lips twitching upward into a half-smile and his eyes brightening again.

I narrowed my eyes suspiciously, confused by his sudden change in attitude. "Why are you looking at me like that?"

"I may have lost my wolf for now, but I've gained something else," he replied cryptically.

"Are you talking about your sanity?" I asked.

"No," Kade said with a shake of his head. "For the next few days, I have complete control," he said calmly.

Control? The idea was laughable in our current situation. We were in an unknown land and had been chased behind a waterfall by giant buzzing insects. And now we were magicless, Kade and the others had no monster abilities, and we were effectively trapped until we attempted to leave in the hopes we could escape the dazra's territory before they spotted us.

I was about to comment that he was delusional because our situation was as chaotic as ever, when he started prowling toward me. Heat flared in his eyes, and it was only then that I understood what he meant. Until the venom from the dazra wore off, he didn't have to worry about controlling his wolf side. He didn't have to worry about controlling himself *with me.*

I gulped, and my body warmed, anticipation making my skin tingle and my heart race. In a few swift movements, Kade had dropped down beside me and pulled me onto his lap. His large arms wrapped around me, and his hard body pressed me against him, molding me to his large form.

His lips crushed against mine, pushing my head back and demanding I respond. Our bond sparked, surprisingly the only thing unaffected by the dazra's venom, but I didn't have time to question why that was. I melted into him, kissing him back and tangling our tongues.

Kade growled possessively, and while the sound wasn't as deep and rumbling as it usually was, my entire being still responded, my desire blazing hotter at the sound. Wetness pooled between my thighs, and I was already aching for him to touch me.

Kade finally pulled his lips from mine, and his voice was gravelly and full of emotion as he said, "That information about our bonds, you shouldn't have kept it from us, Mahare. You might not want to admit it, but you're ours now, and you're mad if you think we'd want to force you away from us." Even without his wolf, his eyes were carnal and wild, like he was desperate to hear that I wouldn't keep secrets from him again.

Regret went through me at the thought. I hadn't intentionally kept the information from them. I was so used to keeping my own secrets that it was now second nature. I was so accustomed to not having someone to talk to, confide in, or make decisions with. Let alone having four of those someones. I hadn't even thought that keeping that information might hurt Kade and the others. I'd just assumed they'd be happy to be free of the bonds, and I hadn't really stopped to consider they might want them to remain. I mean, I knew they held affection for me, but the bonds tied our *lives* together. If I died, they died, and I struggled to believe they could want that.

But... *You're ours now.* The possession with which he'd said those words made my throat sore, and I swallowed thickly. "I know" was all I managed to squeeze out.

Kade's hand brushed gently against my cheek. "If you want to break the bonds, we'll face it together, but we would *never* force you."

My eyes watered, and I couldn't speak with the emotion clogging my throat. Kade's hands trailed lower, sliding between my breasts, and I sucked in a sharp breath.

"Don't keep anything like that from us again," he said, and his pleading stare was so intense I couldn't look away.

"I–I won't," I said, my throat tight.

The sheer relief on Kade's face from those small words shattered me. I knew then I couldn't keep Cara from them. Not when she was such a large part of my life. Not when she could be the reason I might have to separate from them.

I wet my lips. "There...is something else I haven't told you," I said slowly. My gaze slid from Kade to Asher and Darian, who were staring at me just as intently, their expressions not judging but listening.

It was a risk to tell them about my sister. What if they knew who she was and she was their enemy? What if they didn't want to lose me that badly that they would risk hurting her? Or what if they'd known she was dead this whole time? Warrick was evil, and Locke was Warrick's son. These were Locke's friends. What if they knew a sinister, dark secret involving Cara and Warrick?

But Kade's, Asher's, and Darian's eyes were full of light as they stared at me. Their gazes were full of...*love. For me.* Even if they hadn't admitted it out loud. The least I could do was take the risk and tell them about my sister. Especially when deep down, I knew I loved them too.

No one spoke as they waited for me to continue, and I sucked in a deep breath, steeling myself. "Back on the island during the Night of the Offering, I *wanted* to be selected," I admitted quietly. "During the previous offering, all those years earlier, my sister was chosen. Cara. And it was my fault. I shouldn't have been spying on the ritual. I vowed to find her and make sure she was all right. She was only sixteen when she was selected, younger than the usual age, and I'll do anything to find her. I have to know if she's alive. And if she's unhappy and wants to leave Katakin." I paused again, my words becoming quiet. "I had planned to leave with her and find a way for us to escape." I took in another deep breath as I finished, feeling as though it had taken significant energy to get those words out.

For a moment, the cave remained silent. My uncertainty and the fears I held simmered on the surface, but deep in my core, I knew these monsters were good. That telling them was the right thing to do.

Kade was the one to speak first. "The friend you told me about. You were talking about your sister?" he asked softly. I'd told him briefly about my search for a friend nights ago after the first time we'd been together, but I hadn't given away any specific details. Now empathy shone on his face, and I knew if anyone would understand my situation, it would be him—the wolf shifter who had lost his own family to the fae. Tears welled in my eyes, and he leaned forward, cradling my face in his hands. "You should have told us. Wecould have been helping you search for her."

A tear slipped down my cheek, and I sniffed. "You'd taken me from my island just like Cara had been stolen. How was I supposed to trust you with this?"

Regret showed on Kade's face, and Asher and Darian wore similar expressions. I knew it wasn't fair to put this all on them. They had explained they had no choice and were forced by the council to play their part in the trials, but they'd still done it.

"If she means this much to you, we will find her, Raine," Darian said, his blue gaze penetrating in the dim light. "I'm not aware of any newbloods named Cara, and I haven't heard of any newbloods who were below selection age when they were brought to Katakin, but we'll find her. Together."

Another tear slipped down my face.

"Who knows? Maybe she's been under our nose this entire time," Asher said with a soft smile.

"So you're not mad?" I asked incredulously.

"Family is everything," Kade replied. "If she's your sister, that's all we needed to know."

"And if I have to leave you?" I said, a slight wobble in my voice.

It was Darian who swallowed then, his Adam's apple bobbing with the motion. "We'll deal with that when we find her. We'll find a way to break the curse, then we'll find your sister."

I blinked rapidly then, trying to keep the rest of my tears at bay. I hardly cried, but I couldn't believe how supportive Darian and the others were being. I gave them a small smile. "Well, that wasn't nearly as bad as I thought it would be," I joked.

Asher gave me a lopsided grin. "Seems we're all broken, sweetheart. No wonder you fit in so well with us."

"I'm not broken," I protested. "I'm..."

"Rare," Darian finished, the word spoken with such tenderness that I was rendered speechless. Goddess, how was it that I was in the shittiest situation possible but at the same time I felt like the luckiest girl in the world? Lifting from Kade, I dropped down onto Darian's lap, my eyes tracking over the siren's gorgeous face. His blue eyes glittered as he watched me, and when I kissed him, he kissed me back like I was his entire world and he would do anything he could to treasure me. Darian's hands tangled in my wet hair, and I surrendered to the salty and sweet taste of him.

When I opened my eyes, Asher was beside us, and Darian let Asher pull me over. My top half lay across Asher, while my bottom half remained on Darian's lap.

Asher's hands ran down the sides of my body as if he was enjoying every curve and every inch of my skin. "Kade might have lost sensation when he lost his wolf, but not me. You've always felt good in my hands, Sharachi, but not like this." His gaze lingered on my bottom lip, desire swirling in his violet eyes. "Let us help you find your sister, sweetheart. The devils know we want to." And then it was Asher's lips pressing against mine, his hands exploring my body as I melted in his arms.

It wasn't long before Asher's gentle kiss became more fevered, and then his hand was squeezing my breast while the other hand cupped the back of my neck. I moaned at his touch, the bond between us sparking and demanding more.

Darian's hand started sliding up my thigh, and goose bumps prickled over my skin. I was still kissing Asher when I felt Kade's presence behind me, his scents of sandalwood and coffee mixing with Darian's sea salt and patchouli and Asher's musk and leather. Darian and Kade worked together to pull off my pants, and then Kade was kissing the side of my neck, adding to the onslaught of sensation taking hold of me.

Asher squeezed my breast harder as his tongue dominated my mouth, and Darian's fingers brushed against my panties. He pressed his fingers against the soft material, right where I needed him most, and I bit my lip as I writhed on his lap.

Kade lightly bit my ear. His teeth dragged at my skin as he pulled back, his attention moving to my shirt. He lifted the material at my back, and Asher broke the kiss so Kade could lift the shirt over my head, leaving me completely exposed except for my panties. I wanted to complain that they were all still fully clothed, but Kade leaned down, his teeth grazing my nipple as his hand cupped the swell of my breast, and the words died in my throat. Darian pulled off my panties, dragging them down my legs, and then his fingers were sliding between my thighs, teasing the bundle of nerves there and making me gasp with pleasure.

Asher gripped my chin, his lips colliding with mine again as I squirmed in their hold, and soon all I could think about were the three males crowding around me and the way they made me feel so alive.

Darian's fingers pushed into me, and my back arched. The males brought me to the edge of my orgasm until I was sure I would explode at the slightest touch, but then they stopped, the three of them pulling away. Moving in tandem, they lifted me to my feet, holding me up despite my shaky legs.

Asher's gaze went to the smooth stone wall on the side of the cave, then he looked at Kade and Darian as a slow smile pulled across his face. Darian and Kade grinned back at him like they understood exactly what he was thinking.

"Do you trust us?" Asher asked, turning his attention to me.

I bit my lip. "I trust you not to hurt me."

His smile softened, and I let them lead me over to the wall. Darian and Kade held me up with my back pressed to the stone. Gripping under my arms, they lifted me into the air, and Asher knelt before me, moving my legs so they draped over his shoulders. He looked like a dark god, and I cried out as his tongue flicked out, and he teased my clit.

"Asher," I pleaded breathily. I wanted to reach forward and bury my fingers in his hair, but Darian and Kade held me still. Right before I was about to climax, Asher pulled back and slid my legs from his shoulders. Lifting to his feet, he straightened and freed his massive, pierced cock from his pants. I nearly whimpered at the sight of it. Asher's hands cupped under my ass, and then he was thrusting into me, his piercings sliding against my inner walls as I cried out in pleasure.

Kade buried his nose into the crook of my neck, breathing me in. "You all right, Mahare?" His voice was so sweet, so gentle that tears pricked at my eyes.

Asher pulled all the way out before pushing back into me, and I gasped, loving how full I felt.

"Harder" was all I whispered back between shuddering breaths. "I want him to fuck me harder."

Kade didn't need to relay the message. Asher thrust into me harder then, his massive cock stretching me almost beyond my limit as he slammed into me over and over.

"You feel too good, sweetheart," Asher groaned, and I rewarded him by clenching my inner muscles around his cock.

"Fuck," he breathed, his face contorting with pleasure.

Darian and Asher reached over to pinch and tease my nipples, and I couldn't last any longer. I exploded, my orgasm rushing through me and making my toes curl. Light flashed behind my eyes, and tingles spread over my skin.

Asher roared his own release a few thrusts later, his muscles locking up as he spilled himself into me. I'd barely recovered from the aftershocks from my own orgasm when Asher took Kade's place against the wall, and then it was Kade between my legs, his huge cock pushing into me.

My body came alive again at the feel of Kade's cock inside me, demanding my pleasure. *Oh Goddess.* I squeezed my eyes shut as he fucked me.

Too much. The males were too much, but I loved it. It didn't take long before I was crying out again, my stomach clenching as my release crashed through me. Kade came a moment later, his hand bracing on the wall above my head as he pulled out just in time to spill over my cunt. He stared appreciatively as his cum dripped down my thighs.

When Kade took Darian's place and the siren moved between my legs, I shook my head.

"I can't," I rasped. "It's too much."

"If you want to stop, we'll stop," Darian replied, his expression earnest as he watched my face.

I swallowed. I shouldn't have wanted more. Exhaustion dragged at me, and if it weren't for Kade and Asher holding me up, I probably would have collapsed to the ground, but it was there. That desire still coiling in my gut. Still wanting the silver-haired male before me.

"No," I said softly. "I want you. I want all of you."

Darian pressed a tender kiss to my forehead. There was a slight sting as he worked his massive cock into me, and then it was all pleasure as he slid in and out of me, teasing me open more. Darian's blue gaze remained fixed on me, and he lifted my arms above my head, his fingers intertwining with mine.

"Even if our bonds are broken, it won't change the fact that you are and always will be ours," Darian breathed.

I stared back at him, unable to speak as he filled me over and over, every thrust like it was a reminder of how perfect I was for them. When a third orgasm rushed through me, Darian came at the same time, our bodies shuddering as pleasure rippled through us, sapping our strength.

When we stopped shaking, Darian stepped back, and Kade and Asher gently lowered me from the wall. When my knees buckled, Kade scooped me into his arms. "I've got you," he said in my ear, his warm breath puffing on the side of my face. I buried my head into his chest, and my eyes fluttered closed.

I barely noticed when Kade lowered me into Darian's arms and into the water. Asher was beside him, and the pair of them cleaned me before lifting me back onto the rock shelf. Kade carried me further back into the cave, and he took off his shirt and used it to wipe the water from me. Then he pulled me against him, resting my head on his chest again.

Darian and Asher came over to us, the two of them dropping down beside us until I was cocooned by the three of them. I let out a contented sigh, and Asher chuckled and kissed the top of my hair. "Get some rest, sweetheart."

CHAPTER 7

~ Raine ~

I wasn't sure how long I'd slept, but when I awoke, Darian, Asher, and Kade were still curled around me. Lifting from Kade's chest, I moved Asher's arm from around my waist and sat up. Rubbing my eyes, I yawned before peering at the dark entrance at the back of the cave.

Darian and Kade awoke at the movement, and I murmured an apology for waking them.

Darian followed my gaze to the dark entrance. "He may not want to see you," he said gently, clearly understanding my intentions. "You can't imagine what it's like for him to be human again. His entire life he's been trying to help his father find a cure for the curse. Now he has a taste of freedom. But it won't last."

I nodded. "He may not want to see me, but I need to see him." While I was with Kade and the others, there had been this nagging thought. This feeling that someone was missing. And I knew just who that male was.

Rising to my feet, I slid on my panties and shirt but left my pants drying, splayed over a rock.

Kade moved up behind me and kissed my shoulder. "Yell and we'll come running." I didn't doubt he meant it. I took a breath and rolled my shoulders like I was preparing for a fight, then I gave Darian and Kade a confident smile and walked into the entrance.

• • • ● • ● • ● • •

~ Locke ~

After the realization that the dazra's venom had made us all human, I'd needed to escape. I'd turned away from Raine and my brothers and disappeared through the small entranceway at the back of the cave.

The winding tunnel reminded me so much of the tunnels back in the mountain in Katakin, and I hated how my body instantly loosened, soothed by the darkness and familiar surroundings. Fuck, I was damaged. My entire life I'd wanted to be human again, and now that I finally had a taste, I was running into the tunnels like a street rat searching for familiar territory.

Without my vampire sight, I was unable to see when it became pitch black, but I kept moving forward, running my hands along the walls and feeling my way. Eventually, the small tunnel led into a wide cavern illuminated by glowing green algae that covered the walls, jutting rocks hanging from above, and boulders on the ground. When I was in the middle of the cavern, I stopped. I stood there, unable to move from the spot.

I stayed like that for a long while, my mind blank and my chest feeling hollow. After some time, my stomach made a strange rumbling sound, and it took me a while before I realized what the sound meant. I was hungry for *food.*

My satchel was still around my shoulders, and I pulled out a small ration of dried meat. Synthetic blood still coated the wrapping, but I'd removed the broken glass after finding the shattered vials, and I unwrapped the parcel, revealing the small strips of meat.

Then I prepared myself to eat. Because I was now *human.* The word echoed in my mind like someone had shouted it into a void and the echo would repeat for eternity. I hadn't eaten since I'd been turned as a boy—nothing besides blood and alcohol had entered my system for two centuries. I sniffed the parcel, and the scent of spiced beef didn't make my stomach roil like it normally would. Instead, my stomach growled again, this time even louder than before.

Saliva pooled in my mouth as I longed to taste the food, but at the same time, I couldn't bring myself to do it. I couldn't risk trying it in case I was dreaming, and I was still the same vampire I'd become when the curse was created. The devils only knew how long I stood there, staring at those stupid strips of meat.

I hardly registered the soft patter of footsteps until Raine stepped into the cavern. I felt the moment her gaze landed on me. The female watched me warily as she approached like she was worried I'd sense her presence and either bolt or attack her. The second idea was laughable. I was much less of a threat now than all the other times she'd been around me. Still, she moved toward me slowly, purposely making her steps loud in what I could only guess was an effort not to startle me. I had to admit that the fact I hadn't heard the steady beat of her heart as she approached unsettled me.

When she was an arm's length away, she stopped, her gaze sliding from the dried strips in my hand and then to my face. "Feeling hungry?" she said, and her voice was light but tentative. Unsure.

Even without my vampire senses, I could scent what my brothers and her had been doing while I was away. The thought didn't leave me with jealousy. All it left me with was regret.

I remained silent, not confirming her guess, but I kept staring at the damn meat strips in my hand. Awkwardly, she turned her attention to our surroundings. "I used to think Katakin was the most beautiful place I'd ever see," she said as she marveled at the glowing algae covering the walls, "but there's something about the fae realm. Every new place we find ourselves in is spectacular."

I didn't disagree with her, but it was hard to focus on the beauty around me. Not when I knew the blood that was on the fae's hands. There was a time when Kade's mother and sister were almost like my own family, and I was as keen to make the fae pay as Kade was.

When I remained silent, Raine's gaze went back to the food in my hand. Gingerly, she reached out, and I let her take it from my fingers.

"It must be strange," she commented. "Being able to eat food again after so long without it."

This time, I looked at her. Seven devils, she was gorgeous. Wearing only her shirt and panties, the female was as tempting as ever. "I don't think I can eat it," I admitted to her. I thought I would be embarrassed saying something as ridiculous as that out loud, but there was something about Raine that made me feel so at ease. Like no matter what I said, she would understand.

Raine held up one of the strips with her hand. "Well, I know it doesn't look that appetizing, but it's surprisingly delicious. You'll have to work your jaw a bit, but that shouldn't stop you."

I wondered if she knew that Asher had dried and flavored the meat himself. My stomach growled again, and this time it was loud enough that if I were back in Katakin, they might have mistaken me for a wolf shifter.

She grinned. "I don't know if you know this, but we mere humans need food to survive. I think your stomach is trying to tell you something."

I arched a brow at her then. Not because I, of course, knew humans needed food, but because she continued to call herself a human when it was clear she was anything but. She'd used magic on multiple occasions now, and it was obvious she was turning into some kind of monster, but she still refused to admit it to herself. In a way, it reminded me of when I'd first turned as a child. I'd wanted so badly to believe it wasn't true. It wasn't until I was ravenous and ripping out the throats of my friends that the harsh truth had become impossible to deny. And she would have to come to terms with it, too. That was, unless we found a way to break the curse over Katakin.

"I'm aware of that," I responded.

"Are you? Because you've been staring at this meat like you're not sure what to do with it," she said, shaking the strip she held up in midair.

"I'm sure I can figure out how to chew again," I replied dryly.

She stared at me skeptically. "All right, then prove it." She lifted the strip closer to my mouth as if she intended to force-feed me like some fucking babe. I glowered, but she just waggled the little strip in my face. "Open wide, big boy, it's your turn to eat some meat."

Fucking seven devils, this female and her sass. I simultaneously wanted to strangle her and crow with laughter at the comment.

Her eyes sparkled with amusement, and she chuckled at her own joke. My eyes narrowed, and I opened my mouth to curse at her, but quicker than I could get the words out, she shoved the strip into my mouth.

"Chew," she commanded like she thought I'd listen.

I went to spit the damn thing out, but flavor exploded on my tongue, rich spices and salt making my mouth water, and the challenging look Raine was giving me made me hesitate. It was like she dared me to spit it out in front of her. Devils, the confidence of this female.

My nostrils flared in annoyance, but slowly I started to work my jaw, chewing on the strip of meat and softening it. I wanted to fucking hate it. I didn't want to be reminded of the things I was missing out on by being a vampire, a monster, but a small groan slipped out of me as the meat melted on my tongue. I chewed faster, relishing the salty flavor as I swallowed and it trailed down the back of my throat.

Raine stared smugly at me. "It's good, right? Goddess, I wish I had the chance to taste food again for the first time."

I couldn't stop myself then. A wolfish smile curved my lips. I could think of something she hadn't tasted yet, and for once I wouldn't have to worry about accidentally succumbing to my bloodlust and draining her dry.

Unaware of my intentions, she had moved on from the topic of food and was busy rambling about how incredible our surroundings were again. The space was romantic, I had to admit. I could imagine fae males bringing their sweethearts to the hidden space to woo them amidst the glowing lights of the algae and quiet ambience of the cavern. Unfortunately for Raine, romancing females wasn't something I was practiced at.

My dark gaze fixed on the side of her face. "Get on your knees," I ordered abruptly, cutting off her latest remark.

She frowned in confusion like she wasn't sure if she'd heard me correctly. "What?"

"On your knees, *beautiful*," I repeated slowly, enjoying the way my nickname for her rolled off my tongue. A nickname that was all too fitting for the delicious female beside me. Glowing light illuminated her naked skin, giving it a silvery sheen and her fiery hair was still damp from the river and clinging to her shoulders and neck.

I expected her to argue. The female was strong-willed, and she could be unpredictable at the best of times, but her gaze slid to the front of my pants, and her eyes heated at what she saw there.

Licking her lips, she hesitated only a moment before slowly moving in front of me and dropping to her knees. I reached down to free myself, and my cock hardened even more at the surprised gasp that left her delicate throat.

She lifted her gaze to my face, peering up at me with those gorgeous amber eyes, and I reached around to tangle my fingers in her long, wet hair.

"Open your mouth," I commanded.

She stared back at my cock and swallowed hard. "I don't know if— "

"Either you take me in your mouth like a good girl, or I'll fuck your ass instead. Your choice, beautiful."

A shudder of anticipation went through her, but her hand wrapped around the base of my cock, and she opened her mouth, taking me in. Fuck, her mouth felt good.

Her tongue teased the head of my cock, and she moved forward, taking more of me. She began moving her mouth and hand in tandem, and I groaned, my fingers tightening in her hair as she had her way with me. I'd intended to dominate her mouth, but Raine took control, her perfect lips tight around my shaft as she licked and sucked, hollowing her cheeks and making me unravel before her.

My body tightened, pressure building as I neared my release. No female had ever made me feel such pleasure. In the past, I only fucked females from behind so that I couldn't see their faces, but not with Raine. She let out a small whimper of desire as she took me deeper into her throat, and when she began to pull back again, I exploded, my gaze fixed on her beautiful face as I spilled myself into her.

When my body stopped jerking, she slid my cock from her mouth and swallowed my seed without a thought. I was still reeling, my breathing shallow and ragged when she stood. Wiping her mouth, she stared at me with equal parts desire and disbelief. Like she couldn't believe what she'd just done. It wasn't regret but...uncertainty.

She turned from me without a word and took a step back toward the tunnel entrance, but my arm shot out, curling around her waist. Coming up behind her, I spoke in her ear, "Where are you going?"

"Well, I assumed—" she began.

"Assumed what? That I'd leave you wanting after you were just on your knees before me?" My voice was deep, my cock already beginning to harden again at her close proximity.

I reached around with my other hand, brushing up her thigh toward her panties, and a shiver worked its way down her spine. Satisfaction went through me at her response. "No, beautiful, I have plans for you," I rasped.

Her breathing hitched, and I hummed against her neck, enjoying the way I could take in her scent without being overwhelmed by the desire to drink from her. Fuck, if only the effects of the dazra's venom would last.

Pulling back, I removed my black cloak and laid it out on the ground, then I motioned for her to sit on it. It wasn't much, I knew, and it was still damp, but it would help against the cold of the stone underneath our feet. A small smile lifted her lips, and she dropped down, her amber eyes watching me curiously.

"This is, uh, nice," she said awkwardly, and I chuckled darkly.

"Lie back," I instructed.

To my delight, she didn't argue, her eyes widening as she lay back on the cloak.

"Now remove your panties," I said as I lowered, moving in front of her.

Her body tensed, and she didn't move.

"If you don't take them off, I'll rip them from you, and as far as I'm aware, you don't have a spare," I pointed out.

She obviously saw the sense in that, because she promptly pulled them off.

"Now spread your legs for me."

Biting her lip, she spread her legs, and I let out an appreciative sound at the sight of her before me.

"Good girl," I praised, and lust flared brighter in her eyes.

Gripping her thighs, I began kissing up her left leg, and she watched me intently, her breathing shallow.

When I'd almost reached the apex of her thighs, I reached out, my fingers sliding along her center.

"Did you think of me?" I asked. "When my brothers fucked this pretty pink pussy?"

My tongue slid up her as I teased her entrance, and I growled, the taste of her in my mouth driving me wild.

"Please," she pleaded, her thighs trembling.

"Did you think of me?" I asked again, my tongue savoring her.

Her body writhed, desperate for more. Desperate for *me*.

"Yes," she breathed quietly, and my dark heart constricted, a warmth unlike anything I'd ever felt seeping into me.

I pushed two fingers into her body, my teeth grazing her clit, and she cried out.

I relished that I could make her feel like this. That I could suck on her clit without having to worry about the irresistible desire to sink my fangs into her thigh and drag her blood into my mouth.

I teased and pleasured her relentlessly until she was almost sobbing with the need for release.

"I want to hear my name on your lips when you come," I told her.

"Please," she begged again.

"Say it," I said, my voice hard. "Say my name, Raine."

She swallowed, her face destroyed by desire, and when my teeth grazed her clit again, my fingers fucking into her so fast I was like a devil possessed, she shattered.

"Locke," she cried out, pleasure demanding everything from her. I kept going until her body stilled, the aftershocks giving way to exhaustion, and she slumped back, her chest rising and falling rapidly as she let out panting breaths.

As I moved from between her legs and came up beside her, she stared at me, her eyes surprised but sated. I couldn't help myself then. I brushed the hair from her face, tucking a strand behind her ear. She stilled at my touch, but she didn't move away. She just stared at me, like she wasn't sure what I would do next.

My beautiful Raine. The adjusted nickname sounded in my head, feeling way too right. She was becoming my light in the darkness, and with every moment she remained close to me, I was finding it harder to deny my feelings for her. I was beginning to realize that this female was mine, and I didn't know how the fuck she was going to survive me when I was a vampire again.

"Locke, there's something else I need to tell you," she said, breaking the silence between us. "Something I've already told the others."

I tensed, my mind going straight to the information the fae had spilled about our bonds. I *had* only been searching for a way to break our bonds just nights ago. Raine needed to be free of us, but...I didn't want to let her go. The idea that she might have broken it without telling us, that she could have left us, had me wanting to rage, as irrational as it was.

"We should make the choice about our bonds together. The five of us," I said.

She was silent for a moment, but then she added carefully, "It's not that. It's about my sister."

CHAPTER 8

It was night when we left the safety of the cave behind the waterfall and risked venturing back into the forest. A part of me wished we could have stayed where we were. We hadn't exactly been safe there, but for a short while, I'd been able to simply enjoy the company of the four males.

Locke walked beside me, paying attention to the forest around us, but I could still feel his hands on my skin and his tongue between my legs.

"It's too quiet," Kade said with a scowl, one hand gripping Prince Azaren, who was slung over his shoulder. "I don't know how humans survive. It's like I'm walking around deaf and blind."

"Sometimes silence is bliss," I responded with a shrug.

Kade didn't look convinced. "We won't hear the dazra until they're already upon us."

"Just keep alert and put your head down if you hear any buzzing," Locke said.

Right. Don't look the dazra in the eyes, I reminded myself.

We moved slower than we had before the dazra attack, but by some miracle, hours passed and we didn't encounter any of the giant insects. I was busy staring at the never-ending trees when something unusual caught my eye. I frowned, moving closer to the tree to get a better look, but when I realized what I was looking at, I jumped back in fright.

"Whoa there, sweetheart. There are easier ways to get my attention," Asher chuckled, catching me before I slammed into him. "Say my name and I'm there," he said with a lopsided smile.

I grinned back at him before tipping my head toward the tree I'd been looking at.

"Well, that is...surprising," Darian said, tightening his grip on the fae books as he moved closer to inspect the tree.

I slid from Asher's arms to step up beside Darian. "That's not... A fae wasn't trapped in the tree, were they?" I asked with a grimace.

Darian didn't answer.

Locke came up on my other side, and his expression hardened as he peered at the feminine face that was protruding from the tree trunk, formed of the same wood as the tree. The eyes were closed as if the female was sleeping, and delicate, pointed ears were only just visible on the sides of her head.

Asher scrunched his face at the sight of it. "Well, that's fuckin' creepy."

Darian inspected the face more closely, clearly not as bothered as the rest of us. "Look at the detail," he mused.

I stepped back, not wanting to stare at the face any longer. In fact, I was quite happy if we moved away from it as quickly as possible.

"There are more over here," Kade called out from a few paces ahead, and I spotted the two other faces on different tree trunks. Like the first face, they all had feminine features, and their eyes were closed like they were sleeping. *Or like they're dead.* A chill went through me at the thought.

I tried to tell myself the faces were only carvings. That a forest fae merely had a sick sense of humor. If we ever met the artist, I would be sure to tell them it was not, in fact, funny. I already felt like the trees were watching us as we passed. The last thing I needed was to see actual faces on them.

Locke nudged my arm, and I followed him as he began walking again. "We should keep moving. Whether those faces are carvings or remnants of beings who have been trapped in the trees, the one who created them might live around here. I can't imagine they'll be too happy to find us."

At the mention of a new threat, all four males moved into position around me protectively as we walked. I pulled out one of my daggers and gripped it tightly. Being turned into a tree wasn't exactly the future I'd envisioned for myself.

The air grew thicker, and an uneasy feeling made my stomach churn, but we didn't see any more faces as we continued forward, nor did we see any tracks or signs of fae living in the forest. By the time sunlight washed over us, I was about to ask if we could stop for a rest when a breeze swept through the forest, rustling the leaves of the trees and making the hairs rise on the back of my neck. Faint whispers carried on the wind, and I tried to make out the words.

Asher lifted his axes, and his muscles flexed. "You hear that?" he asked us.

"It's like the forest is talking," Darian responded with a nod.

My face blanched. "But the trees can't be alive, can they?"

The crackle of a leaf sounded on my right, and I whipped my head in that direction, but there was nothing there.

"We're being watched," Locke said from beside me as the whispers became louder and my head grew light. *What now?* I was starting to hate this forest. Locke and the others swayed, their eyes fluttering closed, and then darkness took me as well.

CHAPTER 9

~ **Raine** ~

I was woken from sleep by the sound of excited feminine whispering. For the briefest moment, I thought I was back on my island, listening to the girls gush about the upcoming moon festival, but then I registered the hard press of the ground against my back and the scents of vegetation and earth. No, I wasn't on the island; I was in the fae realm with Locke and the others, and we weren't alone.

Adrenaline spiked through me, but I was careful to remain still. Slowly, I cracked an eye open just enough that I could make out the three slender figures hovering over me and my monsters. Dressed in gowns of apple green, the figures, who appeared to be female, bent over Locke and the others. The males were still unconscious, and the fae tugged at their clothes and openly admired their bodies.

I stayed silent, hoping the fae would give away some information. I had no idea what powers the fae had, whereas I, on the other hand, had none thanks to the dazra's venom still in my veins.

"Holy sugar plums! Geralda, look at this one's biceps!" squeaked the smallest female, who was pointing at Asher. Her bright-green hair trailed behind her head in soft curls and a tinge of pink stained her cheeks. "They're almost as thick as my head," she added with a giggle.

"Forget about that," drawled a female with sharper features and green hair that was cut into a bob. She was crouched and leaning uncomfortably close to Darian, and I had a sudden possessive urge to tell her to back the fuck up. "Check out this one's massive —" she began.

"Would you both stop perving on the brutes!" snapped the third female. "All your squealing and ogling is going to wake them up." From the hard expression on this fae's face, and her deep, reprimanding tone, I guessed that out of the three, she was the one who usually made the decisions.

The female with the green bob whom the other fae had called Geralda rose to her feet and planted her hands on her hips. "They won't wake for at least another hour when our magic wears off. You worry too much, Katia."

"And you don't worry enough," chastised the female, who I now knew was named Katia.

The smallest female canted her head as she stared at Locke's sleeping face. With his long black lashes, pale skin, and sleek raven-colored hair, he almost looked like a masculine doll while he slept rather than the predator I knew he was. "I'd hardly say they're brutes. They're so handsome," she said dreamily, and just the idea that she was lusting over Locke had me clenching my fist at my side.

At least I now knew the magic would wear off before too long. The fae would get a rude awakening when Locke and the others came to their senses.

Katia jabbed the smallest female's side with her finger. "What did I say, Frey?"

"Ouch!" the female named Frey complained, rubbing at her assaulted ribs. "What? Even *you* can't deny they're sexy. It's been so long since we've had decent company. What if they're nice?"

Katia rubbed at her temples in frustration. "Can't you see what they are?" She pointed accusingly at Locke's exposed ears. "They're not nice. They're *humans*."

"H-Humans?" stuttered Frey as she took a startled step away from Locke. "Wait..." A horrified expression crossed her face. "You don't think they're the ones who killed King Jazrec, do you?" Her wide green gaze swiped from Katia to Geralda like she expected them to have all the answers.

Katia sighed heavily. "No, they can't be. Everyone knows Queen Izla cursed the humans who killed her father. They must have come from somewhere else. But that doesn't mean they're not dangerous."

Frey shook her head in disbelief. "Are you sure they aren't fae using glamours?"

"And who would glamour themselves to look human here? Being human is a death sentence," Katia said harshly. "No, we must send word to the king."

At that moment, Locke's finger twitched. *Wait, was that—?* Kade shifted slightly, and his dark brows lowered, his eyes moving beneath his eyelids. Thankfully, Katia and the other fae didn't seem to notice. If the males came to, I was sure the five of us could take on the three fae. The fae had magic on their side, but I hoped the element of surprise would work for us. Even Darian and Asher were showing subtle signs that they were regaining consciousness, the small twitches of their bodies signaling that they would soon wake.

Frey walked between the sleeping males, seemingly too distracted with her thoughts to notice what was happening. She frowned as her gaze slid to something a short distance away, and I knew the exact moment she'd spotted the prince. Her face contorted with surprise, her eyes widening to resemble small moons and her jaw falling open. "It can't be," she squeaked as she scurried away. I realized then that Kade must have dropped the prince a little before he'd blacked out.

Geralda and Katia gasped as they followed Frey's line of sight, and they sprang forward, following after the smaller female.

"The crown prince!" Geralda wailed a moment later.

I couldn't see what they were doing now that they were out of my line of sight, and I tensed, ready to dart to my feet. *C'mon, guys. Wake up,* I mentally willed Kade and the others.

"He's still alive. Thank the gods!" Katia exclaimed with a relieved sigh. "Oh, this is much worse than I thought."

"What have they done to you?" Geralda asked with a shaky sob, and I could only guess her comment was directed at the prince. A beat passed, and her voice was cold when she added, "He's been brutalized."

"No," Katia replied darkly. "He's been tortured."

"Tortured?" Frey squeaked.

"Come on, my Prince. You need to wake," Geralda said, and my heart began to race. If they went to attack me or the others, I'd have to act, but I didn't have a weapon. My gaze flicked to where the fae had taken our weapons and collected them into a pile a few yards away. Too far. They were too damn far.

I clenched my fists even tighter.

"That one's awake!" Geralda shrieked abruptly, and my heart leaped to my throat as her green gaze collided with mine. She lifted her hands, and magic prickled through the air.

Oh fuck.

I rolled to my side a split second before a tree speared out of the ground right where I'd just been, growing upward until it resembled the other massive trees around us. If I'd remained there, the plant would have pierced through my chest and carried me upward with it.

Trying not to dwell on the fact that I'd almost just died, I jumped to my feet.

"This isn't what it looks like," I said, trying to defuse the situation.

Geralda's green eyes glistened with anger, and her hands remained outstretched in front of her.

"Geralda, what are you doing!" Frey said in a panicked whisper.

"Humans took our King Jazrec and Queen Izla, and now they're trying to take our crown prince. Well, I won't let them," Geralda seethed. Gone was the playful demeanor of the fae I'd first seen when I'd awoken. Now hatred made her top lip curl, and she puffed out her chest as she glared at me.

"We didn't torture him!" I said, my eyes pleading with them to believe me. "We saved him!"

Geralda's expression hardened, and she flicked her hand. More magic prickled in the air, and a muscled chest slammed into me from the side, pushing me out of the way.

Locke kept his arms wrapped around me protectively as we fell to the ground, and his strong scent of cedarwood, ash, and spice helped calm my shaking hands. I gaped at the giant tree that now grew in the space where I'd just been standing. It had grown so fast that if Locke hadn't pushed me out of the way, I would have been speared by the damn thing.

"They know the prince is with us. They're going to tell the king," I gasped, and Locke clenched his jaw so tightly it twitched.

"No, they're not," Asher said with a casual grin that didn't meet his eyes. Kade and Darian were also awake, and the three of them moved in front of Locke and me as we climbed to our feet.

"We won't let you hurt him anymore!" Geralda screamed, angry tears welling in her eyes.

Asher lifted his hands with his palms out in a placating gesture. "Now, now, we weren't the ones who did that. Well, maybe Kade here gave your prince a few bumps on the head, but—" His words were cut off as he dodged a wooden arrow that Katia had seemingly created out of thin air and launched at him. Fury glistened in Katia's eyes, rivaling the hatred emanating from Geralda.

Frey whimpered and dropped down to clutch at the prince. Reaching into her pocket, she lifted something and waved it under his nose. "My prince, you must wake!" she cried.

"We just need to make them understand," I insisted, but Locke's black eyes were unkind as he glared at the fae females.

Two more trees sprouted out of the ground, and this time, it was Darian and Kade who narrowly avoided being speared. Asher darted to the right, dropping low to avoid another arrow from Katia and only stopping when he reached the pile of weapons.

"Catch," he barked and tossed weapons to the rest of us.

Frey whimpered again, and Geralda snarled with anger.

Soon a dozen trees were sprouting out of the ground courtesy of Geralda's wrath and accompanied by Katia's arrows.

We all sprang into action, the scene turning to chaos as we defended ourselves against the fae. Locke sliced his sword through an arrow that was aimed at his face. "We need to shut this down," he said coldly as if we'd all simply been playing this whole time.

Kade cracked his neck. "Couldn't agree more," he growled, his teeth bared even though he had no fangs.

Like the males had danced the same dance a thousand times, they moved fluidly and efficiently, circling around the fae females and dodging the arrows and trees. Within moments, Kade had Geralda kneeling before him, her hands gripped behind her back. Asher had Katia in a similar position, and Frey had let go of Prince Azaren and was backing away from Darian, fear shining in her green eyes.

"We're not the enemy," Locke said as we approached the fae females.

Katia kept her lips tightly pressed together, but Geralda snarled, "King Chalir will have your soul for this. You will see."

"You don't understand. We came here to return the prince—" I started, but Geralda wasn't listening.

Katia's head tilted to the side, and her mouth opened and began moving, though I couldn't hear her speak any words. The trees around us began to sway as though affected by some unnatural wind, and the faintest sound of whispers carried through the forest, fluttering the leaves and making the hairs stand up on my arms.

"Kill our prince if you must, but know that retribution will be ours," Katia seethed. "We fight another day, narelas," she added, and this time, as if those last words were a command, all three fae females closed their eyes and bowed their heads.

Kade, Asher, and Darian moved back as the fae transformed, their bodies hardening and growing into silver-white trees that rose high into the air. Thin branches burst from their trunks, and vibrant green leaves sprouted in bushy patches. The females' faces molded into the wood, forming into the same faces we'd seen on the tree trunks not too long ago.

"Well, that's not something you see every day," Darian mused.

CHAPTER 10

"So I'm guessin' that didn't go well for us," Asher said as he craned his neck to look at the top of the tree Katia had transformed into. "Do you think they can still hear us?"

"Anything's possible in this place," Kade growled, circling the tree that used to be Geralda.

Darian ran a hand over his silver hair, smoothing the long, tousled locks back into place. "One thing is certain: the fae king now knows we have Prince Azaren. Or if he doesn't know yet, he will soon." Darian moved to grab the remainder of his weapons which were still on the ground, and I did the same.

Locke's dark gaze landed on Prince Azaren, who was starting to stir, likely roused by whatever Frey had waved under his nose. "I think it's about time we extracted some information from our guest. If he is telling the truth about the effects of the dazra's venom, he should be without his power for a while yet."

"Just because he doesn't have access to his magic doesn't mean he can't cause trouble," Kade growled, clearly not impressed with the idea of talking to the fae.

Asher's gaze swiped from Kade to Locke, but he moved to crouch next to Prince Azaren. Gripping the front of the prince's shirt, he yanked the fae up and delivered a sharp slap to his cheek. "Wakey, wakey, sunshine."

When Prince Azaren's eyes blinked open, Asher let go of the prince's shirt and let him drop to the grass. Groaning, Prince Azaren slowly lifted onto his elbows. He squinted against the sunlight and lifted a hand in front of his face before focusing his attention on Asher, who was still squatting close by. "Water," he rasped, wincing when he tried to swallow.

Locke dug into his satchel and tossed a canteen at the prince. It hit Prince Azaren's chest, and he snatched it up and pulled off the lid before drinking greedily. Water dripped down the fae's slender chin, and when he'd drained the last of it, he let out an appreciative sigh. "Gods, how long have I been out?" He passed the canteen to Asher. "And was that really necessary?" he added indignantly, his attention going back to Locke.

Locke stepped closer to the prince, and his hand rested on the hilt of his sword at his side. "If you so much as look like you're concentrating too hard and trying to access your magic, I won't hesitate to end you." His words were cold and harsh, and I had no doubt Locke would uphold his word.

I wasn't sure if the prince assumed Locke was bluffing or if he was simply too concussed to care what came out of Locke's mouth, but he didn't seem the least bit fearful when he nodded his head in an exaggerated manner. "Yes, yes, I'm dead if I use my magic. You needn't worry, as I still feel the dazra's venom in me suppressing my powers. Besides, I'm an enoram. Now, if you'll kindly help me up." He directed the last part at Asher, who looked a little baffled by the request.

When Asher didn't move to help him, Prince Azaren twisted onto his side and slowly lifted to his feet. His legs wobbled unsteadily, his knees almost knocking together, but when he remained standing, he grinned proudly and straightened. Even with the cuts and bruises over his body, somehow the male still had an air of importance about him. "I see you were able to leave the cave without another incident with the dazra," he commented as his emerald gaze raked over us, then he turned his attention to the clearing we were standing in. Undoubtedly, he was trying to determine our location in the forest.

"What is an enoram?" I asked, genuinely curious as to why he thought explaining such would help convince us he wasn't a threat.

Prince Azaren's gaze slid back to me. "An enoram is someone who doesn't believe in the use of violence for any reason. I've never used my magic to harm a soul, and I'm not about to start now."

"No violence?" Asher asked in horror, acting like the prince had just spluttered some forbidden curse word. "Now where would be the fun in that?"

"I believe there are always other methods that will harbor more favorable results. True power lies in the pursuit of knowledge and enlightening others," Prince Azaren replied earnestly.

"How noble," Kade sniped, still glaring at the prince like he was imagining driving a dagger through the fae's heart.

Locke motioned to the prince's bloodied clothes. "And I suppose the monster from whom you stole your clothing was not harmed when you liberated him from his attire."

Prince Azaren shrugged casually. "I found the clothing hanging on a balcony when I made my way through your city. I said I didn't believe in violence, but I never said anything about stealing. And speaking of stealing..." His words trailed off as he peered around us, but he soon spotted the four fae books scattered close by. Darian had dropped them when the forest fae had knocked us out, and no one had picked them back up. Kade tensed as Prince Azaren moved to collect the fairy tales, but Locke shook his head, signaling for Kade to let him be.

Prince Azaren bent to pick up one of the books, and he brushed some dirt from the cover. "Though, I dare say taking the books wasn't stealing but rather reclaiming seeing as they rightfully belong to my family." He frowned then as he stared at the other three books still on the ground. "Where are the rest of them?"

"They're safe," Locke answered, taking a step forward. "Cooperate and help us find a way to break the curse over Katakin, and you can have them back."

Prince Azaren stilled, and his eyes flared wide with panic. "No, you don't understand," he said with a shake of his head. "Those books are priceless. You need to tell me where they are. I brought them here, and if they get into the wrong hands—"

"Correction," Asher said butting in. "Locke and Raine brought them through the portal, not you."

"Only because your *friend* here rendered me unconscious," Prince Azaren retorted, staring at Kade with annoyance. Kade simply stood there with his arms crossed, his brow forming a hard line.

"Our friend here saved your life," Locke pointed out. "The quicker you tell us what we need to know and we deliver you to the fae, the sooner we'll tell you the location of the other books. So if they're as important as you say, agree to the terms."

Guilt seeped into me as I thought of where the other books were strewn around the forest floor, surrounded by murderous toadstools. I mean, they had to be reasonably safe, right? Unless some forest animal decided to have a snack or it started raining, that was. In any case, I rationalized that if the prince wanted us to keep the books safe, then he shouldn't have created the portal near the death fungi.

"Wait, you want to deliver me back to the fae?" Prince Azaren asked in surprise, pulling me from my musings.

"Like I said back in the cave, we're here to find a way to break the curse over Katakin," I explained. "If we can stop a war from breaking out while we're at it, that would be great."

"Raine," Kade growled my name in warning, but I pressed on.

What did it matter if the prince knew our intentions? He was likely the only fae who could help us. "If you are truly against violence, then prove it. The citizens of Katakin have suffered for centuries. Help us remove the curse and make them human again, and they won't be a threat anymore. There is no need for war." Realistically, I knew asking Prince Azaren to help the monsters of Katakin after he had just been tortured by Warrick was ridiculous, but there was something about the prince that made me believe his story about being an enoram. And what better way to avoid violence than to prevent a war?

Prince Azaren studied us all for a long moment before answering. "I can help keep you alive and out of my father's dungeon, but I can't promise to provide you with the secrets on how to break the curse. What my aunt did had never been done before, but I will try my best to find an answer in our ancient tomes. Some of the works detail information about forbidden magic and may be of use." He paused then, his face growing serious. "But then you must tell me where my missing books are. The pages must not fall into the wrong hands. Not everyone in this realm is as honorable as I."

It didn't escape my notice that he said "the pages" rather than the books or the stories. *What is on the pages of the books?*

"Agreed," Locke said without hesitation.

"Now about that part where you said you could keep us out of your father's dungeon," Darian said. "We encountered some friends of yours quite recently."

"Yes, I gathered I wasn't the only fae you'd had the pleasure of speaking to in the last while," Prince Azaren said with a sly smile, his gaze flicking to where Katia, Geralda, and Frey still stood as giant trees.

"What are they?" Kade asked, curiosity getting the better of him.

"Dryads, of course," Prince Azaren said like the answer was obvious. "Otherwise known as spirits of the forest. Kind fae who help protect all you see around you."

Darian ran a hand down his chest like he was checking his stars were in their proper places, hidden in their pouches. "Those kind fae just attacked us and have sent word to King Chalir of our existence. I am sure they believe us to be your torturers and kidnappers."

"How long will it be before your father comes for us?" Locke asked.

I had thought the prince would be glad to hear his father was coming to get him, but he only looked even more fatigued. "Dryads are wonderful fae, but everyone knows they are the biggest gossips of the forest. It shouldn't be too hard to change the story. I can't be certain how long it will take for word to reach the king, but the dryads can use the trees to pass messages, and I suspect guards could arrive at any moment."

"Then I guess we'd best be expectin' company," Asher said as he pulled out his axes and twirled them in the air.

"What are our chances of evading him?" Kade asked.

Prince Azaren shook his head. "If you had your monster abilities, perhaps there would have been a chance. But without them..." He trailed off before saying, "None."

Locke and Kade shared a look, but Prince Azaren started speaking again. "You *have* lost your abilities, haven't you?" he queried. "Or was it only him?" He tilted his head toward Asher.

When no one answered, he added, "If you were all stung by the dazra, it could work to our advantage. My father will assume you're human."

"I'm not so sure that's a good thing," Darian said. "Your dryad friends didn't seem too pleased by the presence of humans in their forest."

Prince Azaren didn't appear concerned. "The fae despise the monsters of Katakin. After all, your human King Adrien murdered my grandfather, King Jazrec. Not to mention, you took my beautiful aunt Izla from us, formerly a princess in our realm but a queen in yours. Still, it's common knowledge that all the humans in Katakin were turned into monsters by my aunt's curse. We've had little contact with any other realms, but the fact you appear human may make my father more sympathetic. He might believe you are also humans who were captured by the Katakin monsters."

I shifted on the spot, feeling uneasy because of the major fault I found in the prince's plan. "But if the magic wears off..."

"I shall try to find the information about the curse before that happens, but it is, of course, a risk," Prince Azaren admitted.

"I don't like this," Kade growled to Locke and the others.

Prince Azaren rubbed his chin. "Don't show any hostility while you are in the castle, and as long as your magic is suppressed, you should be safe. Once I've given you information about the curse, you can tell me where my missing books are located. When the books are in my hands, I can create a portal to send you to Katakin."

It sounded too simple. Much too easy to be possible. Darian and the others looked as skeptical as I felt, but Locke canted his head. "If you betray us, you will never learn the location of your books," he reminded Prince Azaren, and the prince narrowed his eyes.

"Then I'd best not betray you," Prince Azaren replied.

It seemed wrong to trust the prince given what little we knew about him and his intentions, but what choice did we have?

With that, our group began walking again, weaving a path between the trees and trekking toward the city. From what we learned from Prince Azaren, King Chalir would find us now, no matter where we went in the forest, but it felt good to be moving again.

Kade and the others refused to let me walk next to the fae, but I still managed to ask him questions about his world, like why he'd chosen to create the portal in a spot near a sea of murderous toadstools. In response to the question, the prince's grin split wide, and he explained that unless they're disturbed, the toadstools are completely harmless. He figured they would be useful if enemies were to follow him through the portal back to the fae realm, and I had to admire his plan.

I was busy asking the prince more about the dryads and how many of them lived in the forest when the air crackled with energy.

Instinctively, Locke, Kade, Asher, and Darian halted and drew their weapons. The four of them took up positions around me, making a misshapen circle, and their bodies hardened. I pulled out two of my knives, knowing I could launch them between the males if I needed to.

Even Prince Azaren looked apprehensive at his father's arrival, and that wasn't doing much for my confidence.

"Here he comes," Prince Azaren announced with a weak smile.

CHAPTER II

~ Darian ~

My muscles tensed as a ring of blue fire appeared a few paces in front of me, growing to become larger than any portal I'd seen before. Armed soldiers exited the ring in double file, their armor chinking and their boots smacking on the ground as they poured into the forest, forming a single neat line as they surrounded our group. Sunlight reflected off the soldiers' silver helmets, and the fae guards took up offensive stances, angling their spears inward.

Hold. My muscles twitched as I forced myself to remain still. My hands shifted slightly, my grip tightening on the hilt of my sword. Seven devils, how my fingers longed to slide out three of my stars and sink them into the three fae closest to me. But I knew my sword would serve me better in close combat, and we were supposed to act like peaceful humans. It made sense that we might instinctively grab our weapons, but ideally, there wouldn't actually be any bloodshed.

Humans. I'd been enjoying my time without my siren abilities, but now, for the first time since the dazra's venom had changed me, I wished I had my power back. With a few notes, I could have entranced the fae soldiers and given us a chance at defeating them. That was, I could have tried. In truth, I couldn't know what powers these fae wielded and whether my magic would have even affected them. The soldiers around us all appeared the same with golden skin; long, lithe limbs; and delicately pointed ears, but I suspected that like the monsters in Katakin, there was a large variety when it came to the powers each individual possessed.

I hoped the prince's plan would work, but all it would take was one strike. If a single weapon was launched in my lovely Raine's direction, I wouldn't hesitate to protect her and kill her attacker. The thought of cutting down a fae soldier brought a small smile to my face. I didn't know Kade's sister and mother well, but I saw how their deaths destroyed him. I'd happily help Kade get his vengeance on the fae if it came to it.

The last fae to emerge from the portal didn't wear the same armor as the other soldiers. Rich sky-blue material lined with silver thread hung beneath plates of gleaming armor that crossed his chest and stomach and covered his shoulders. The picture of a flying dazra was etched onto the fae's breastplate, the image of the insect large and imposing, and the arrogant smile on the male's face made it easy for me to guess he was the leader of our welcome party.

The fae stopped just beyond the circle of warriors, his penetrating gray eyes assessing each of us before fixing on Prince Azaren. One hand rested on the pommel of the sword at his side while his other hand hung on to his weapons belt. He gestured with his head to the soldiers closest to him, and they lifted their spears and moved back, clearing a space for Prince Azaren to walk through.

"My prince, your father the king was most relieved to hear of your arrival back in Zalei," the fae said, his bright-blue lips forming a smile that lacked any true warmth. "He has been most concerned by your absence."

Prince Azaren gave us a reassuring nod before striding forward. As soon as he had exited the circle, the soldiers took up their positions again, sealing the circle once more. "Captain Pezar," the prince replied, giving the fae a tight smile of his own. "I see he was so concerned he didn't even bother coming here to greet me himself."

"There is good reason for the rule against portals to Katakin," Captain Pezar said, ignoring Prince Azaren's comment. "It is fortunate you were able to escape with your life. We would have been so...saddened in the event of your death or your failure to return home."

I was all too aware of the political games played among the Katakin monsters, and now it seemed we had walked into a game created by the fae. Whoever this Captain Pezar was, I was getting the sense he wasn't to be underestimated.

"I am sure you can understand your father is preoccupied with another matter," Captain Pezar continued. "There was another rebel attack last night, and our war general wasn't there to assist."

Rebel attack? I tried not to look too interested in their conversation, but if there was unrest in the fae realm, it could help our cause.

Captain Pezar's accusatory stare bore into Prince Azaren, but the prince didn't blanch. "I do not doubt that as captain of the guard, you were more than able to assist in the matter in my absence."

"Indeed," Captain Pezar confirmed, jutting out his chin and puffing out his chest.

A proud gleam shone in the captain's eyes, and I resisted the urge to sneer at the male's posturing. It was clear he thought too highly of himself, and I couldn't stand the sight of him. If I wished to see such behavior, I would have stayed with the House of Saceris. But even more troubling was the fact the captain acted like Prince Azaren was his subject rather than his crown prince. I had assumed Prince Azaren held great power in his realm. Enough power to keep us out of the dungeons and away from the executioner's block.

Watching the males before me had me doubting the prince's plan. My gaze slid to where Raine remained still in the middle of our smaller circle. She watched the prince and the captain intently, her beautiful head slightly cocked to the side and her mind working just as hard as mine was.

I focused on the weight of the cool steel in my hands. Whatever happened here, I was ready.

"Well, now that's confirmed, as you can plainly see, I am in need of medical attention and a soak that lasts the better half of a century," Prince Azaren said jovially, bringing my attention back to him. "If you'll kindly release my friends, I'd very much like to be back at the palace." He beamed at us then, his eyes lighting up like we weren't monsters who'd repeatedly rendered him unconscious but rather friends whom he held in high esteem.

Captain Pezar's brows slammed down, and his gaze cut to us. "Friends?" he asked skeptically. "We were led to believe these mere *humans* were the ones who tortured and kidnapped you. Rumor has spread that they were hoping to collect a ransom for your return."

There was a beat of silence, and then Prince Azaren burst into laughter, the abrasive sound ringing through the trees.

Captain Pezar stiffened, his chin jutting out further and his back so straight it looked positively painful.

"Did you hear that, Raine? Pezar here thinks you kidnapped me," Prince Azaren said when his laughter had died down.

Raine's brows lifted, the female caught off guard when the captain's attention fixed on her, but she quickly adjusted her reaction. "Told you I look fierce, my Prince," she responded lightheartedly, her lips forming an amused grin.

My Prince. My eye twitched with annoyance.

Captain Pezar's focus remained on her, his expression still suspicious, and my irritation grew. Resisting the urge to launch my sword into one of the fae captain's eyes, I relaxed my features, molding my lips into a smile of my own. "We are resourceful, it's true, but kidnapping isn't among our list of achievements," I said calmly as I sheathed my sword. I could sense the hesitation of my brothers, but they followed my lead, lowering their weapons as well.

"And what *would* be in your list of achievements?" Captain Pezar asked icily, then he wrinkled his nose and sneered. "Smelling like swine?"

"Rescuing the Crown Prince of the Kingdom of Zalei from torture by the monsters of Katakin and returning him home," Prince Azaren said, his serious tone like a lash slapping across the captain's face.

Captain Pezar jerked his head toward the prince. "You can't honestly expect me to believe these humans are—"

"Heroes," Prince Azaren declared. He pulled his shoulders back, and it was the first time I'd seen him act like the prince he was. "These humans were also captured by the Katakin monsters, and they helped me escape. We were in the dungeons together, and if it weren't for them, I would no longer be here. A monster had almost bled me dry, leaving me without access to my magic, but these honorable souls rescued me."

Heroes? Honorable souls? I arched a brow at that, but I had to admire the prince's act.

"I am sure King Chalir would want us to show gratitude to the ones who saved my life," Prince Azaren continued, and he directed his next words to the soldiers surrounding us. "So lower your weapons, unless of course, you do not respect the life of your prince and wish to be tried for treason."

A moment passed, but then the soldiers all stood up their spears and knelt with one knee on the ground while they lifted their free arms above their heads. "May the prince shine," they chanted in unison, and I didn't miss the way Captain Pezar's top lip curled at the show of loyalty.

Spinning around, Captain Pezar faced the portal. "Oh, I look forward to hearing you explain to your father why you created a forbidden portal to Katakin and landed yourself in that situation."

• • • • ⬤ • ⬤ • ⬤ • • •

Exiting the portal, we emerged into some kind of large sitting room. Oiled portraits lined the walls, hanging in delicate silver frames, and various velvet armchairs were arranged around the space. A group of beautiful fae were waiting for us when we arrived, and they gushed over Prince Azaren, one of them almost fainting at the sight of his battered body.

They glared at us as they led the prince away with murmured promises that they would take him to the jewel and restore him to good health. I didn't know what this "jewel" was, perhaps a healing device of some kind. Either way, the prince's well-being was out of our hands.

The rest of us had to surrender our weapons, and Kade and Locke had to give up their satchels, then we were ushered down a series of long corridors and into a large, extravagant bedroom. I frowned at the two double beds.

"This was the best we could do on such short notice, unless you'd rather the cells? The *lady* will occupy the next room," Captain Pezar explained.

Kade looked ready to tear the captain's head off for even suggesting we separate, wolf shifter or not, and the rest of us moved closer to Raine.

"King Chalir has requested the arrangement, so unless you wish for your first council with the king to be about you wanting to defy his wishes, I suggest you move back," Captain Pezar added, his eyes sparkling like he wanted us to continue to resist.

I clenched my jaw.

"It's all right," Raine said slowly, like she wasn't keen on being away from us either. "It's only the next room. I'll be fine."

Kade's nostrils flared, and his fists clenched, but Raine smiled at him. "Try not to break anything," she said and left the room.

Captain Pezar eyed us as if he was disappointed we didn't create more of a scene. "Guards will escort you and your lady friend to a private dinner with the king in three hours," he said, and then he promptly left the room, followed by the guards who'd been escorting us. The last guard closed the door behind him, and I didn't need to check to know there were guards stationed outside.

"I don't fucking like this," Kade growled and began stomping back and forth across the length of the bedroom. Locke strode to peer out the window at the other end of the room, and Asher dropped onto the closest bed.

"Better a fine room with comfortable beds than the dungeons," I pointed out. "And we still have this, remember?" I rubbed my chest. "If anything bad happens to her, we'll know."

Kade clenched his jaw before speaking. "We can't be sure they're taking her to the next room. If they hurt her—"

"If we want to get information about the curse, we need to stay out of chains," Locke said. "Darian's right. We'll know if she's in danger. If we feel the slightest hint of pain in our chests, I'll happily help you destroy this place to get to her, but for now, we wait. From what the captain said, we'll see Raine again at the dinner in three hours."

Asher let out a low whistle. "Do you think Sharachi's room is as fine as this, because damn."

"It's better than the forest," I agreed, hardly showing appreciation for the opulent room we found ourselves in. Every surface appeared to be lined with silver down to the lush cushions covering the chaise lounges near the far wall.

A door was situated on the right side of the room, and I opened it to find a gleaming water closet equipped with a large ceramic bath. Getting clean wasn't the most important thing we needed, but after recent events, I wasn't too proud to take advantage of our situation.

"For now, we are guests in the palace. We need to give Prince Azaren a chance to bring us the information about the curse. Until then, we have a dinner to attend in a few hours," I said, turning away from the bath.

"And what if he doesn't come through?" Asher questioned. "It's obvious he wants the books, but I still don't understand why he would help us. We all know things will take a bad turn for us once our abilities return and they realize we're monsters. I don't intend to end up with my head severed from my body, and I sure as fuck ain't goin' to let that happen to Sharachi."

"If it comes to it, we'll take matters into our own hands and search for the information about the curse on our own," Locke said. "But without knowing the layout of the castle and what powers each of the fae have, and without our monster abilities, even I have to admit it would be difficult. For now, we go along with Prince Azaren's plan."

"Agreed," I replied. "And on that note, I must get some of this grime off me so I can feel like a dignified being again."

"Dignified? You're not the one with your ass crack hangin' out," grumbled Asher.

Fine garments had been left on the ends of each of the beds, and I snatched one up and tossed it to Asher. "Seems like you're in luck." Then I grabbed another for myself and disappeared into the washroom. The bath was already filled with warm water, and I stripped out of my clothes, eager to step in.

CHAPTER 12

The silver cloche covering the plate before me was so shiny my reflection stared back, and I found myself looking at a strange version of the woman I'd once been. A silver dress with long, pointed sleeves and intricate beading clung to my body, and I'd arranged my hair into a simple braid that hung over one shoulder. *Of course it had to be a dress*, I sighed internally.

True to his word, hours earlier Captain Pezar had escorted me to the room next to the one Kade and the others had been placed in. It was a lavish space with a single four-poster bed and elegant floral wallpaper, but it was empty without my monsters. Still, I'd tried not to think about how our separation unsettled me, and I'd focused my attention on my next tasks.

The dress had been laid out on the edge of the bed, and I didn't need to be a genius to understand it had been left for me to wear. It wasn't a practical outfit, but I'd been glad to have something else to change into. There'd been a not-so-pleasant smell in the room, and I was starting to suspect it might have been coming from me.

After trying to peer out of the frosted window that only provided a blurred view of the fae kingdom beyond the castle, I'd allowed myself to bathe and dress in preparation for our dinner with the king. The water was glorious, but the longer I'd been away from Darian and the others, the more my stomach had twisted with unease. Honestly, I'd been downright ecstatic when Captain Pezar had arrived to escort us all to dinner.

Though we had only been apart for a few hours, Asher and the others had visibly relaxed when they'd spotted me, their gazes frantically sliding over my body like they were desperate to drink me in and check I was unharmed. My lips had twitched upward in amusement, but my heart had swelled at the attention. *Goddess help me if I ever need to separate from them completely.* Did one need their sanity to live? That was a problem for another day if it ever came to it.

The long dining table we'd been taken to was situated in the middle of a great hall, and I sat on one side of the table in between Asher and Locke. Kade, Darian, and Prince Azaren sat opposite us, and King Chalir was positioned at the head. The monsters had all obviously taken advantage of their time in the room like I had, because they were all bathed and dressed in fine silver suits, and they looked sexy as sin. Asher's and Locke's scents of musk, leather, cedarwood, and spice swirled around me like a delicious cocktail, making my mouth water.

Even Prince Azaren looked regal and fit for an audience with the king, with his pressed suit and spiked blue hair that was no longer thick with blood. The fae who'd fussed over the prince when we'd first arrived at the castle clearly hadn't been joking when they'd promised to restore him to health. There wasn't a single mark to indicate he had ever been tortured or carried unconscious through the forest. *Good for him.*

Moving light reflected from above, glittering over the cloche, and I turned my attention to the large, glowing statue of a fish hovering in the air above the center of the table. The piece of art hung suspended as if held by invisible strings, and the fine detail of the creature's eyes and scales made it appear real. As I stared, the blue mass began twisting and shifting, remolding into the sculpture of a bird of prey taking flight.

Four smaller sculptures hovered in each corner of the room, and these changed in time with the larger statue as if they were all responding to the same command. It took me a moment to realize the sculptures were entirely made out of water that must have been manipulated by magic, and a shiver swept through me. *If fae can manipulate water to create such beauty, I hate to wonder what else they are capable of.*

"Ah, now those were gifted to me by the water fae a century ago. Just some of the many mesmerizing wonders in this palace," King Chalir said, drawing my attention back to him. The fae king had entered the dining hall shortly after us, along with another half a dozen guards, and a herald had announced his long string of names, most of which I'd already forgotten.

King Chalir appeared older than many of the other fae in the room, with lines marring his forehead, but he was attractive with striking cobalt-colored eyes and a chiseled jaw leading to a prominent chin. A silver crown encrusted with sparkling gems sat atop his long white hair, and two fae females stood at either side of his chair, pawing over him like he was their purpose for existence.

The females had entered with the king, and I'd first marveled appreciatively at their shimmering clothing which was an artful display of silver mixed with bright pinks, yellows, and greens. That was, until I'd realized the fae were actually naked and those clothes were *literal* art. The colors had been painted onto their skin to mimic the appearance of tight-fitting garments, and the moment I understood those silver circles on their chests were actually nipples, my gaze shot to Asher beside me. Of course, he pretended he hadn't been looking, and I shook my head at him with a grin. Locke acted like the females were invisible,

Darian merely looked curious, and Kade looked like he wanted to rip their heads off. I figured that was better than them lusting over the females, so I took it as a win.

"I imagine you haven't seen anything so refined," King Chalir added condescendingly, and for a moment, I thought he was talking about the pretty fae female who was trailing her manicured fingers down his muscled chest. Then I realized he was talking about the water sculptures. *Right.*

"They are spectacular," I replied, forcing a smile to my face despite his irritating tone.

"And they are just one of the treats you get to experience tonight," King Chalir said with a calculated smile. "My son has explained how you heroically rescued him from the monsters, so tonight I intend to show you my appreciation." He turned then and signaled with his hand to the closest servant on his right. In response, a ring of fae dressed in plain white garments stepped forward in unison at the king's command and lifted the cloches from our plates.

I sucked in a sharp breath, and Asher and Locke stilled beside me. *What the hell?*

"My favorite delicacy," King Chalir chuckled.

I gaped at the tiny baby toadstool on my plate, its red spots unmistakable where it sat nestled in a salad of rich greens, alongside thinly sliced pieces of meat, and colorful, clear balls that created an artistic pattern. Locke, Kade, and Darian had the sense to keep their expressions neutral, but Asher winced like he thought this very moment was another penance for crushing one of the little fungi under his boot in the forest. If it weren't for my own panic, I would have grinned at him.

My first thought was that the king was trying to kill us. I mean, he still had his soldiers lining the walls, so clearly he wasn't taking any chances with us, and I couldn't be certain whether he believed Prince Azaren's story. Across from me, the prince's green eyes sparkled like he knew exactly what I was thinking. He smiled reassuringly as if to say I had nothing to worry about, but I still couldn't be sure that the king wasn't trying to hurt us. Like hell was I going to eat that toadstool.

"My chef tells a story with every plate of food he serves, and this one is my favorite. I asked him to prepare it specifically in honor of you, our new guests," King Chalir explained. "Known as the Happy Death, these toadstools are native to our kingdom and dreadfully poisonous if eaten raw, but once they're cooked, they make the most exquisite dishes."

Dreadfully poisonous? My stomach roiled.

As if to prove his point, I watched in horror as King Chalir used his fork to stab the toadstool on his plate and slip the fungus into his mouth. As he closed his eyes, a look of ecstasy crossed his face, and he moaned like one of those pretty fae females was doing more than just stroking his arm and sitting on his lap.

The servant who'd removed the cloche from King Chalir's plate beamed at the king's display of appreciation, and I guessed he was the chef who had created our dishes. He stared at the rest of us expectantly, and Locke and the others started picking at the food on their plates, purposely avoiding the toadstools and swallowing the meat and greens. When the chef's gaze fixed on me, I placed a piece of meat in my own mouth and chewed. "Mm-hmmm," I mumbled, smiling awkwardly around the mouthful. The fae continued to watch me, his gaze flicking from the toadstool on my plate and back to my face.

Oh, hell no. I gulped, knowing exactly what the chef wanted me to do. *Can a person be thrown into the dungeons for not eating the king's favorite meal?* I couldn't risk finding out. Close to gagging, I slid my fork under the toadstool and steeled myself.

Before I'd lifted my fork off the plate, Darian cleared his throat loudly. The chef's attention went to him as he speared his toadstool and popped it into his mouth. He barely chewed before swallowing. "Possibly the best thing I've ever eaten," he said politely, giving the chef his most charming smile.

Pride filled the chef's face. Seemingly satisfied with the response, he snapped his fingers at the other servants, and the fae all turned as one, the group of them filing out of the room and leaving us to finish our meal. I shot Darian a grateful look, and he winked at me. *Yep, I'm going to owe him for that.*

Beside me, Asher grimaced and placed his toadstool in his mouth. Like Darian, he barely chewed before swallowing it down. King Chalir was busy whispering to one of the giggling females beside him, and I knew it was my chance. In a quick movement, I lifted my fork, flinging the toadstool to the side.

The spotted fungus rose into the air and landed with a thud...right in the center of Asher's previously empty plate.

Oops.

Asher whipped his head toward me, but King Chalir was now the one staring at him expectantly just like the chef had been previously staring at me. "I, uh— I was savin' the best for last," Asher mumbled to the king and shoved my toadstool reluctantly into his mouth. "Mmm...so delicious," Asher said, giving the king a thumbs-up, and I didn't know whether to be horrified or snort with laughter. I'd intended to flick the toadstool onto the floor, not onto Asher's plate! The second King Chalir wasn't paying attention to Asher, he narrowed his eyes at me, and I just knew he was planning an epic punishment for me. *Welp.* Still, the bright side was that I didn't have to eat one of the creepy little fungi. *Worth it.*

"So I have to ask. How *did* you manage to rescue my son?" King Chalir said when we'd all finished eating.

Prince Azaren paled at the question, and panic went through me for the second time. We had no clue what story Prince Azaren had told the king. Was this a test?

"When you've been held captive for long enough, you start to pick up on the patterns," Locke replied coolly. "Like when the guards swap shifts and serve rations. It was simply a matter of timing and good luck."

King Chalir looked thoughtful as he held Locke's stare. "Luck, was it? And why *were* you all captives? My son didn't say."

Fuck. It was definitely a test.

Locke's expression remained passive as he returned the king's stare. "The monsters took us from our home—a small island that had been our haven for centuries. They came from the water, great beasts with tusks and tails. We didn't stand a chance." A hint of anger entered his gaze, and if I hadn't known better, I would have thought the emotion was genuine. "They didn't say why they took us, but I suspect we are the last ones left."

It was a lie woven for the benefit of the king, but emotion clogged my throat, and I struggled to swallow it down. Locke had almost told *my* story, and when my gaze connected with Locke's, there was an apology in his onyx eyes.

A beat of silence passed as the king's gaze weighed heavily on us, but when King Chalir spoke next, his voice was softer. Kinder. "That is...unfortunate. As the ones who rescued the Crown Prince of the Kingdom of Zalei, I will ensure you are each given land and residence here so you may have a fresh start. You have my gratitude and respect. Your life here won't ever be what you lost, and the fae aren't often trusting of humans, but it's something."

"You are extremely generous, your highness," Darian said graciously.

King Chalir turned to Prince Azaren then and let out a long sigh. "It is terrible about your past but fortunate you were there to save my son. I can only hope he now realizes how foolish he was to risk everything to go to that abomination of a place. Curiosity always has been Azaren's biggest flaw, that and his unyielding determination to pursue peace even when violence is the only remaining course of action."

I frowned, confused that the king would think the pursuit of peace was a weakness. I mean, wasn't that what kings were for? To keep the peace and ensure their people were safe and fed?

"It is fortunate," I agreed, feeling the strange need to defend Prince Azaren. "Your son is a great fae, and one day he'll make a great leader."

King Chalir scoffed, not hiding his disbelief at my statement. "Since I appointed Prince Azaren as war general, he's attended one out of five meetings and is absent more than he is present during all matters of conflict. This latest attack by the Forgotten Fae being just another incident. It's lucky Captain Pezar was able to lead the soldiers."

"Forgotten Fae?" Darian asked curiously.

At first, I thought the king would shut down at the question, but he simply waved his hand like the Forgotten Fae were common knowledge.

"They call themselves the 'Forgotten Fae'. Their name is a statement. They say they fight for the fae who have been forgotten by the kingdom," Prince Azaren explained grimly.

King Chalir's face hardened. "They are a group of rebels who are determined to take over my kingdom and send us into darkness."

"I don't think—" Prince Azaren began.

"They came into my room while I was sleeping and attempted to assassinate me," King Chalir spat, cutting off his son. "They will pay for their crimes."

Prince Azaren looked like he wanted to say more, but he kept his lips sealed.

The king took a calming breath and pinned his son with his stare. "When I was unable to find you and that old scholar in the library finally divulged your plan to portal to Katakin and search for those useless ancient books, I had feared the monsters might have already captured or killed you. Then our soldiers would have had to go to war once again. Given recent events with the Forgotten Fae and your safe return home, it is a relief that was not the outcome."

Prince Azaren continued to remain silent, and I found myself sympathizing with the prince. I still didn't understand the importance of the books, but I did understand that the prince was unhappy with his life and he was hoping those books would change something. *Was he secretly working with the Forgotten Fae?* It didn't make sense. If the Forgotten Fae were planning on assassinating the king, then they were clearly okay with violence and not friends of the monarchy, both things that would go against what I knew about Prince Azaren, but there was more going on here than I understood.

King Chalir stood and pushed back his chair. "I have discussed with my advisers, and there will be a grand party held tomorrow night in your honor. Times are fragile, and it will also be good to remind the fae that we are stronger than ever and they do not need to worry about the Forgotten Fae or the Katakin monsters. Servants will ensure you're appropriately ready for the party. Over the following days, I will see to it that you're set up with homes and given the resources for you to begin your lives. Now I must retire for the night, but I trust my son will stay with you for the remainder of the evening." He paused to stare at Prince Azaren before continuing, "My chef has prepared more courses, and I imagine you are famished after your long journey. Again, I thank you for saving our crown prince and my only son. Now if you'll excuse me."

The two fae females turned to leave with the king and his horde of guards, but before they did, their gazes flicked from Prince Azaren to Darian, Locke, Kade, and Asher like they were sad to be leaving the dinner. No doubt they'd been hoping to get more gossip out of us all. Or maybe they weren't as infatuated by the king as they made it seem. In any case, it wasn't until the king and his escorts were out of the room that I felt as though I could breathe easily again. I just hoped the next course didn't include toadstools.

CHAPTER 13

~ **Raine** ~

A thud sounded somewhere in the darkness of my room, and my eyes snapped open. My heart raced as I twisted my body and slid my hand under my pillow, grabbing out the knife I'd stolen from my dinner plate hours earlier. It was a bread knife that wouldn't do much as a weapon, but it felt good to have the cool sting of metal in my hand. I scanned the room, my gaze darting from the long drapes covering the window to the closed door that led to the washroom.

It was late when we'd left the dining hall, escorted by half a dozen guards. We'd stayed only as long as we had to until the chef finally stopped bringing out more plates of food. Alone in my room, I'd changed out of the dress and slipped on the nightgown that had been left on the bed for me. The material was loose and comfortable, but when I tried to sleep, the gnawing sense that something was missing made it impossible to drift off. I knew it wasn't a "something" but a "someone." *Four* someones, to be exact.

And now I was alone in my room and hearing strange noises. *Great.* More thuds sounded, but the noises were muffled like they were coming from the room next to me. *The room Locke and the others are staying in.* Slipping from my bed, I pressed my ear to the decorative wallpaper, listening intently.

This time, I could swear I heard grunting. *What the—?* I scowled. *If I find out they've taken fae females back to their room, I am going to make them regret it.* As if they'd heard me, the noises abruptly stopped, and silence filled the room. Grumbling under my breath, I pulled back from the wall and slowly climbed into bed, knowing full well that any chance I had of sleep had now been successfully obliterated. I had just slid beneath the covers again when a rattling sounded in my room. Not next door but somewhere close. Whipping my head to the side, I gaped as the window opposite the door creaked open, and a large form fell into the room, landing with a thud as it got tangled in the long drapes.

Ho-ly Goddess. I darted backward off the bed, clutching my knife and ready to stab someone.

"Well, that was fuckin' graceful," the lump groused, and the warm tones of the male's voice had my stomach flipping.

Is that—?

"Get the fuck out of the way so the rest of us can get through," growled another voice from outside the window. "There's not much for us to hold on to out here." Goddess, I knew those voices. *Kade. Asher.*

"If I had my powers, I could have simply entranced the guards outside our room," Darian pointed out. "It's like we've been turned into primitives."

"If we had our abilities, I could tear them to shreds," Kade added, and I could just imagine the dark smile on his face as he said it.

"Would you both shut up," Asher grumbled, standing with the drapes still over him. He cursed, trying to yank them off him but somehow making them wind around him even more.

"You're making enough noise to wake the entire castle, brother. I don't think our silence will make a difference," Darian responded.

There was a long-suffering sigh, and I rushed closer, barely containing my laughter as I helped detangle Asher. I half expected the guards outside my door to barge in, roused by the commotion he was making, but by some miracle, it was silent outside my room. *Maybe the guards fell asleep?* It was late, after all. In any case, I tried not to think about it and focused on freeing my monster.

"Hi, sweetheart," Asher said with a lopsided grin and a flushed face when he finally managed to step away from the now-torn drapes and peered down at me.

I resisted the urge to roll my eyes. "What the hell are you doing?"

He shrugged his broad shoulders and stepped forward, brushing torn threads of fabric from his skin and the undershorts he wore. "You didn't think we'd leave you unprotected all night, did you?"

Unprotected? I stared at him in disbelief. "You seem to forget not too long ago, I survived my entire life without you four."

Darian jumped through the window and glided into the room, assessing our surroundings. "He means to say, none of us could sleep while knowing you were on your own, lovely. At least this way, we might now be able to get some shut-eye."

My cheeks heated, warmth going through me as I thought of what he'd said. *They couldn't sleep knowing I was alone?*

Kade crouched as he landed in the room, and he strode straight to me, curving his arms around my back and shocking me with a crushing kiss that left me breathless. When he pulled back, he growled, "I had to know you were all right. Come find me when you get sick of these two."

I hadn't even had time to answer when he released me and prowled back to the window, disappearing from sight. I ran over in time to see him finish scaling the side of the castle, his fingers only just gripping the bricks and his feet finding small crevices. He leaped the last distance to their window and pulled himself back into their room. I didn't dare look at the drop to the ground below.

Swallowing, I turned my attention to Asher and Darian. "So you two, huh?"

"Yeah, we agreed," Asher said with a nod.

I frowned. "Agreed?"

"Let's just say tonight you're ours," Asher replied with a wolfish grin. "Now get your ass back in the bed so we can get some sleep."

Sleep? My brows rose. It wasn't exactly what I was expecting when he said I was theirs for the night.

Leading the way, Darian slid onto the other side of the bed. When I didn't move, Asher hooked an arm around my belly and lifted me into the bed, plopping me in the middle of the mattress and climbing in after me.

"I know how to get into a bed," I griped, but Asher only chuckled as he settled beside me, tucking me into his chest protectively. Darian moved closer to my other side, the monsters surrounding me with warmth and hard panes of muscle. *Fuck, was it always so hot in here?*

And then the asses simply shut their eyes as if they were serious about going straight to sleep. *Unbelievable.* I stared at the darkened ceiling, wondering whether it might have been easier to sleep without them after all. Time crawled by, and I squirmed between them, unable to keep still.

With the scents of musk and leather and sea salt and patchouli filling my lungs, my body screamed for attention, and I needed to get away just so I could breathe. A plush reading chair sat close to the window, and I tried to wiggle free, determined to sleep there instead. Asher's arm tightened around me, and his lips found my ear. His warm breath tickled the side of my face, and my breathing became shallow.

"Because of you, I had to eat two of those mushrooms tonight, Sharachi," he accused in my ear, and goose bumps raced along my skin. "I've never tasted anythin' so damn—"

"Delicious?" I supplied breathlessly.

"Squishy," Asher finished with a sound of disgust, though a smile curved his lips. "And now we're goin' to tease you until you wish you'd eaten it." His hand reached under my nightgown, his fingers brushing over my belly, and I sucked in a sharp breath.

"I meant to throw it onto the floor," I defended. "It's not my fault—"

My words were cut off as he slid his hand upward, cupping my breast firmly and flicking his thumb over my nipple.

Darian moved on my other side, leaning down and pressing soft kisses to my collarbone. My body melted at their touch, and I forced myself to take a few slow breaths.

"It just landed there," I said, finishing my sentence. "I hardly think it's worth torturing me over."

"Torture?" Darian asked, lifting his head and giving me a sensual smile. "No, darling, torture was trying to sleep knowing you were over here in this huge bed by yourself."

I gaped at him. "I didn't get to choose where I slept!"

"You didn't fight against the arrangement either," Asher said, moving his hand to my other breast.

I wanted to curse at their stupidity, but deep down I couldn't help but wonder whether this was still really about the fact I'd kept the information from them that Prince Azaren might be able to break our bonds. I mean, they'd acted like they'd forgiven me back in the cave behind the waterfall, but this was ridiculous.

"Actually, you're right," I said, clenching my jaw. "And now I'm going to fight against *this* arrangement. Tonight I *choose* to sleep on the damn couch."

But when I went to move, Asher didn't release me, and Darian's smirk was devilish. "Not until your punishment is over, lovely," Darian said as his hand trailed up my bare thigh, gliding beneath the nightgown.

"And when will it be over?" I asked.

"You'll see," Asher said with a grin, and then Darian's fingers were sliding into my panties and swiping up my center. I gasped as his fingers pressed against my clit, massaging the bundle of nerves and making desire pool between my legs. *Oh yes.* At this point, I was starting to think that if this was punishment, I needed to put myself in this situation more often.

I writhed as the monsters teased me, the pleasure building in me until I was sure I would explode, but before I tipped over the edge, they stopped in unison, not giving me the release I desperately needed. *What the actual fuck?*

They waited until the feeling had crashed down before playing with me again, toying with me until I was squirming again on the bed. Darian watched as his fingers slid in and out of me, his face filled with such desire that I knew he was torturing himself as much as he was torturing me. "You're so perfect," he murmured like he was in awe, and I didn't have it in me to feel embarrassed. I wiggled my hips, begging him to drive his fingers in deeper, even though he was already pushing them in as far as they would go.

"More," I pleaded.

"What's that, sweetheart?" Asher asked with a shit-eating grin that made me want to snarl at him.

"I need more," I gasped.

When Darian pulled his fingers out again, I twisted to the side, flinging my leg over Asher's torso. I yanked his undershorts down, and his cock sprang free, his piercings glinting in the dim light.

Seriously never going to get used to that.

Asher grinned at me like he knew exactly what I was thinking, but his grin fell away, his face contorting with pleasure as I slid onto his cock and began bouncing up and down like my life depended on it.

"I thought we were only going to tease her," Darian said with amusement from beside us.

Asher glared at him. "You try fuckin' stoppin' when she feels this damn good," Asher groaned, and I grinned at the both of them.

I rocked my hips against Asher as he drove deep, and I cried out as stars burst behind my eyes, relief washing through me as I finally found my climax. But Asher and Darian weren't done with me yet.

Cradling his arm around my back, Asher flipped me so my back was on the bed, and Darian moved toward my head as Asher continued to fuck me. I took Darian's cock in my mouth, relishing the taste of him as Asher pounded into me, reigniting my desire and making me clench around him as pleasure built in me again.

The next time I came, Asher and Darian both came with me, the pair of them spilling into me as their muscles locked up and their bodies jerked as they found their release. When they moved back, I swallowed and stared at the ceiling as Asher tucked himself next to me again, and Darian draped an arm beneath my breasts.

Darian pressed a soft kiss to my sweaty brow. "You don't understand what you've done to us, do you, lovely?" he asked lightly, and I kept silent, not sure if I was supposed to answer.

CHAPTER 14

~ **Kade** ~

I flexed my back, hating the navy-blue suit that pulled uncomfortably against my skin. Raine, my brothers, and I stood close to the raised dais situated at one end of the massive ballroom we were in. On the dais, King Chalir lounged on his silver throne as brightly painted fae females fed him morsels of food from small silver platters. The sight was sickening, and I scowled, turning my gaze away from the fae leader.

Above our heads, fae acrobats flew across the room, springing from swinging bars and holding on to one another as they twirled and spun. The movement kept catching my eye, and every time, I jerked my head upward, ready to defend against the fae.

My muscles twitched as a shadow fell over me, the fae acrobat free-falling into the air until another fae grabbed onto their arms and the pair of them swung to perch on a high platform. Clapping came from some of the finely dressed fae spread across the glossy ballroom floor.

"Relax, Kade," Asher said, nudging me with his arm. "The fae think we saved the prince. We won't need to fight anyone tonight."

But my scowl only deepened at his comment. When King Chalir had arrived in the ballroom and addressed the crowd, he'd made a big show of parading Prince Azaren around and declared we were the prince's rescuers. That we were to be treated as heroes in Zalei. But I didn't want the fae to think I was some kind of angel to their prince. I wanted them to see me as the monster they feared those in Katakin to be. As they'd seen my mother and sister to be. I wanted to shift and destroy the ridiculous party we'd found ourselves at. The fae were merciless and hateful, and to stand there while the fae females ogled me curiously from afar was making my skin crawl. If they knew what we truly were, they wouldn't have been staring at me like they wanted me to seduce them and take them to my bed.

Raine's hand landed on my arm like she understood the rage coursing through me, and my fury cooled to a manageable level. "One night," she said to me quietly. "You only have to endure one more night."

I breathed in, dragging in her scent like it was my tether to sanity. Her smell of coconuts and steel was weaker now that I was without my wolf, but it still had the same effect. I longed to pull her against me. To disappear from this place and take her somewhere I could protect her, away from the fae, but that wasn't part of our plan.

Before we'd been escorted to the party, the five of us had agreed to behave for the night and try to blend in. When the party was over and we were taken back to our rooms, we'd hunt down Prince Azaren and try to get answers about the curse. If he didn't provide them, we'd scour the castle, trying to find them. The dazra's venom would wear off soon, and we were out of time.

A fae server with pale-yellow eyes and translucent wings folded behind their back came past with a tray of food, and Raine and Asher each took a serving. The chocolate had been shaped into small roses, the petals artfully carved and sprayed with edible glitter, and they both shoved them into their mouths at the same time.

Raine's eyes fluttered closed, and she moaned as she chewed. Asher looked like he was enjoying the dessert almost as much as she was.

My brows slammed down, and I leaned closer to Raine. "Stop moaning like that," I growled and glared daggers at the nearest fae. "The fae are already staring at you. You don't need to draw more attention."

Raine opened her eyes and canted her head as she peered back at me. "The fae are staring at all of us," she pointed out. "We're the first humans some of them have ever seen. We should probably be thankful none of them have attacked us." She was right about that. While the king had announced we were to be honored, the fae who didn't look like they were lusting over us were giving us wary glances. I was confident none of the fae would defy the king and attack us at his party, but I could sense the hostility from some of the fae. We weren't safe in Zalei.

"That's not what I mean, and you know it," I replied.

Raine stared at me for a moment longer. "Fine, but the next time that tray comes around, you'd better grab me some of those roses for later, where I can moan in peace."

Asher grinned. "We don't need chocolate to make you moan, Sharachi."

She glared at him, but a smile teased her lips.

Prince Azaren approached us then, and he stopped casually between Darian and Locke. I hated the fae prince as much as I hated the fucking rest of them, but there was something about him that didn't make me want to tear him apart like I did the others. His shoulders dropped, his muscles relaxing in a way that was at odds with his rigid posture when he spoke to any of the fae.

"I hope you're ready, Prince Azaren," Locke said quietly to the fae, and Prince Azaren regarded him.

"As ready as one can be," he responded cryptically with a sigh, and I glowered at him. The sooner he told us about the curse, the sooner we could leave this fucking place.

• • • • • • • • • •

~ Raine ~

A gorgeous fae female stalked over to our group, her hair hanging in dozens of small, long braids around her face and falling to either side of her pointed ears. Gemstones glittered on her green velvet dress that brushed along the floor, and her smile was polite like she'd practiced it in the mirror a thousand times. None of the other fae had approached us despite the fact we were the supposed rescuers of their prince, and I had to wonder why she was different.

Not sparing the rest of us a second glance, she fixed her attention on Prince Azaren. "My beloved, there are more guests you should speak with," she said, her voice high and lilting. "They've dearly missed their war general and their prince."

Beloved? My brows rose in surprise. *Is the prince...betrothed?*

Prince Azaren deflated, exhaustion sapping the vibrancy from his face, but he nodded dutifully. "Yes, I suppose they would have."

The female's gaze slid subtly to the side, and I frowned when I realized the king was staring back at her. The cold and calculating look he gave her made me think the pair had some kind of agreement, and I was reminded that we really had no idea what we'd stepped into in the fae realm.

When Prince Azaren took a reluctant step forward, I moved to block him. "Prince Azaren," I said in the sweetest voice I could muster. "You promised you'd honor me with a dance. You know, after saving your life and all."

He stilled and blinked at me in surprise. "You wish to dance the Fazea?"

A group of fae were dancing to a lively tune in the middle of the ballroom, their odd, jerky movements and shaking bodies completely different from any dance I'd ever seen, and I could only guess he was referring to whatever it was they were doing. I suddenly regretted my decision to lend a helping hand and tried not to show just how badly I did *not* want to join them.

The fae female narrowed her eyes at me like she was daring me to say yes. Well, now I *definitely* had to.

"The prince has been absent for a number of days and almost died," she said indignantly. "It's important that he show strength in this time of—"

"Yes," Prince Azaren blurted, his emerald eyes sparkling as he smiled at me. "I did promise you a dance, didn't I?" He turned back to the fae female who still had her mouth open like she couldn't believe he'd just interrupted her. "One dance, Alessa, and then I'll resume my duties as the prince. It's the least I can do for the ones who saved me."

The fae female, Alessa, promptly shut her mouth. If you could kill someone with a glare, I'm pretty sure Alessa would have killed me right then. Honestly, she looked like she wanted to gouge my eyes out, which seemed like an overreaction, but what did I know? Without uttering another word, she huffed and spun around, stalking back into the crowd around us.

Prince Azaren lifted his arm, an invitation for me to link my arm with his, but Kade stepped between us. "Raine," Kade growled in warning. "We're not leaving you alone with him."

"I'm going to dance," I replied in exasperation, stepping around Kade and taking Prince Azaren's arm. "You're welcome to join us if you like."

Darian gave a friendly smile to a pixie who gawked as she flew past him. Distracted, she flew into the back of a larger fae and went tumbling to the ground. Darian took a step forward to help her, but the pixie shot back into the air and was out of sight before he could offer his assistance. Grimacing, he turned to us again. "It's not an entirely bad idea. It would look better if we acted as though we were trying to fit in with the fae. This is supposedly going to be our new home, after all."

Asher grinned and slapped Kade on the back. "Dancing it is, brother."

Kade looked like he wanted to tackle Asher to the ground, his muscles wound so tightly it seemed almost painful, but he clenched his jaw as Prince Azaren led us closer to the dance floor.

As we walked, Prince Azaren glanced at me from the side, and his lips quirked into a knowing smile. "You don't need to save me from Alessa," he said quietly. "I'm well aware of the duties I must perform."

I tried not to think about how all the fae were staring at me like I was some kind of alien. I mean, Katakin was bad enough. Couldn't a girl get a break? "Save you? How do you know I don't just want to dance?" I asked, shrugging it off.

He studied me like I was as fascinating as one of the books he'd desperately wanted to reclaim from Katakin. "Well, it seems I owe you yet again. These parties can be a little..."

"Soul suckin'?" Asher supplied with a bored expression, and I tried to smother my grin.

Prince Azaren eyed him. "I was going to say 'draining.'"

We'd reached the other dancing fae then, and if I hadn't regretted my decision to suggest the activity before, I definitely would have now. I couldn't even explain why I'd wanted to help the fae prince escape his duties for a while. Maybe I still felt guilty for watching Kade and Locke render him unconscious all those times. In any case, I was committed now.

Kade, Locke, Darian, and Asher formed a half circle around me, and Prince Azaren positioned himself across from us. I took solace in the fact that at least the fae behind me wouldn't see my crazy moves because my monsters were blocking me from view.

Prince Azaren abruptly started shooting his arms and legs out like he'd lost his mind, and laughter burst out of me before I could clamp a hand over my mouth. A few nearby fae glared daggers at me, and I coughed, clearing my throat.

"What, not to your taste?" Prince Azaren asked with a grin.

Some of the fae were still glaring at me, so I started awkwardly moving my limbs, trying to match his movements. "Oh, it is," I said, nodding vigorously, then winced when I accidentally punched my other arm as my limbs flailed around. "But I don't think I could ever master such an expressive dance."

His smile grew wider, and I tried not to think about the four monsters who had moved closer behind me and were watching us intently. *Oh, I'm definitely going to hear about this later.*

I shook and moved my body closer to the prince, sure that almost all the fae females in the ballroom were glaring at me now. From the way they'd fawned over him all night, it was clear if the prince wasn't yet betrothed, he had plenty of potential candidates. With the music loud in our ears, I leaned closer to him, hoping no one else would hear. "So when are you going to hold up your end of our deal?"

Prince Azaren's gaze darted around us cautiously, but before he could answer, King Chalir stood up on the raised dais and lifted his arms.

Immediately the music and chatter quieted, and we all stared up at the monarch. Unease went through me, though I couldn't explain why.

"My fair fae of Zalei, how wonderful it is to see you here tonight. It brings joy to my heart to see you all celebrate the return of Prince Azaren, my eldest and only son. But now I must admit it is not the only reason I invited you here. Tonight I have a special treat for you."

He'd barely finished speaking when at least a dozen guards fully dressed in silver armor jogged into the room, lining the walls. A hand gripped my waist, and I flinched until Darian's scent wafted over me. Kade, Locke, and Asher were crowding close around me now as well, and my heart picked up its pace. "If this goes badly, you run, hide, and do whatever you need to do to survive," Darian whispered in my ear, his words so quiet I almost couldn't make them out. A tremble worked through me. *If this goes badly.*

But the king had announced we were heroes, and the prince had just been dancing like we were friends. I tried not to let my thoughts spiral and kept my focus on the king who looked wholly impressed with himself.

His expression hardened, his eyes shining with hatred and cruelty I hadn't seen there before. "As you've no doubt heard by now, two nights ago a member of the Forgotten Fae infiltrated this castle and tried to assassinate me in my very bed." I didn't think it was possible, but the ballroom became even quieter then like the fae had stopped breathing altogether. "Yes, those rumors are very true, but what you don't know is that I captured my attacker, and tonight, I will show him what happens to traitors who dare try to take what's mine."

An uproar of chatter exploded across the ballroom, and the king gestured to the guards closest to the doors. At his signal, the doors flung open, and another two guards dragged a ragged figure between them, their hands hooked under the prisoner's arms.

The male's head was down, long dirty-blond hair hanging over a beaten face, and blue blood dripping from his pointed ears. Angry dark bruises marred his skin, and a few of his fingers hung awkwardly as if they'd been broken.

The guards brought the prisoner to a halt in front of the dais and dropped him to the floor.

Darian's hand tightened on me, and I resisted the urge to lean back into him, suddenly not wanting the king to know how I felt about the siren.

The prisoner slowly lifted to his knees like every movement was agony, and though I knew he was a traitor, my heart clenched at the sight. He swayed in the position and lifted his head to stare at the crowd. Despite his injuries, his topaz-colored eyes were alert and defiant as he peered up at the king.

"This traitor wanted to destroy everything we've built," King Chalir said, his voice booming across the ballroom now. "The Forgotten Fae wish to take what is ours. To ruin the lives of our children and take what our ancestors left us. He came into my bedchamber in the middle of the night and planned to slay me while I slept like the dishonorable worm he is."

Boos and angry shouts erupted from the fae around the ballroom now as they voiced their displeasure at the criminal in their midst.

It wasn't hard to picture the prisoner sneaking into the castle to kill the king. Even now, his expression was fearless. Like he'd already given himself up to the idea of death.

"Enjoying the show?" said a smooth, slick voice with dry amusement.

I jolted, my head tilting to the side, but no one appeared to have spoken, and they all had their gazes locked firmly on the Forgotten Fae. "What—?" I began in confusion, but the rest of my sentence trailed off as I realized no one had spoken aloud.

Darian and the others were watching the fae grimly. Even Prince Azaren looked displeased, though I could tell he was trying to hide it.

"Hopefully it will be over quickly," Darian said softly to me as if he thought I was about to ask what was going to happen to the prisoner, and I bobbed my head in agreement, realizing that I must have imagined the voice from earlier.

Turning my attention back to the prisoner, I almost reeled back in surprise when I found his topaz-colored eyes were fixed on *me. What the hell?*

"You shouldn't have left us," that same smooth voice spoke again, and I cocked my head, finally understanding but still not quite believing that it was the prisoner who was speaking to me. In my freaking *mind.* Panic crawled up my throat, and I tried not to react. Tried not to show the fae I'd heard him.

"He's going mad without you," the fae continued speaking in my mind. "But I'm sure you already know that. He'd like the red hair. It suits you. Though, I'm not sure why you decided to get rid of the glamour. If we hadn't spent so much time together back then, I would have hardly recognized you."

When I still didn't respond, he continued, "When the real fight comes, just remember you're the one who picked the wrong side. What is it the king calls you? His *jewel*." A laugh that was almost maniacal sounded in my mind, and the hairs stood up on the back of my neck. "We'll see how he treats his jewel when war is at the castle gates."

I couldn't keep silent any longer. Nothing the prisoner was saying made any sense. Why was he telling me all this?

"Get out of my head," I snarled in my mind. "I don't know what you're talking about. What war?"

But that laughter continued in my head, and the prisoner simply kept staring at me like he was determined that my face would be the last thing he saw when the king took his life.

I didn't even hear the king give the order. One moment, the fae was staring at me, and the next, his body was slumped over as a fae with white hair and swirling gray eyes stood over him, holding his hand over the prisoner. Power crackled in the air, and the prisoner's back arched, his head flying backward and his muscles tightening.

The laughter in my mind abruptly cut off, and the next words I heard were faint and pained. "Tell Xander I have no regrets. We couldn't know the king would—" The voice cut off, silence filling my mind as the fae standing over the prisoner yanked his hand back. As he did so, a long stream of silver light flew upward and threaded between his knobbly fingers, like the fae had ripped the prisoner's soul from his body. My breathing became rapid, sweat coating my skin. I couldn't explain the way my chest caved. Couldn't explain why my throat tightened, but sadness overcame me. Somehow, I knew the prisoner didn't need to die, and whoever this Xander was, I hoped one day I'd get the chance to pass on this fae's message.

Darian and the others shuffled closer to me, their muscles bunching with tension as we all watched the prisoner's body fall, lifeless, to the ground.

The fae who had been standing over the prisoner made a fist with his hand, and the light tangled in his fingers disappeared like it was simply snuffed out.

A heavy silence filled the ballroom, but the sound was shattered by the king's clapping. I flinched against the abrasive noise, but slowly, others around the ballroom began to clap until the applause was so loud it stung my ears.

"Clap," Prince Azaren said beside us, and I didn't even have the energy to glare at him. Lifting my trembling hands, I brought them together in slow, measured movements. The sadness inside me turned to anger, and I kept staring at the fae who had taken the prisoner's white light. His *soul*, if my suspicions were correct. Rationally, I knew the emotions likely weren't my own. If the prisoner could implant thoughts in my mind, it made sense that he could place emotions there as well, but I couldn't shake it off. Prince Azaren clapped like he'd just witnessed some amazing feat, but a tinge of sadness marred his gaze.

By some mercy, the king finally stopped clapping, and the ballroom quieted again. Relief filtered through me, though I still couldn't explain why.

"As long as I rule, the Forgotten Fae will not succeed in destroying this kingdom," King Chalir declared, and there was another round of applause. "They will never break us. Like the dazra, we will protect our home and render our attackers powerless against us. Now let's get back to the celebration!"

At that, the king lifted his goblet, draining the liquid, and around the room, there were cheers as others did the same. It was then that I wondered whether the fae might be worse than the monsters.

CHAPTER 15

I couldn't get the Forgotten Fae's voice out of my head. His words had imprinted on my mind, and I kept replaying them over and over. *When the real fight comes, just remember you're the one who picked the wrong side.* The fae had stared at me like he knew who I was, though I'd never seen him before in my life.

Locke's dark gaze swept over me with concern, and he turned to Prince Azaren, who was about to stride past him. "We've stayed here long enough. It's time for you to uphold your end of the bargain, *Prince.*"

Prince Azaren didn't cow at Locke's harsh tone but simply peered out of the great stained-glass windows that lined the ceiling. Hours had passed since the Forgotten Fae prisoner had been executed, and the guests were starting to dwindle.

Prince Azaren gave Locke a curt nod. "I have one other person I must speak with, but meet me in the hallway in a few minutes."

Turning back to me, Locke pressed his hand against the small of my back, leading me toward the doors, and our group waited in the hallway for the prince to join us.

"Damn, when I said the party was soul suckin', I hadn't meant it literally," Asher commented as we waited, and Locke glared at him, gesturing subtly with his head to the guards stationed along the walls.

I didn't have it in me to grin at the joke. Not after what I'd seen. Thankfully, we didn't need to wait long for Prince Azaren. Mere moments later, the prince strode through the doorway, that princely smile still fixed on his face like it had become permanently molded to his skin. "Well, that was quite the celebration, don't you think?" he chirped, clapping his hands together, and the rest of us just stared at him.

I was about to open my mouth and say something stupid when Darian forced a smile onto his face. "A fine introduction to your kingdom, Your Highness."

It was then that I noticed the way Prince Azaren's gaze kept sliding to the guards. *Right.* The show wasn't over yet.

"Now, my friends, I am sure you must be thoroughly worn out from the festivities. Let me escort you to your rooms," Prince Azaren declared, his lighthearted voice echoing along the hallway. Indicating with his arm, he began ushering us down the hallway in the direction of our rooms.

We traveled down two more hallways, and I was lost in my thoughts when Kade whirled on the prince. "This isn't the way back to our rooms. Where are you taking us?"

Prince Azaren pressed a finger to his lips, his gaze darting nervously up the deserted hallway. In a hushed tone, he replied, "If you want the answers about the curse, you'll keep quiet and follow me."

Kade clearly wanted to argue, but Asher elbowed him in the side, and he begrudgingly followed after the prince as we were led along a number of other passageways that wound through the castle. We moved in precise bursts, sometimes stopping to wait around corners and statues before we'd dart forward again, and I had to give Prince Azaren credit for getting us through the castle without encountering any more guards.

Eventually, we were taken into what appeared to be a sitting room, much like the room we'd first been in when we initially arrived at the castle, but at the back of the room was an arched doorway that led to a curved flight of stairs.

I'd expected Prince Azaren was taking us to a secretive location where we could talk privately, but when we reached the bottom of the staircase, my mouth dropped open in surprise. A grand library spread before us, towering rows of leather-bound tomes lining the walls and wide stone columns reaching high to the ceiling.

Dimly lit lanterns cast a white glow into the darkness, illuminating the polished wood shelves and velvet reading chairs scattered throughout the space.

None of us spoke, but Locke's chest expanded as he breathed in, like he was savoring the scents of aged parchment, stained wood, and ink.

Prince Azaren led us across the glossy stone floor to a private room at the back of the library complete with two chaise lounges, floor-to-ceiling bookshelves, and a short table that held a single glowing lantern.

When we were inside the room, Prince Azaren closed the door. "We can talk freely now," he said with a long sigh. Darian pulled me to one of the couches, and Asher plopped down on my other side. Kade stood behind us with his arms folded, and Locke circled the room, eyeing the tomes neatly arranged on the shelves.

Darian folded one leg over the other. "As lovely as our surroundings are, couldn't we have done this back in one of our rooms to avoid suspicion?"

"We could have," Prince Azaren replied. "But I wanted to be certain no one would hear us. These rooms adjoining the library are silent spaces. When the door is closed, the magic activates, and no one outside can hear what is said within. It's intended so fae can read and research without being interrupted by others who use the library."

Locke turned from the books he'd been browsing and raised a brow as if the idea intrigued him.

"If that's true, you'll have no problems tellin' us what the fuck happened back there with that fae prisoner," Asher said as he casually placed one of his large hands on my thigh. "That wasn't like any execution I've seen."

My chest tightened as I once again thought of the Forgotten Fae and the message he'd asked me to pass on. For a moment, I wondered whether I should tell Prince Azaren about it, but then I dismissed the thought. Prince Azaren was a royal, and the Forgotten Fae clearly hated the monarchy.

Prince Azaren's expression shuttered, and I could tell Asher and the others were as shocked by his reaction as I was. "It's a long story," he said wearily.

"Then give us the short version," Kade growled.

Prince Azaren swallowed, but he nodded as if he had already intended to explain it all to us. "How much do you know about what happened to my aunt?" he asked carefully.

"She married Katakin's human king, King Adrien," I said, reciting what Kade and the others had told me nights ago.

Prince Azaren leaned forward, resting his elbows on his knees and threading his fingers together. "Yes, well they were happy for a time. Or so I'm told. For a while, fae say it was the treaty that kept our two kingdoms at peace, but it was obviously more than that. Queen Izla loved King Adrien, and it was her love for him that kept the fae at ease. I was only young at the time, but I've heard the story told by numerous scholars and members of the fae court. Queen Izla had plans to unite our kingdoms and believed we could learn from each other, but just when she had almost persuaded some of the fae to resettle in Katakin, King Adrien betrayed her and all the fae by killing my grandfather, King Jazrec. He traveled without the queen and slew him here in this very castle. The treaty was broken, and the trust that had been built was shattered. As the king's only son, my father, Prince Chalir, was crowned as king, and the fae looked to him for answers. For retribution.

"My father roused only a small portion of the fae army, confident that the humans stood no chance against our power. He led them through three portals, ready to annihilate the humans for their treachery and rescue my aunt, but by the time our soldiers were organized and made their way through..." Prince Azaren paused, shadows crossing over his face. "Well, by then my aunt Izla had cursed those in Katakin, and while the humans may not have stood a chance against the fae, the monsters proved to be a different foe entirely, their powers and cruelty taking the fae completely by surprise. The loss of life was...regrettable, and Izla was gone, rumored to have escaped through a portal.

"Many of the members of the group we call the Forgotten Fae are family members of those who lost loved ones that day. They blamed my father for such a reckless attack. King Chalir tried to mobilize the remainder of the fae army and strategized with the war council on the best path to victory, but there was an outcry from our citizens when word spread that Queen Izla was no longer in Katakin and there was an army of monsters in that foreign land.

"The fae wanted to rescue their princess, but with everyone gone, the Forgotten Fae argued for the portals to be closed. They didn't want the extra loss of life. As a general rule, the fae are a peaceful race. We don't seek out conflict, and there are those who also blamed my grandfather, the late King Jazrec, for traveling to Katakin and connecting with the humans in the first place. For offering my aunt to be the human king's bride.

"After a number of small, coordinated protests, King Chalir eventually had to concede that the fae wouldn't go to war. The Forgotten Fae basically forced his hand to stop the violence, and King Chalir has resented them since. To keep the peace, King Chalir agreed that no fae would ever travel to Katakin and risk opening a portal that the monsters could exploit to reach us. When Izla never arrived in Zalei as expected, King Chalir sent soldiers to Katakin only a handful of times and always in secret. Just long enough to see whether the fae could detect my aunt, but they never could."

Kade ground his jaw. "That's not all the fae have done when they've visited."

Prince Azaren's brow wrinkled in confusion at Kade's comment, but he kept on with his story. "Over the centuries, there have been vast periods of peace for the fae, but the group called the Forgotten Fae has only grown, the seed of dissent having been sown so long ago. A few months ago, my father found a large outpost of the rebel fae and sent his soldiers to destroy their camp in the hopes it would force them to split up and reintegrate into society, but his approach was all wrong, and now their supporters grow by the day. It's no longer only about the slaughter all those years ago. It's become about the belief that there shouldn't be a monarchy at all."

I stared at Prince Azaren in disbelief. "The Forgotten Fae don't want a king?"

"In simple terms," Prince Azaren said with a grim expression. "News of the execution you saw tonight will not be received well by the Forgotten Fae. Ellis was a well-known member of the group, and brother to one of the leading members, Xander. The Forgotten Fae have never tried to assassinate a member of the royal family, and I suspect Ellis had foolishly acted on his own." He let out another long breath. "But none of this is your problem, and it isn't why I brought you here. I can feel the dazra's venom has almost worn off, so that must mean you will all gain your abilities again soon. You can't be here when that happens. If all goes well, you won't be returning to your rooms at all."

"The books," I asked quietly. "If you knew the risk you posed by opening a portal to Katakin, why search for them?"

Prince Azaren leaned down and pulled out a book from under the couch he sat on. I could only guess he'd left it there earlier, and I had to wonder why he'd felt the need to hide it. The book wasn't like the ones he'd saved from Katakin. The cover was made of pure silver instead of leather, and there was no translation inked under the foreign letters that were the title. The only thing I could make out was the author: *Sharou Zanae.*

Locke leaned closer like he was as curious about the book as I was. "The author," he asked. "Who is this Sharou?"

Prince Azaren's lips tipped upward into a soft smile, and he ran his fingers fondly over the engraved cover. "My aunt," he said quietly.

My brows rose practically to my hairline. "Wait, Sharou Zanae *is* Izla?"

Prince Azaren gave me a wry grin. "She had a sense of humor. Sharou means 'common' in ancient fae, and Zanae means 'writer.'"

"I get that the books hold sentimental value for you," Asher commented. "But what has this got to do with our curse?"

Prince Azaren opened the book on his lap, turning to the first page. "Aunt Izla read many of her stories to me when I was young. I always assumed they were made up, and they are, but it was the last time I saw her when she admitted her stories are more than simply fairy tales."

"What do you mean, they're more than just stories?" Darian asked with a frown.

"Years ago, on that last night I saw her, Aunt Izla gave me this book. She asked me to hide it but wouldn't tell me why. All she said was that if it all goes wrong, the answers are hidden in her stories, and in this book in particular. As a child, I had thought she was intentionally scaring me as some kind of game, and it wasn't until I was older that I realized it was so much more than that. Every story of hers holds instructions. A hidden code. The secrets to creating curses."

I leaned forward even more, hoping to get a better look at the first page even though I couldn't read the text. My gaze slid back to Prince Azaren. "Why did she keep it a secret?"

"Curses are forbidden among our people," Prince Azaren replied. "The magic of the fae is usually self-sustaining. We draw our power from within to project it outward. With a curse, we use our magic to take something from another or place a perversion on them that isn't always visible to the naked eye. Thousands of years ago, the ancient fae figured out the secrets around curses and effectively used the magic to destroy one another. Centuries ago, Izla found a number of the ancient scrolls. My grandfather, King Jazrec, ordered for them to be destroyed, but from what I can tell, Izla couldn't bear to eradicate a part of our history. She burned the scrolls but weaved the secrets as codes into various books she wrote. I don't think she ever intended to use the magic but wanted us to remember the errors of our past. Undoubtedly, she knew the results could be disastrous if the secrets about curses fell into the wrong hands, but the scholar in her couldn't help but document them. I can only guess she brought some of her books to Katakin so she could further study them and keep them somewhere she could protect them. Obviously, she thought they were safest in plain sight."

"Why didn't you leave them in Katakin, then?" Asher asked. "The monsters probably can't break Izla's code. Locke should know. He's read those books a thousand times."

Locke glowered at Asher, and Asher lifted his hands in a gesture of peace before resting a hand back on my thigh.

Prince Azaren shifted uneasily on his chair. "I've long suspected that there are fae within the kingdom who are creating curses, whether they realize it or not. I've spent years studying the curses in Izla's books, if only to prove they are still happening today, and hopefully help those who have been afflicted. I'll admit I was desperate to have my hands on Izla's remaining works. Plus, I had no idea how advanced the Katakin monsters had become and worried about what would happen if you did by chance figure out the secret behind the books and decipher her code.

"In hindsight, it probably was a mistake to bring the books here, but it's done now. I'm not sure what would be worse: the Forgotten Fae getting a hold of the books or my father. I don't think King Chalir would turn away from the chance of using a powerful curse as a weapon if given the opportunity. But, so far, he still believes the secrets in those ancient scrolls are gone, and I've managed to convince him that I traveled to Katakin on a foolish mission to try to see if I could find my aunt. Most everyone thinks she's dead seeing as no one could detect her when we visited Katakin in the past, but I've always believed she's still alive. My father thinks I made an emotional decision in pursuit of family. Though, I'm not sure if he'll continue to believe that once you have all returned to Katakin."

The reality of why Prince Azaren wanted the books in the forest so badly came crashing down on me, and I suddenly panicked that they might not be there.

"We still don't know how to break *our* curse," Kade growled impatiently like he couldn't care less about the fae and their struggles. The edge in his voice was enough to get Prince Azaren flicking through the pages of the book in front of him.

As he did so, magic rippled through the room, and Prince Azaren tipped his head back and smiled as his eyes sparked brighter. Wings shot out of Locke's back, and he frowned as he lifted his clawed hand to touch the fangs that protruded from his mouth. Kade cracked his neck and smiled darkly as his ears shifted to wolf form and then back.

"Oh fuck!" Asher cursed, jumping off the couch as his tail speared through his pants and horns grew on the top of his head.

Only Darian and I were the ones who remained without access to our power. "Guess you were right about the dazra's power wearing off soon," I said. "Darian and I were the only ones stung more than once."

Prince Azaren rolled his neck and smiled. "Yes, well, I'm sorry I don't have a more helpful answer for you."

"How do we break the curse?" Locke prompted like he was even keener to know the information now that he was a vampire again.

Asher sat back down beside me, and Prince Azaren cleared his throat. "The code Izla used with the other books mostly all followed a similar pattern, but it wasn't until I visited Katakin that I was able to crack the code for this one. I spent most of the night trying to piece it all together, but I think I have the answers you're looking for. From what I can tell, this curse is intended for a single being, not an entire kingdom, and it clearly went wrong when Izla tried to use it. For obvious reasons, I won't tell you the secrets to how she created the curse, but I'll share what I've gleaned on how to break it. That is, I'll tell *her*." He stared directly at me then, and my eyes shot wide. "I'm an empath," he said, "much to the disappointment of my father. It's why I know I can trust you with this. Your friends, I can sense their anger and hatred for the fae, but not you. You're like a neutral party."

Kade took a step toward the prince, the violent intent clear in his eyes, but Prince Azaren quickly added, "I'm not going to hurt her. I'll simply imprint the secrets into her mind."

"No." Asher's voice was as cold as ice. "We have no guarantee you're even telling us the truth. For all we know, you could be embedding something else into Raine's mind."

"It's true you'd have to take me at my word," Prince Azaren responded, "but it's the only way I can pass on the information, and of the five of you, I trust her the most."

I let out a shaky breath, not feeling at all flattered by his comment and hating the situation I was in. *This is why you shouldn't be nice to people*, I grumbled internally. I was all for breaking the curse on Katakin, but I hadn't thought it would mean I would have to let a fae mess with my mind.

Kade gripped the back of the couch, his fingers digging into the velvet. "We could torture you and force you to imprint the information on another one of us."

"You could," Prince Azaren agreed. "But if you allow me to share it with Raine, you'll know the information is correct. If you torture me for it, I'm just as likely to implant something very different. I won't give the secrets of the curse to simply anyone. Aunt Izla kept the information hidden, and I won't be the weak link that shares it with the first monster who tortures me for it."

Kade cursed, and the rest of us tensed. There was a long beat of silence, and Prince Azaren waited as we thought it over.

I placed my hand on Asher's, rubbing my thumb soothingly over his skin. "It's just a bit of information. I'm sure I'll be fine," I said.

"No," Asher said again, his body rigid, and I bumped him with my shoulder. I wondered whether he was thinking about his mother. Did he think I'd somehow go crazy if Prince Azaren messed with my mind?

"We came here to find a way to break the curse, and we're not leaving without it. He's given us no reason not to trust him, and I'd rather know I have the real information than risk Prince Azaren scrambling one of your minds," I said.

Asher's face paled, but he said nothing.

"If you're the one with the information, you'll be more of a target when we return to Katakin," Darian commented.

"Not if no one else knows," I pointed out.

Asher flipped his hand over, and he entwined his fingers with mine. Glaring at Prince Azaren, he said, "If you hurt her, I won't just kill you. I'll make you suffer for centuries." There was a lethal edge to his voice that I'd never heard come from Asher before, and it was fucking scary. Even Prince Azaren seemed taken aback despite his bravery moments before.

"We'd take turns torturing you," Locke added, and Prince Azaren's face grew even whiter.

"Do it," I urged the prince, snapping him out of the staring competition he was currently having with my monsters. "Implant the information in my mind."

Prince Azaren nodded slowly, and he seemed to recollect himself before sliding his gaze to me. "It's a good thing my magic has returned; otherwise, we would be having a very different conversation right now. You need to close your eyes, relax your body, and let me in."

"Right, relax. Because it's not like I just invited a fae to poke around in my brain," I grumbled lightheartedly, but no one laughed.

Coming over, Prince Azaren crouched before me, placing the book on the table behind him. A beautiful illustration of a winged beast was depicted on the left page, and for some reason, I found the drawing soothing as I placed my life in the literal hands of a fae I hardly knew. Sighing, I gripped Asher's hand tighter and closed my eyes.

Prince Azaren took my other hand in his, and our skin had barely touched before my fingers began to tingle and heat.

"This shouldn't take long," Prince Azaren said. I felt the very moment our minds connected, and then his magic was weaving like blue light into me. Images and words flashed behind my eyes, but they moved so quickly I couldn't focus on a single one.

"Almost done," Prince Azaren's voice sounded in my head. More images flashed, and then it abruptly stopped, though I knew the information was still in my mind, the roots having been sown into my memory. I expected Prince Azaren to stop the connection then, but he lingered in my mind like he was trying to dig deeper. "Your bonds." The words floated softly in my head before the connection was cut off.

I gasped, my eyes snapping open as I stared at Prince Azaren.

"What about the bonds?" I asked him, questioning him out loud about what he'd said in my mind.

His green eyes were wide and round, and he stared at me like I'd grown a second head. "The information about how to break the curse is there," he said like he had to focus to get his lips to move again.

"Are you all right, lovely?" Darian asked me with concern, but I ignored him.

"You felt something. When you were in my mind," I said to Prince Azaren. "What did you find out about our bonds?"

Prince Azaren shook his head like he was still struggling to believe whatever he'd just discovered. "I–I can't be certain."

"What's she talking about?" Locke asked, coming closer.

Prince Azaren fidgeted with his fingers. "I was wrong about your bonds."

"What do you mean, you were wrong?" I asked him.

"You haven't been cursed," he said with a disbelieving shake of his head. "Well, you have, but it's like the curse has been changed. It's more like a blessing of some kind."

"Yeah, right," I said with a sarcastic smile. "You make it sound like it's one of Goddess Falia's miracles."

"Not Falia," Prince Azaren said softly, and his serious expression had the smile falling from my face. "Whether it's a curse or some kind of blessing, all I can tell is that at its heart, the magic is about protection. I think these four have been bound to you to protect you, and the magic wasn't placed over you with ill intent. If anything, I'd say it was made from...*love*."

"So it wasn't Warrick?" Locke murmured with confusion, and I remembered our theory that the bonds had come about because of Warrick's experiments on me.

"The magic is ancient, so similar to the curses I've been studying but also completely different," Prince Azaren commented.

I was busy contemplating what the prince had said when a ghostly, cloaked figure walked right through the wall like a wraith, emerging from the middle of the bookcase. Before I could cry out, the figure launched an ice dagger through the air, and I watched in shocked horror as the weapon speared into Prince Azaren's back. He let out a pained noise as he blinked wide eyes at me and wobbled in the air before slumping onto my legs.

Locke went for the cloaked figure, but the assassin was gone, vanished back between the books before the vampire could reach him.

"Assassin!" Kade cried, his growl vibrating around the room as he shifted, and Asher and Darian were both crowding around me and Prince Azaren.

The weapon was buried deep in Prince Azaren's back, but the ice blade was melting rapidly. The faster it melted, the more blood poured from the wound. "We need to get you to a healer," I said to Prince Azaren, hoping he would tell me how I could help him. Where were those fussing fae when he needed them?

A gurgling noise came from Prince Azaren's throat. "They can't get Izla's books."

The books! We still hadn't told him where the other books were. "You held up your end of the deal," I told him frantically. "The other books you rescued from Katakin. They're in the forest near where you created the portal. We only left them because we'd disturbed the toadstools and couldn't carry them."

His head bobbed, and I couldn't be sure if he was nodding. "The king's jewel," he rasped, a trail of blood dribbling down his chin. "She can heal me."

The ice spear had melted entirely now, and I pressed my hands to the wound, trying to stop the bleeding.

"Who's the jewel? Where can we find her?" Darian asked him, but Prince Azaren didn't respond, his head unmoving where it rested on my lap.

"He's bleedin' badly," Asher said.

He bent to lift the prince off me, but the door burst open with a crash.

Three fae marched into the room, fully dressed in armor. "They're monsters!" one of the fae shouted, but I was still staring at the prince in horror. Blue blood covered my fingers, and my hands shook violently.

There was a crack as Locke killed one of the fae and tossed their body to the floor, but then searing pain clamped around my neck as a ring of fire started squeezing off my air supply.

"Kneel!" a female fae commanded. Her long auburn braid reached her hips, and she stared at us with hatred as she kept her hands outstretched. "If you struggle, I'll end you here and now."

Kade growled like he was going to attack, but then the pain around my neck became so intense I let out a pained cry.

"Stop!" Asher shouted. "We'll kneel!"

Slowly Locke and Darian lowered to their knees, and Asher helped me move Prince Azaren from my lap to the couch before we did the same. Kade shifted back to his human form and knelt close to Darian. Rings of fire burning around each of our necks.

"They've killed the prince," a fae guard said to the female with auburn hair. "We need to alert the king!"

"Raine," Darian wheezed, trying to reach for me, but then the world went dark.

CHAPTER 16

~ Locke ~

My eyes peeled open, and thick steel bars appeared in my hazy vision. I lifted my head from the stone floor and climbed to my feet. My wings sagged toward the ground as I swayed on the spot, and I staggered over to the bars, mostly to have something to hold on to.

The moment my hands touched the metal, pain raced up my fingers, and I jerked backward, falling with a jarring thud onto my ass. "Fuck!"

I shook my head, trying to clear it, but all I could focus on was the deep ache in my body, the telltale sign of bloodlust. It had been days since I'd last fed, and now that the dazra's venom had worn off, I craved blood like a newly turned.

Where are the others?

My gaze swiped around the cell I was in, but I scented her before my eyes found her curled, unconscious, against the far wall. *Raine.* Kade and the others were nowhere to be seen, but Raine was in the cell *with me.*

I stumbled for her but stopped myself after two steps. Every instinct in my body was screaming at me to sink my fangs into her soft flesh and drink until the ache within me subsided. Grinding my jaw, I fought against the urge.

Fucking bastards. Our fae captors didn't know what they'd done by placing us in the same cell. She couldn't be around me while I was like this.

I staggered closer to the bars, careful this time not to touch them, and peered down the empty hallway. "You can't leave her in here with me!" I yelled, hoping to get the attention of the prison guards. "She'll fucking die! She's not a monster!" The faint thudding of two separate heartbeats came from somewhere down the rows of cells, but no one answered me. A long string of curses left my lips, and I peered back at Raine's unmoving form. The little female's heartbeat was weaker than usual, but it was steady.

My breathing grew ragged as I fought against the bloodlust that was taking over my every thought. For days, I'd been able to live without the curse. I'd been able to eat food and enjoy living rather than having to obsess about controlling my cravings. But not now. Now I was right back where I started. The hunger in me was so primal, so deep, that I wanted to howl in agony.

Memories of when I'd first turned into a vampire as a child came rushing at me, and I slumped to my knees, my head hanging down. Every suppressed memory of when my father had conducted experiments on me tormented my mind, driving me back to that dark place I'd been in two centuries ago.

A shudder rippled through me as I remembered when Warrick had trapped me in that stone room with a group of other newly turned children.

Demons, shifters, goblins, they were all there. They were all orphans, and some of them were my friends. Warrick began by running tests to observe our strength, speed, and any abilities we had. He would inflict pain on the shifters to see how fast their bodies would contort and shift as they instinctively changed into their more powerful forms. He would break our bones, shattering our shins to see how fast we would heal. But despite the pain, none of us cried.

After weeks of experimenting, eventually he stopped sending us rations of food and blood. The large room had no windows and no escape. I held out as long as I could until the bloodlust took over me. Then one after another, I drained them dry, and they weren't able to stop me. Some of them were too frightened and confused to use their own abilities, but others fought back. Not that it mattered in the end. With every soul I took, my strength grew, and soon it wasn't just the bloodlust that was controlling me. It was the desire for power. By the time there were only two of us left, I'd become a creature without any shred of humanity.

Garan, a young boy who'd been turned into a gargoyle, managed to survive until the end. He was larger than the others, and his exterior was made of stone, making his blood almost undetectable, but I knew he had to die. That was what Warrick wanted, I'd realized. To pit us against each other until there was only one left.

But Garan didn't go down easy like the others. The pair of us fought for hours, our clumsy, newfound strength evenly matched. We pounded into each other, claws scraping against stone and fists smashing against ribs until we were heaving on the floor. That was when Garan hit me with the images.

Using his gargoyle abilities, Garan transferred images into my mind. Spoken words couldn't break through to the monster I had become, but those images penetrated into my core. At first, Garan showed me images of the other children, the other monsters. Of what I'd done to them. Once a day, curls of black smoke would creep under the door, and Warrick would remove the corpses while we were unconscious. There was no evidence of my cruelty once we awoke other than the blood smearing the floor, but Garan remembered, and he assaulted me with the memories.

The endless stream of images eventually sowed the seeds of guilt, but it was when Garan showed me images of myself that I finally managed to reach out and grasp onto the remaining shred of humanity that had been buried deep within me.

Garan and I hadn't been friends before the change, but he'd seen me playing with the other children when we were human, and he flooded my brain with images of my smiling face as I played innocently, running around on the cobblestones playing tag, and sharing treats from the local candy shop. For hours more, he plagued my mind with image after image, and eventually, I was able to see through the fog of hatred, violence, and bloodlust. Because of Garan, I was able to recapture parts of the boy I'd once been, and once that happened, my head was clear enough that together we were able to come up with a plan. While Warrick had been using his experiments to learn about us and our abilities, it also taught us to understand what we were. And I learned a particularly useful piece of information: vampires didn't need to breathe.

I couldn't send images back to Garan, so instead, in the far corner, I wrote two small words on the stone floor using my own blood as ink. It read, PLAY DEAD. I pretended to drink Garan dry until he fell limp to the ground, his gray body remaining still on the floor. Gargoyles had hearts of stone, and Garan was able to slow his heart rate until it was barely detectable. We hoped Warrick wouldn't realize Garan was still alive until it was too late.

That night when black tendrils seeped under the door, I pretended to fall unconscious, and when Warwick entered the room and went to collect Garan's body, I attacked. I couldn't know whether Warrick would set me free after Garan's death, and in any case, I now had enough humanity that I was determined to save the gargoyle's life. My fangs sank into my father's neck, tearing deep. Garan, who had only pretended to die and had held his breath when the black smoke came, rose from the ground and slashed at Warrick's body with his long claws.

Warrick managed to fight us off, throwing us both across the room, but we landed near the doorway and were able to scramble through and lock the door behind us before Warrick could follow. Oh, how I relished the sound of my father's angry bellows. Neither Garan nor I stayed to find out what would happen next. We fled into the city and remained in hiding for the weeks that followed. I later learned that Warrick had been freed from the cell by his goblin assistant, Gosren.

It was my mother who found me first, and she eventually convinced me to return to the House of Nesarin with the assurances that she wouldn't let my father treat me so poorly again. I refused at first, but when she started to threaten the lives of others if I didn't comply, I went back, if only to ensure no one else was harmed because of me and my parents. Warrick never did try to experiment on me again, and he never spoke about Garan and me locking him in that cell, but over time I learned about his mission to find a way to break the curse. Warrick exploited my interest, and before I knew it, I had become another tool in his arsenal. I always understood he was manipulating me, but my desperate desire to be human drove me to keep working for him. As long as I wasn't hurting other monsters, I could tolerate his requests. His orders.

But then he wanted me to take over the House of Nesarin. The cruelty of the monsters in that house almost matched Warrick's, and I despised the idea of being their leader. I'd befriended Kade, Asher, and Darian in the weeks when I'd been hiding in the city, and I still caught up with them frequently.

So when Warrick had begun pressuring me to fight for my place as alpha of the House of Nesarin, I'd left the house entirely.

And after all that, now here I was, once again fighting my bloodlust while trapped with someone I cared about. Except this time, it was worse. Because this time it was *Raine.* An angry cry burst from me, and then I was on my feet, running at the steel bars.

Pain zapped through me as my body connected with the metal, and I jerked and shook as I fell to the ground.

"Locke, what the hell are you doing?" croaked a feminine voice, and Raine came over to crouch beside me.

She went to place her hands on my chest, but I snarled at her.

"Get away from me!"

She stayed where she was, but I could see the uncertainty shining in her eyes as she stared at the long fangs protruding from my mouth.

"You need to calm down," she said softly. "We'll find a way to get out of this."

I chuckled darkly. "You think I'm worried about the fae?"

She eased back a little, and I suspected it was likely due to the wild look in my eyes.

"You need to stay away," I said more calmly than I had before. "I can't control the bloodlust."

Her face paled, but a determined look overcame her. "You won't hurt me. You've had the chance to do that countless times over, and if you were going to, you would have by now."

"You don't understand," I said with a shake of my head. "I haven't experienced bloodlust like this since I was first turned."

She noted the strain on my face, but her expression still didn't reflect the terror I knew she should be feeling. "You drank from Darian back in the forest," she began, but I didn't like where she was heading.

I remembered when she'd found me drinking from Darian's neck. I'd been about to release him as I'd taken just enough from my friend to keep myself going, but when her scent of coconut had filled my senses, my fangs had buried deeper into my siren brother. I'd dragged more of his blood into my mouth, knowing he could handle it, to stop myself from lunging for her instead. Darian hadn't complained about how much I'd taken from him, but I knew he'd felt the after-effects, and guilt had eaten at me the next day.

"I'm not going to drink from you," I growled. "If I start, I won't be able to stop. This wouldn't be like it was with Darian. I would kill you."

Raine still didn't turn from me. Instead, she pressed closer again and lifted her hand to brush her red hair over one shoulder, baring her neck to me.

"So quick to beg for death," I sneered. "What happened to the human who wanted to do anything to save her sister?"

She bristled at my comment, her eyes narrowing on my face. "I *will* find my sister, but we won't be able to escape with you behaving like this. If Darian could trust you, then I do too. Take what you fucking need."

I glared at her, hatred burning in me because she was openly taunting me so brashly. Why? Why was she so different from everyone else? I was showing her my most ugly, unredeemable self, yet she was rewarding me with her trust. Had I been an ignorant male, I would have chalked it up to stupidity, but I now knew Raine too well to think that. She was giving me a chance. A chance to survive. And hopefully a chance for her to survive too.

"I refuse to let the fae kill us," she said, her eyes burning with fire. "If they think we killed Prince Azaren, then we'll be the next ones with our souls ripped from our bodies. I fucking need you to have your wits about you so we can focus on how we'll get out of this together."

She was right. There was no way my head would be clear enough to even come up with any semblance of an escape plan while I was stuck in this bloodlust state. Garan had managed to get through to me with his images, but Raine didn't have that power. I had to do this. For her. For my brothers. And for my fucking self.

In the span of a heartbeat, I was kneeling before her. She flinched at the sudden movement, but she didn't back away. "I–I trust you, Locke," she said, letting an unusual vulnerability enter her tone.

"You shouldn't," I replied, and then I was grabbing her, my fangs clamping down on the exposed flesh of her neck as I gripped onto her thigh with one hand and grasped her shoulder with the other, pulling her closer to me. A small gasp escaped her, but as I drew her blood into my mouth, my venom entered her bloodstream and her body relaxed, becoming easily pliable in my fingers. Her gasp turned into a moan, and I sucked harder, overcome by my thirst as Raine's blood slipped down my throat, the warm liquid like sweet nectar and the taste more intoxicating and addictive than anything I'd had before.

I forgot who I was holding. My mind became overrun with bloodlust, and it was just me, the victim in my arms, and the craving for blood that had consumed my mind. I gripped the body I held tighter, my claws starting to dig in as I hollowed my cheeks and dragged my victim's blood into my veins, desperate to take everything they could give me. Pain bloomed in my chest, but I ignored it. I wanted to drown in my victim's blood and consume her until there was nothing left. Power washed through me as her blood flooded my system, and still I drank.

The pain became more intense, but I fought through, determined not to let it stop me from taking what was mine. *My* victim. *My* blood. More power flowed through me, and the pain in my chest increased until it felt as though my chest was on fire. I pushed through the searing agony, snarling as I feasted on the female in my arms.

"Locke," a quiet, drowsy word fell from my victim's lips, and then she was silent again.

Locke. The word meant nothing to me.

The pain in my chest increased until it felt as if someone was cleaving at my heart, stabbing at my flesh, and ripping apart my rib cage. I released my victim, yanking my head back with a frustrated hiss. The female's head slumped forward, her chin falling toward her chest and her red waves gleaming in the dim light. *Red waves. Searing pain.*

A long moment passed as I stared at that silky hair, as I felt the power running through my veins, and as I breathed in the scents of coconut and steel. *Raine. My beautiful Raine.*

Fuck. FUCK! The pain in my chest was like an inferno dancing around my heart, no longer a strange nuisance that was keeping me from finishing my meal but a warning that was blaring through my whole body, reminding me that I was murdering the very female I was bonded to and meant to protect. The female who had become as much a part of our group as Kade, Darian, and Asher. And the only female I'd ever imagined spending my cursed eternity with.

My claws retracted, removing from Raine's skin, and I swiftly carried her to the metal cot by the wall. Gently lowering her, I brushed the hair away from her ghostly face and let out a string of curses.

I wasn't willing to let her die. No. She would fucking live, and I'd make sure of it.

Using one of my claws, I slashed a line across my left wrist and pressed it to her lips. "You need to drink, beautiful. If you don't, you'll die. And I know you don't want that."

Blood dripped onto her lips, but she didn't move. Her eyes remained closed and her breathing shallow.

"Fuck!" I opened her mouth and created a fist with my hand, dripping blood onto her tongue. "Drink, damn it."

I couldn't be certain it would work, but her blood had given me strength, so I hoped mine would do the same for her. I lowered my wrist to her mouth again.

This time, there was movement. At first, it was only the brush of her lips against my wrist. The movement was barely detectable, and I wouldn't have noticed if I hadn't been watching her so carefully. Then again. More movement. Her eyelids fluttered before closing, and she opened her mouth wider, her tongue darting out to lick at my cut.

"That's right," I purred my encouragement, trying to remain calm in spite of my hammering heart. "Drink," I instructed her again, and this time, she leaned her head forward, her lips sealing around my wrist as she began to suck and take my blood into her mouth.

"Good girl," I praised as I stroked her hair with my other hand. As she drank, color returned to her skin, the pain in my chest beginning to lessen, and soon she was grabbing hold of my arm as she drank greedily. I let her take from me until the pain was gone from my chest, and when I could feel my own strength starting to drain away again, I pulled my wrist away.

Raine's lips were stained with black, and she blinked up at me with wide eyes like she'd only just realized what she'd been doing. I waited for the look of disgust. Waited for her to recoil from me now that she was lucid, but she surprised me by licking her lips. "Well, I can see now why you wanted blood so badly," she said with a small grin, and just seeing the life in her eyes made my heart crack with relief.

She took in my position, my body leaning over her and my fingers still tangled in her hair. Lust sparked in her amber eyes, vibrant and wanting, and I couldn't help myself. "Fucking beautiful," I murmured, and then I was curving down and pressing my lips to hers, my tongue diving into her mouth like I was desperate to taste my blood on her lips. She returned the kiss, her hands winding behind my back and her nails digging into my shoulder blades. My mouth left hers, and I began kissing down her neck, my movements almost as frantic as when I'd been desperate for her blood.

"I thought I'd killed you," I said, my voice hoarse as I kissed her collarbone.

Her fingers dived into my hair as I continued to make my way lower. When I lifted the skirt of her dress and began kissing between her thighs, she let out a gasp. "I don't know if you know this, but I'm bonded to four badass monsters who won't let me die," she squeezed out with panting breaths.

"I hope those lucky bastards know what they're doing," I commented with a sly smile as I slid her panties down her legs and threw them to the floor. Standing, I undressed, letting her see every inch of my hardened muscles and bare skin, and then I was moving back between her thighs.

When my fingers slid up her center, she was more than ready for me. She sucked in a sharp breath at my touch, her eyes glazing with desire. Leaning down, I grazed my fangs lightly up her thigh as I slid a finger into her, and she trembled at my touch, a moan squeezing from her throat. Fuck, I would worship her.

"They seem to know what they're doing," she said breathlessly, and I chuckled darkly.

Moving over her, I teased her with the tip of my hard cock, and she gasped, her legs opening even wider for me. "Fuck me already," she urged, and I didn't hold back. My cock glided into her, and her face scrunched with pleasure, her mouth opening like she was letting out a silent scream. *So fucking beautiful.* Her body felt like it was made for me, and my throat tightened with an unfamiliar emotion. A desperation that I couldn't quite place. I was still high from having drank her blood, but I knew it was more than that. Her muscles clenched like she was trying to keep me inside her, and I got the distinct feeling that even though I was the one on top, she was the one claiming me. The one accepting me, even after I'd nearly taken her life. Faster I slammed into her.

"You know what I want to hear," I rasped, and she wet her lips.

"Yes," she breathed.

"Say it."

"Locke," she whispered.

Fuck. I loved the sound of my name on her lips as I filled her.

She cried out as she shattered, her nails digging deeper into my back, and I roared as I found my own release, an unusual satisfaction settling over me as I spilled into her.

When we stopped jerking, I slowly pulled out and dropped beside her, staying on my side so we could both fit on the narrow cot. Pulling her to me, I rested my head against her fiery hair and breathed her in. I hadn't thought it was possible, but this female was saving my dark soul. I already knew she was mine. I'd known it the first time I'd tasted her, though I'd tried to deny it. But it was now that I realized I was *hers* too.

Her amber eyes were drowsy as she stared up at me with a smile. "So now about that escape plan..."

CHAPTER 17

~ Raine ~

I dropped onto the edge of the metal cot and watched as Locke continued circling our cell and checking for weak points. We'd both been over every inch of the space and whenever we touched the walls or the metal bars facing out into the passageway, magic would crackle against our skin, zapping pain up our fingers.

Locke touched a low brick that jutted further out than the others, but he yanked his hand back and cursed a second later.

Leaning my head to one side, I rubbed at my temple and tried not to think about the pulsing pain in my head. Every time I'd touched the enchanted walls, the pain had increased, until it had become a dull ache that never left me.

"Stop," I told him with a weary sigh. "We're sealed in. However they've enchanted the cell, we're not getting out until someone opens the door."

Locke ignored me and kept pacing and prodding the walls, but then he shot to the bars and tried peering down the passageway.

"We're about to have company," he growled.

I jumped to my feet. "What?"

"I can hear at least three of them," Locke added as he took a few steps back. "Just keep quiet and let me do the talking."

I knew what he was really saying: *Keep quiet so their attention remains on me.*

Locke cocked his head like he was listening, and soon I heard it too. The scrape of footsteps on the stone floor and the jostling of metal keys. When King Chalir came into view, he wasn't alone. Three fae soldiers stood with him, including a female soldier with long auburn hair and hatred shining in her hazel eyes. The one who'd been there when we were captured. When I'd gained consciousness in the cell, the fire around my neck had disappeared, and there was no wound to suggest it had ever been there, but I could still remember the searing pain. The fae soldier smirked as if she knew I was thinking about what she'd done to me.

King Chalir stopped in front of the bars, and his expression hardened at the sight of us. It was the first time

I'd seen him without his painted fae females pawing at him. *No wonder he looks so agitated.*

"Torez. Zandras," he said to two of the soldiers. A male soldier, Torez, and Zandras, the female soldier with the auburn hair, lifted their arms. The magic crackling around our cell disappeared, and almost in the same instant, searing pain curled around my throat, the agony driving me to my knees. Locke managed to stay standing, fighting against the pain. He staggered toward me and tried to rip the collar of fire from my neck, but his efforts only made the pain worse as the fire burned hotter.

"Stop," I croaked, and his panicked gaze lingered on me before he swiveled back toward the king.

"Let her go," he snarled, but King Chalir ignored him.

"I knew there was something strange about Azaren's story. Humans escaping those monsters? Those beasts? I was a gullible fool for believing him." King Chalir's brows lowered, and he took a calming breath, his expression becoming thoughtful. "That son of mine always was too soft. I'm sure this was your plan all along. To pretend to be his saviors so you could finally gain access to our world."

"We *did* save your son," Locke said coldly.

"I can only imagine you intended to assassinate me after you murdered him. Just like your human king did to my father," King Chalir continued, acting like Locke hadn't spoken.

"The Forgotten Fae are the ones who stabbed Prince Azaren," I blurted, my words turning into a coughing fit as the ring around my throat tightened.

"You're killing her!" Locke shouted, and King Chalir watched us for a moment before nodding at Zandras. She flicked her wrist, and the ring of fire around my throat became smaller again. Tears leaked from my eyes, and I tried to control my erratic breathing.

"My soldiers tell me there was no evidence to suggest anyone else was in the room besides you five monsters and my son," King Chalir commented conversationally.

Locke peered back at me before turning to face the king again. "What have you done with our friends?"

King Chalir waved a hand in the air. "There really is no point torturing you monsters. I could never believe anything that came out of your mouths, even if it *was* the truth."

"Whatever you think happened," Locke growled, "at least know Raine had nothing to do with it. She was a prisoner like Prince Azaren, and we brought her along to help sell the story. As you can see, she's still human." He twisted to the side, indicating to where I had staggered to my feet. While the fire had lessened, the pain in my neck was still unbearable, and I fought to keep down the bile that started rising up my throat.

King Chalir scoffed in disbelief, though he regarded me again before saying, "If she is, then that is most unfortunate. For your crimes against the crown, all five of you will be executed in the morning."

Executed? I didn't know why fear hollowed out my gut. It was exactly what I'd expected the king to say. At least I knew Kade, Darian, and Asher were alive. *For now, that is.*

Locke's hands fisted at his sides as anger rolled off him. "Then you'll be murdering an innocent." He wasn't trying to claim that we were all innocent. He was only trying to save me, and I found it irritating as hell.

"There are always regrettable casualties during times of war," King Chalir replied coolly.

I took an unsteady step closer to the steel bars. "What do you mean, *war*?" I rasped.

King Chalir smiled, but there was no warmth in the expression. "I should be thanking you, truly. For over a century, I've wanted to march on Katakin. To get vengeance for the deaths of my father and sister and rid us of the abominations Izla created. Now that you've brought violence to our home, the fae will have to act. Even the Forgotten Fae won't be able to stop what's coming."

"Assassination was never our intention," Locke seethed. "We came to stop a war, not start one. The only battle you should be focused on is the one you're waging against your own kind."

But it was obvious that nothing we could say was going to change King Chalir's mind.

"You monsters are the reason there was ever dissent among the fae to begin with. When your soul is being torn from your bodies, just remember *you're* the ones who infiltrated this castle and came into my home," King Chalir responded, his face reddening with anger. "And when you're paraded before the fae, and they see how powerless you are to stop me from taking your lives, they'll finally understand their fear for the monsters of Katakin is unfounded. Your race is but a perversion of the fae. A cruel and twisted imitation of our kind. My sister cursed you all as penance for your crimes, but I'll be the one to eradicate you once and for all."

I wanted to point out that from what I'd heard, Izla had only intended to curse the human king, but nausea overwhelmed me, and the room began to spin. Locke caught me before I fell, and all I heard were Locke's words to the king, "You'll suffer for this," before I was thrown into darkness once again.

CHAPTER 18

~ Raine ~

A high-pitched ringing sounded in my ears, and I forced my crusted eyes open. Groaning, I squinted against the blinding light coming from above. I tried to lift a hand to shield my eyes, but cold metal bit into my wrists, keeping my arms by my sides. *What the hell?*

"Thank all fuckin' seven devils, sweetheart, we were startin' to worry you weren't gonna wake."

I turned my head to the side to see Asher strung up beside me, his body pinned to a thick steel slab with his arms and legs spread and shackled close to the steel. Beside him, Darian and Kade were held in similar positions, and Locke was restrained in the same manner to the other side of me. The five of us were all in a line, our steel slabs connected to a wide platform, and before us stood a sea of well-dressed fae who gawked, booed, and cursed at us. Around the fae, beautiful buildings made from silver and glass towered into the air, the balconies and tiled rooves covered with vines, greenery, and a kaleidoscope of color.

"They moved us outside while we were unconscious," Asher commented, his violet eyes lacking their usual mirth. "I was the first to wake after they'd placed us here."

A fae in the crowd threw something in Asher's direction, and a ball of fire smacked into the steel above his head. The ball exploded, bits of ash clouding the air, and burning embers fell down the side of Asher's face. The skin beside his right eye and most of his cheek turned an angry shade of red, but he healed quickly, the skin smoothing and returning to its normal color.

"Least I have my healin' abilities back," Asher said with a grin, but I couldn't return his smile. My chest heaved as I failed to control my breathing, fear making my heartbeat thunder in my ears. Gritting my teeth, I tried to yank both arms free, not caring when the metal cuffs rubbed painfully at my wrists.

"The restraints have been laced with the same magic as our cells," Locke said, his eyes as black as night. "The magic is weakening us, stopping us from using our abilities. I can't break the cuffs."

"So what do we do, then?" I asked with a shaky voice. I'd assumed we might be able to escape in the time when we were being led from our cell to our execution. But we were already here, on display, and ready to be slaughtered.

"Kill the monsters!" a fae female in the crowd spat at us, and I tried to ignore her.

Locke's expression hardened, but there was a trace of fear in his onyx eyes as his gaze traveled to my restraints and settled again on my face. "I don't know," he admitted quietly.

I swallowed and peered at the hundreds of fae who'd turned up to watch our execution. Some stood on the balconies of the surrounding houses, gripping the barriers and enjoying the higher view, while the remainder of them crowded the street, jostling and pushing against one another. A line of soldiers stood before the platform we were on, their silver armor gleaming in the sun, but none of the fae tried to get past them. Despite the hate-filled gazes and angry faces of the fae, a wide gap remained between us and them, and it didn't take me long to figure out why.

No one wanted to get close to the monsters.

Some of the fae clung to their children, their arms trembling, while others gripped weapons and held up their hands, ready to assault us with their power and steel. We were the ones in chains. The ones without power, yet they were afraid of *us*.

Kade let out an enraged howl that rattled the glass of the nearby buildings, and the fae flinched, their pointed ears twitching at the noise. Even a few of the fae soldiers before us twisted their heads around to ensure he was still restrained. *All right, so maybe they're right to be afraid.* Somewhere a child cried, and instead of feeling satisfied that Kade was terrifying the fae, I just felt sick. Because we weren't monsters. Not in the way they saw us. But Warrick was.

I thought of what would happen if the fae attacked Katakin. I couldn't know who would win. I still wasn't sure of what power many of the fae possessed, but what I did know was that Warrick's outliers wouldn't show mercy, and neither would the alphas. There would be a massive loss of life on both sides, and I couldn't let that happen. I didn't want my soul sucked from my body, that was a freakin' given, but getting free wasn't only about us.

Closing my eyes, I searched for any indication that the dazra's venom had worn off. When I'd accessed my magic during the battle with the outliers in the ballroom, it had been like a spark buried deep in my mind. One I'd had to focus on to make my power grow. But now when I searched, it was as if there was a blank hole where my spark should have been. I growled in frustration.

Footsteps thudded on the wooden platform, and I snapped my eyes open as King Chalir strode into view followed by a fae with white hair and swirling gray eyes. A shiver went through me as I recognized the fae who had executed the Forgotten Fae prisoner at the king's celebration.

Lifting his arms, King Chalir waited for the fae to quiet. When silence settled over the sea of faces, he bellowed out at the crowd, "Citizens of Zalei. Not long ago I was standing before you announcing the safe return of my son, the Crown Prince Azaren, war general of our armies. I embraced our human guests, said to be the rescuers of my son, and granted them a place of honor among our kind."

He took a dramatic pause before continuing, his face becoming grave. "But I have come to learn that I was deceived, as was my son. For these humans are in fact monsters who disguised themselves. They are abominations sent from Katakin to infiltrate our home and assassinate the royal family and all those in a position of power. From there, I believe they planned to open portals around the city and create gateways allowing more of their kind to enter Zalei and ravage and conquer our fair land."

A ripple of gasps and whimpers of terror swept through the crowd, and I glared at the king, internally cursing him for his lies.

King Chalir lifted his chin. "For nearly two centuries, I had accepted that we would not be able to enact justice for the death of my father, King Jazrec, and my dear sister, Princess Izla, queen to the once human realm of Katakin. Above all else, I have pursued peace, sitting idly, sated by the knowledge that the monsters could not reach our world. But now the beasts have shown they are not happy to leave us be. They have come for your prince, *my son*, and they will come for everything else we hold dear. This morning, we start the day by executing the monsters who tried to assassinate my son, but once our army is assembled, I plan to march upon Katakin and eradicate the monsters entirely so we shall never have to fear them again!" He shouted the last part, his face reddening with emotion, and the fae roared in response, showing their support and cursing us.

I peered out at the crowd of fae and noticed a hooded figure standing in the shadows of a nearby building. Even with the distance, I recognized the cloak. *The Forgotten Fae who tried to murder the prince. The one who created the ice dagger.* As if they could feel my stare, the fae slunk behind the building, disappearing from sight.

King Chalir stepped back from the front of the platform and went to stand at the side, and the fae who'd sucked out the prisoner's soul at the party not long ago moved toward us, his tall, thin frame and swirling gray eyes making him seem more like a reaper than an executioner.

He stopped at the front of the platform, pivoting to face us, and though he looked in our direction, his gray eyes appeared unseeing and devoid of life. Lifting his hands, he stretched out his knobby fingers, and Locke, Kade, Darian, and Asher all struggled at their restraints, their muscles bunching as they fought to get free.

"Go to war against the monsters of Katakin and you will all be slaughtered," Locke snarled at the crowd. "You have no idea what's waiting for you on the other side."

But the fae didn't stop shouting obscenities at us, and the executioner didn't drop his hands.

Asher jerked and strained against his cuffs. "We'll get out of this, Sharachi," he said to me, but my attention snapped forward as the executioner fae's magic reached out to all five of us at once. The fae's tendrils of power were like talons that dug into my body and tore through my flesh to grip my very essence. I gasped and squeezed my eyes shut as my entire body screamed in pain as a part of me felt like it was being ripped away.

Kade's roar and Darian's hiss of pain filled my ears, drowning out the thudding of my heartbeat.

"Raine," Locke rasped, his voice a ragged whisper. I opened my eyes, but my gaze never made it to the vampire. Five streams of shimmering white light were flowing through the air from our bodies toward the fae with the gray eyes, the light beginning to wind around the fae's bony fingers. The fae's face was scrunched, strain pulling at his brow, but he held us there.

I fought through my agony, desperately trying to find the spark of power within myself. I knew it was hopeless. Even if the dazra's venom had left my system, the enchanted cuffs would still nullify my magic, but I had to keep trying.

"See, these monsters are no different from any beings!" King Chalir jeered from the side of the platform. "They can be killed just as easily."

I ignored the tears leaking down my cheeks and fought against the white light that was now shining behind my eyes. *The cuffs. If I can break the restrain—* My thought trailed off as more of the fae's power flowed into me and a piercing noise assaulted my ears. It took me a moment to realize I was screaming. Kade howled with me, the sound primal and full of anger, and I couldn't hear any of the fae now. I wasn't sure if it was because we were drowning them out or if they had grown silent.

My scream ended, and my head sagged, my chin dropping to my chest. I focused on sucking in slow breaths through my nose. *Goddess, we're about to die.* I thought of the secrets about the Katakin curse now buried in my memory. Thought of my sister, and of the four monsters who had fought to protect me. It was strange thinking the fae would take my life when throughout my childhood it was the monsters I'd feared.

Locke was silent beside me now, but I couldn't lift my head to see if he was still alive. I couldn't—

A spark flared in my chest briefly before disappearing. *Was that—?* I struggled to focus my mind. To fight against the fae's power and my weakening state. Another spark briefly lit up inside me, like the flame of a candle lighting up in a chasm of darkness. *Yes.* It was impossible, but it was there. Power rushed through me as the dazra's venom wore off completely, my magic no longer a spark but licks of flame. I didn't know why the enchanted cuffs weren't stopping my magic, but I almost sobbed with relief as I reached for it. Goose bumps prickled over my arms, a cold chill settling into my bones as my soul continued to be yanked from me, but I didn't hesitate to let my power loose.

The cuffs restraining my monsters and around my arms and ankles dissolved into sand, and that was when the real chaos began. Asher caught me before I hit the ground, his thick arms wrapping around me protectively and his touch gentle like he was afraid I'd come apart in his grip. A growl ripped through the air, and Kade's wolf shot toward the executioner fae, reaching him in a few powerful strides. The fae's gray eyes shuttered as he was torn apart, blue blood splattering across the platform, and the white light that was winding around his fingers sprang back into the five of us. I sucked in a sharp breath as the agonizing pain in my body vanished, and warmth sank into my bones, my strength returning.

That was when I noticed the mournful song winding through the air. Darian stood at the front of the platform, an enchanting melody coming from him as he entranced the crowd of fae. To the side of the platform, Locke glared at King Chalir as he squeezed his clawed hand around the king's throat. The king was the only fae who hadn't been entranced by Darian's power.

"Try to use magic and I'll snap your neck," Locke snarled, his voice filled with the promise of death.

Kade's massive wolf form tossed the remains of the executioner fae's body from the platform, and he stalked toward the king, his golden eyes narrowed on the ruler of the fae realm. King Chalir's eyes widened with fear as the wolf bared his bloodied teeth.

"Create a portal to Katakin," Locke ordered, and tipped his head toward Kade. "Or I let him have you."

King Chalir's nostrils flared, his face growing redder.

Darian was backing up in our direction now as the entranced fae started moving toward him.

Locke gripped King Chalir's neck tighter, but the king kept his lips sealed.

"Do it," Locke snarled. "And if the portal leads to anywhere other than Katakin, I won't just kill you. I'll make sure Kade here keeps you alive for days until you're begging for death."

Kade growled, the rumbling sound vibrating through the platform, and King Chalir swallowed, his face growing pale. With shaky hands, he reluctantly lifted his arms, a look of concentration crossing his face, and then a ring of blue fire was forming in the air before us.

Enchanted fae were climbing onto the platform now, their lust-filled gazes fixed on Darian.

"Release them," Locke barked at the siren. "Let's go."

Locke dragged King Chalir into the portal first, and I had just enough time to see Darian release his hold on the fae before Asher carried me into the portal.

CHAPTER 19

My ears popped as we emerged from the portal, and Asher carried me out onto a cobbled street. Tall, dark buildings surrounded us, the gray stone lit by lanterns with flickering blue fire, and I could only guess we were somewhere in Katakin City. Locke stood a few steps away, a clawed hand gripping King Chalir's neck while the other hand clasped the king's shoulder. Kade and Darian exited the portal after us, striding forward like angry gods. Kade was back in his human form, and his golden gaze flicked from me to the king.

"Let me kill him," the wolf shifter growled, his eyes flashing with anger.

"As much as I hate to say it, we must return King Chalir," Darian drawled. "We don't need the fae thinking the Katakin monsters murdered another fae royal."

"You heard the king," Kade countered. "War is coming now. Nothing is going to change that."

Locke studied King Chalir like he was considering killing the fae ruler himself, but then he dragged the king closer to the portal and bared his fangs. "Whether you believe us or not, we didn't attack Prince Azaren. That was the work of a Forgotten Fae assassin. If you insist on sending your army here, it will be a massacre." He paused then, studying the fae male. "But you already know that, don't you?" Locke went to push the king into the portal, but he paused again. "Close the portal as soon as you return to your realm. I don't think I need to explain what will happen if you don't." And then he was hurling the king through the ring of blue fire.

As soon as King Chalir was gone, Kade was at my side, and Asher let the wolf shifter lift me into his arms. It was like he knew Kade needed me more than he did in that moment.

"I *can* stand," I groused, but Kade's only response was to crush me to his chest as his shaky fingers brushed over my body. His nose dipped to my hair, and he breathed in deeply.

"I thought I'd lost you, Mahare," he said as his golden eyes tracked over my face.

"Nope, still here," I said with a weak smile.

"Least the king ain't a complete idiot," Asher commented, and I peered over in time to see the last flickering flames of the portal disappear.

"We need to get off the street," Locke said coldly, bringing our attention back to the city. "We're in Borren's territory."

Kade had only taken one step when his head jerked upward and his ears shifted, forming points. His ears twitched, and his brows lowered as he lifted his nose into the air and sniffed.

"What is it?" I asked, but his gaze collided with Locke's, alarm flashing in his eyes as he shouted, "We're not alone!"

Two monsters lumbered out from behind a building. Thick black veins ran over their massive ash-gray chests and along the bands of muscle on their misshapen arms, and when they roared, their fanged mouths opened so wide they could swallow my head whole. Each of their meaty hands ended in three long claws, and two small red eyes glowed atop their bald heads. One of the monsters let out a strange, keening sound, and as if it was a signal, more monsters appeared, swarming from all directions. They came from between buildings and jumped from rooftops like they'd been waiting for us.

My heart stuttered. "Outliers," I breathed as Kade quickly lowered me to the ground.

"We can't seem to get a fuckin' break," Asher commented as the four of them circled around me protectively. "And the fae think *I'm* ugly. Just wait until they see these bastards."

Darian's lips twisted. "They will be surprised indeed."

Locke glared at the outliers. "We knew there might be trouble when we returned. Looks like Warrick has been busy while we were away."

As the closest outliers reached us, Kade and the others launched into action. Locke's claws raked in deep across the chest of an outlier, while Asher's fist smashed into another creature's face. Darian darted and spun, delivering short, sharp blows to various places on an outlier's abdomen before performing a roundhouse kick that sent the beast flying.

I jumped back from an outlier that tried to grab my arm, and the creature's claws tore through the silken skirt of the fae gown still clinging to me. Opening its massive mouth, the outlier roared, its rancid breath rushing at my face and saliva spraying on my cheeks. *Fuck.* And then Asher was barreling into the monster, pushing it away from me.

Another outlier advanced from my other side, and Locke came up behind the beast, ripping its head clean from its body. But as soon as one outlier fell, there were three more to take its place. All around, the outliers advanced, coming at us from all sides. Kade, Locke, Darian, and Asher fought hard, but without their blades, it was harder to deal killing blows.

"Stay close to Raine!" Locke shouted, but his voice was quickly drowned out by the outliers' roars and the sounds of battle.

An outlier smacked a meaty arm across Darian's chest, and the siren went flying to the side. He rolled along the cobblestones as he landed, but before an outlier could crush his skull with its large, clawed foot, Darian opened his mouth and a spine-chilling tune poured out of him. As one, the outliers turned to focus their attention on the siren, and Asher, Kade, and Locke went on the offensive, working efficiently to bring the creatures down.

An outlier who had managed to block its ears, drove its fist into Darian's chest, and the siren's tune sputtered out. Freed from their trance, three outliers ran at me, aiming for a gap that had opened up between Kade and Asher. Their red eyes locked onto my face, and I backed toward the door of a darkened building, panic building in my throat. If I could just find a blade or another weapon. Even a kitchen knife would do! Grasping the door handle, I twisted my wrist, but the door didn't budge, the wood remaining hard against my spine. *Oh fuck!* Kade and the others growled and snarled as they fought the monsters coming at them from all angles. Kade was in animal form now, his wolf raging as it ripped apart the outliers swarming him.

Magic, Raine! Use your stupid magic! I didn't need a weapon; I *was* a damn weapon. Sweat streamed down my forehead as I tried to find the spark. *Come on!* But the three outliers were too close. Claws reached for me, ready to tear me to pieces, when my magic flared to life, reaching for the outliers in front of me.

A rumbling came from the cobblestones beneath my feet, and then a small portion of the street in front of me disintegrated to sand, and water rushed through the opening, crashing into the outliers and pushing them backward. The water cocooned the beasts as they thrashed, the liquid diving into their noses, throats, and ears. Their bodies swelled as they filled with water, ballooning until they exploded, water, blood, and flesh spraying in all directions. *Well, that got the job done*, I thought with a disgusted wince.

Locke, Asher, and Darian peered over at me, their brows raised in surprise. Asher gave me a toothy grin, the expression looking almost crazed given his face was slick with black blood. Locke took a step in my direction, but five more outliers attacked from his right, taking his attention away from me.

I rolled my shoulders, setting my sights on the massive pile of outliers that were crowding around Kade's wolf. Taking a breath, I focused my mind, but a warm hand clamped over my mouth in the same instant that an arm wrapped around my middle, pulling me backward.

My startled cry was muffled as I was yanked into the building behind me. The wooden door shut as quickly as it had been opened, and I started to buck and struggle. The hand removed from my face just long enough for someone to wrap a gag over my mouth.

"We need to get her away from here," a feminine voice said behind me, and I frowned. *Where have I heard that fucking voice?* I still hadn't figured it out, when strong hands gripped under my arms, and I was pulled through the house, the shadowed furniture passing in a blur. Within a matter of seconds, I was yanked out of the back of the building and pulled across a street and into another dwelling. We crossed at least six streets, moving through multiple houses before my kidnappers paused again.

A figure stepped into my line of sight, and I glared at my captor. *Kasey.* One of Zacal's wolves. One of the ones who used to torment Kade. The one I would have killed if Kade hadn't stopped me.

She gave me a cruel, fanged smile. "Oh, how I've waited for this," she growled, and faster than I'd seen her move, her hand cracked across my cheek, forcing my head to the side. Pain flared all the way up to my eye, but I gritted my teeth. Strong hands still held under my arms, keeping me steady, and I twisted my head to glance at the two burly-looking males holding me before turning my attention back to Kasey.

Claws peeked from the wolf shifter's hand, but as she pulled back to strike me again, an ear-splitting growl shattered through the city, rattling the buildings and lampposts.

"Kade," she snarled through clenched teeth.

Low, rumbling growls came from the males holding me, and I smiled like a maniac at the thought of Kade's wolf tearing these three apart. *Then again, why should he have all the fun?* I thought of my magic. I'd been so panicked I hadn't even thought of using it while they'd dragged me away.

I focused on the power flowing through my veins and thought of my three captors. Magic swelled inside me, making my body tingle.

"We need to hurry!" Kasey snapped at the males, a hint of fear in her voice, and then pain erupted in my skull, and the world went black.

CHAPTER 20

~ **Kade** ~

Raine had been taken from us. One moment, she'd been near that fucking building, using her magic to obliterate outliers, and the next, she was gone. Fear and fury exploded inside me, and I let out an enraged growl as my wolf teeth tore through the outliers attacking me from all sides. The creatures swarmed at me and my brothers like rats pouring from a sewer, and a sickening feeling twisted in my gut. This had been Warrick's plan all along. His outliers hadn't been waiting for *us*. They'd been waiting for Raine.

"We can't let him fuckin' have her!" Asher yelled as he drove his fist forward, smashing through an outlier's rib cage and tearing out its heart.

Locke's fighting was wild, his claws slashing through any outlier that neared, and when a space had cleared around him, he launched into the air, his wings flapping as he rose above the rooftops. Pain bloomed in my chest signaling that Raine was in danger and she'd been hurt, and I howled in frustration. Snarling and snapping, I fought through the mass of outliers, leaping over the creatures and running to the building where I'd last seen her.

Traces of coconut and steel led into the house, and I smashed through the door, stepping over the splintered wood as I followed her scent. My nostrils flared as I breathed in, and I snarled as I also picked up the scents of three other wolf shifters. Grunts came behind me, and I turned my head to see Asher and Darian had fought their way to the building and were coming after me. Baring my teeth, I sprinted through the house, flying past the furniture as I let my nose guide me. Asher and Darian ran close at my heels, and the growls of the outliers faded away when they didn't follow us.

Deep down, I knew it was a bad sign the outliers weren't pursuing us, but I pushed onward, my powerful body carrying me through building after building and up multiple streets as I raced after my Mahare. Locke followed from the air, but I knew if he'd spotted her, he would have come down by now. *Fuck.*

Veering around the corner of a building, I stopped abruptly when Raine's scent trail ended in the middle of a narrow alley. A splash of red blood colored the cobblestones, and another guttural growl rumbled from my chest. I paced the area, hoping to pick up her scent again, or even the scents of her kidnappers, but it was as if the group of them had vanished into thin air.

Asher cursed as he came up behind me, and he brushed a bloodied hand over his horns. "Where is she?"

Darian's chest heaved, and his sharp blue gaze darted around the alley.

Locke, who had been circling the skies above us, landed a few paces away, and his face was the picture of wrath. "I can't find Raine from above, but those outliers only respond to one master. This is Warrick's doing."

The pain in my chest was constant, but it hadn't become more intense, indicating that she wasn't too badly harmed. We still had time to save her.

"We should go back and follow the outliers. Surely they'll lead back to Daddy," Asher suggested.

"We need weapons," Darian pointed out. "We won't be any good to our lovely Raine if we're dead."

"You'll need more than that," a female voice purred, and all four of us tensed, ready for a fight, as a female figure dropped from a nearby rooftop. Lyr walked slowly, her hips swaying as she approached us, and two of her mates flanked her. I eyed Nic's ghostly face and Soren's crimson wings, the soft red feathers ruffling in the breeze.

I should have detected them, but Lyr and her mates were known for their stealth, and I was much too riled up about Raine's disappearance to beat myself up about it now.

"What do you know?" Locke asked, his body deathly still.

Lyr's pale gaze assessed the four of us in turn before she answered, "She's been taken to one of Warrick's new locations." She tilted her head toward Soren. "He spotted Zacal and his wolves taking her into one of the mansions Warrick's recently acquired."

Locke bared his fangs. "You saw them take her?"

"You four might be suicidal, but I intend on keeping my head," Soren replied, lifting his hands in a placating gesture. The male with red wings had once been one of Queen Izla's personal guards, and while I knew he was a formidable fighter, it had been a while since I'd seen him engaged in combat. In any case, why *would* he try to save Raine? Aside from Lyr showing some interest in her, I couldn't see any reason for Soren to risk his life.

Locke still looked like he wanted to tear Soren's head off for not doing anything, but Lyr planted her hands on her hips. "If you're going to be an ass, we'll leave, but if you want our help in saving your mate, then you might want to put your fangs away."

None of us commented on the fact that Lyr had called Raine our mate. We had yet to mark our red-haired goddess, sealing her as ours, but I'd long since accepted she was our mate. And when she was willing to accept it too, I'd be all ready to make her mine in every sense of the word. But first, I had to save her.

Darian crossed his arms and frowned. "Why would you help us?"

Lyr turned her attention to him. "You're not the only ones interested in her well-being. While you were all away doing whatever the hell it was you hoped to achieve in the fae realm, the rest of us were here fighting. Zacal has been spreading rumors about how you all sided with the fae, so I hope it was worth it. Warrick and his outliers all but run the city now, but the old vampire seems to have forgotten we're all monsters just as he is."

I shifted back into my human form, my bones cracking and ears popping. "What does this have to do with Raine?" I growled.

"Whatever monster she's turning into," Lyr began, "I believe she's the key to defeating Warrick and this curse, and there are others who agree. She's the only one who wasn't turned by the curse within a matter of hours or days, and her magic is already more powerful than any other monster in Katakin."

My brothers and I kept silent, weighing our limited options. None of us tried to deny Lyr's claims.

"We've been watching Warrick's for nights and know where he's keeping her," Lyr added. "Trust me, you need us. And we need her."

I didn't want Raine mixed up in whatever rebellion was brewing among the monsters, and allowing Lyr to help us would leave us in her debt, but I couldn't deny we needed the information. Not to mention the extra muscle would be useful when we retrieved Raine from Warrick's clutches.

I shared a look with my brothers, but it was Locke who spoke next. "Tell us where she is."

· · · · ● · ● · · ·

I crouched low beside Asher and Darian in my wolf form, my ears folded back and my senses on high alert. We were in a small city house that Lyr had discreetly acquired nights ago, and I peered through the glass window, surveying the massive building across the street. According to the tiger shifter and her mates, Warrick had claimed four abandoned mansions since we'd been away in the fae realm, and the one across the street was the one Warrick visited the least. Located in the far west of the city, the old mansion stood three stories high, the building still standing despite the crumbling brick and smashed glass windows. A wide stretch of dead grass surrounded the mansion, and a tall iron gate wrapped around the entirety of the estate.

Two outliers guarded the angled ash-gray roof, the large creatures scampering along the tiles in random quick bursts. The color of their skin was a shade of gray identical to that of the tiles, making it hard to spot them unless they moved. I thought of Locke, who would soon be swooping down from above, and hoped for his sake that there weren't more outliers up there than we realized.

Another dozen outliers, similar to the ones we'd encountered not long ago in the city, guarded the entrances and exits of the house and stalked the perimeter of the estate. But it wasn't the outliers that had me baring my teeth.

Zacal's wolves prowled the grounds, moving between the outliers and helping guard the mansion. A low growl slipped out of me at the sight of the wolf shifters of the House of Worzel working alongside Warrick. There was a time when the wolves had honor and integrity. A time when the members of the House of Worzel would never have turned their backs on their own kind.

Lyr had warned us about the alliance between the wolves and Warrick, but the sight of it still made me want to rage. I had no problem tearing apart the outliers, but the wolves...? I let out a long breath through my nose. *If they try to stop me from getting to Raine, they've made their choice.*

"If Lyr's intel is correct, the mansion is mostly empty," Darian said quietly. "But it'll still be a fight for us to get through those doors."

Asher flexed his back and tightened his grip on the axes in his hands. Lyr and her mates had armed Darian, Locke, and Asher to the teeth, but I opted to rely on my stronger wolf form.

"Don't know 'bout you, but the fight couldn't come soon enough," Asher groused. "How long do we have to wait? Who knows what Warrick is doin' to Raine in there, and I'm lookin' forward to seein' the vampire's head roll."

"Any moment now," Darian assured him. "We must wait for the signal."

I still wasn't entirely sure why the tiger shifter and her mates were helping us, but I couldn't worry about it now. A loud bang followed by a chorus of shouts and howls came from the left side of the mansion, and that was our cue.

As the outliers and wolves ran to fight Lyr and her mates from the side entrance, we sprang into action. Leaving the cover of the small house we were in, I sprinted toward the iron gate, my powerful body flying over the cobblestones. Asher and Darian sped after me, but I didn't wait for them as I bunched my haunches, leaping clear over the gate and landing with a thud as my large paws connected with dead grass. Half a dozen outliers still guarded this side of the building, and the beasts screeched and lumbered toward me. I snarled and lunged for the closest outlier, my jaws closing around its meaty arm. Before I could tear the limb from its socket, another outlier grabbed hold of my tail, throwing me back toward the gate, and I dug my paws into the ground as I landed, maintaining my balance.

Darian and Asher dropped down on either side of me, the pair of them crouching low, and we fought off the outliers. We'd only managed to bring them down when six more outliers streamed out of the mansion.

"So much for the buildin' bein' empty," Asher commented grimly as the three of us ran to attack the monsters. Darian spun and lunged, using his speed and agility to carve his sword into the outliers, and Asher cleaved into them with brute force, his strength an even match with the giant beasts. I tore my teeth into the creatures, ripping limbs and shredding throats.

A body fell from the roof, bones cracking as the limp outlier slammed into the stone steps at the front of the mansion, and I looked up, expecting to see Locke standing at the edge of the rooftop. In the moment of distraction, an outlier lifted me off my feet, a clawed hand wrapping around my furry neck and squeezing.

I jerked my head from side to side, trying to work myself free as the outlier opened its huge toothy mouth, ready to swallow my head whole. Swinging my body, I lifted my hind legs, scraping my paws down the outlier's abdomen and letting my claws slide in deep, cutting through flesh. The outlier snapped its mouth shut, and its hold on me loosened. I slipped from its grasp, falling to the ground before lunging and tearing the beast apart.

As I tossed the outlier's head away, the pain in my chest intensified like acid was eating its way to my heart, and I growled and slavered, driven wild by the physical reminder that Raine needed me.

"Get her!" Asher roared from somewhere behind me, and I twisted my head back. Outliers and wolves circled around Asher and Darian as the duo fought back-to-back, their blades gleaming in the moonlight. My demon brother sank an ax into an outlier's throat, and his gaze locked onto mine. "We've got this!" he shouted, but he grunted when a wolf sank its teeth into his right leg. I'd foolishly hoped that when it came to it, the wolves wouldn't fight us, but they moved alongside the outliers, not holding back.

I hesitated, my gaze sliding to Darian, who took down another outlier. "Go, Kade!" the siren yelled, and as the pain in my chest increased, it was all the encouragement I needed.

Shooting forward, I aimed for the door of the mansion, but three wolves darted from the side, moving into my path. Kasey, Tristan, and Zacal faced me in their shifted forms as heavy rain started falling from the sky, soaking into my fur, and running into my eyes. I growled a warning at the wolves and curled my lips to expose my fangs, but they only snarled back at me, their snouts wrinkled and bodies taut. Zacal stood ahead of the others, asserting his dominance, but I wasn't willing to submit to the inferior wolf anymore. I wasn't that same broken wolf, the one so weighed by guilt that I let them take out their anger on me. No, I was an alpha, and nothing and no one was going to stop me from saving Raine.

Straightening my legs, I rose to my full height and filled the air with my dominant scent, then I let my growl build in my throat before the sound crashed through the air. Kasey and Tristan instinctively lowered their heads, but they quickly lifted again, determined to resist me.

I wasn't willing to give them a second chance. As I charged forward, it took all but a few moments before Kasey and her mate, Tristan, were on the ground, bleeding and bruised but still alive. Zacal was the last wolf before me. I expected him to cower and submit now that it was clear I wasn't backing down, but his copper eyes glinted. I snarled, ready to dart forward and clamp my jaws onto his throat, but a body crashed into me from the side. Claws raked across my chest as the outlier's powerful arm sent me sprawling.

Before I could rise, the outlier stood over me, slamming a heavy, clawed foot onto the side of my rib cage and pressing down, holding me in place.

Zacal shifted then, his body molding and changing as he stalked toward me until it wasn't a wolf but a male in human form standing a short distance away. He smirked smugly as he peered down at me, a self-satisfied expression on his face.

I scratched my paws against the mud as I tried to lift from the outlier's foot, but the creature held me still.

"Now there's the Kade I remember," Zacal sneered. "The pathetic alpha scrabbling in the dirt without a house or his pack behind him." Zacal peered over at where Asher and Darian were fighting to get to me, and his smile stretched wider. "Oh, how proud you were to become alpha of the House or Worzel all those years ago, with your grand ideas of family and honor. Your mother doted upon you, and your sister was as fierce as you, all too ready to act as your second. But all it took was the guilt of their deaths and you crumbled, turning your back on the wolves." He paused then, nodding to the outlier who pressed harder on my chest. I gnashed my jaws, snapping at the air as my ribs came close to breaking.

Zacal's face hardened. "How I've wanted to kill you, but I couldn't before now. Not when you always submitted, leaving me with no choice but to allow you to keep breathing. But now that Warrick and his outliers rule this city, there's nothing to stop me."

His gaze flicked to where Kasey and Tristan lay unmoving, and when he turned back to me, cruelty twisted his face. "Think of it this way. Now you'll finally get to see your mother and sister." He cackled at that, and I fantasized about the thousand different ways I could make the wolf suffer.

Kasey blinked her gray eyes open, her bloody muzzle shifting almost imperceptibly as she regained consciousness.

Zacal's laugh died off, turning to a snarl, and he continued, "Oh, you signed your death notice the moment you took over as alpha of the house, eager and brimming with possibilities. I knew my goals didn't align with yours. You would have found a way to push me from the pack and drive me to one of the lower houses, and I couldn't allow that. I'll admit it has been bothering me that you didn't know the true reason for your grand fall from power." Zacal laughed. "I guess now that you're about to die it's only fitting that you know I'm the one who pulled you from that pedestal the wolves put you on.

"Oh yes, when Warrick approached me with an opportunity, I was all ears. It seemed your sister had learned of his early experiments to create the outliers, and she had plans to find you that night and share the information. Instead, Warrick unleashed one of his creatures, and we silenced your sister and the other wolves who witnessed the event, including your mother."

I growled, anger coursing through me at Zacal's admission, but he shrugged as if he felt no remorse for the wolves.

"Warrick had little control over the outliers back then, so there was more bloodshed than expected, but the end result was as intended. Warrick destroyed the outlier and disposed of its body, and all I had to do was spin some tale about the fae attacking and disappearing back to the fae realm, and you were crushed by the guilt of their deaths. I didn't even need to call in my favor with Warrick to have you expelled from the pack. You can imagine my delight when you stepped down of your own accord, leaving me to take over the house."

My nostrils flared as I pawed furiously at the muddy ground, snapping and growling as the rain pelted down on us. *It wasn't the fae. Zacal and Warrick are responsible for the deaths of my family and the other wolves. It was a fucking planned attack.* The truth settled into my bones, and I howled in both anger and anguish.

Zacal signaled to the outlier, and the creature reached for me, its clawed hands aiming for either side of my head. Before it grabbed my fur, a silvery gray blur slammed into the outlier, pushing it off me. Kasey growled as she sank her teeth into the outlier's shoulder, and I was up in an instant.

Zacal had barely shifted into his wolf form when my teeth sank deep into his neck. Snarling, I ripped out his throat, and he fell limp to the ground. Tipping my head up, I howled as I stood over him, rage and revenge singing in my bones. The black wolf, Tristan, lifted weakly to his feet and limped over to Kasey. The outlier she'd fought was down, but Kasey lay bleeding, her breathing labored.

She shifted into human form, and black blood gushed from a deep slash that stretched across the length of her stomach. Tristan shifted to human form, and he frantically pressed his hands to the wound, trying to stop the bleeding. Blood flowed between his fingers, pooling onto the ground, and he let out a pained whine.

"Kasey," he rasped, his voice tight, and his angry glare found me.

"Don't," Kasey wheezed. "It's not Kade's fault we've been so blind."

Kasey peered at me, and for the first time since that night when my family was murdered, she didn't look at me with loathing and anger. "I never knew Zacal helped kill the wolves. My brother's death..." Blood gurgled from her mouth, and something rattled in her chest when she took a pained breath. "All this time, I blamed you, and I couldn't see through my anger. Z-Zacal was half the alpha you would have been." She coughed, and a tear leaked from the corner of her eye. "We've been lost for so long. Save our pack...Alpha. Go and find your mate."

Alpha. In the past, I'd detested the word, the title, but now it made my chest swell and my ears straighten. I'd killed Zacal while he was in wolf form, and that made me alpha of the House of Worzel again. I'd stepped down before. I'd submitted to Zacal publicly and removed myself from the pack, but here I was. Rightful alpha to the pack once again.

"If what Kasey says is true, the wolves need to know that our alliance with Warrick was built on a lie," Tristan growled quietly. "The vampire must pay for what he's done."

I nodded. Oh, I planned to make Warrick suffer.

Digging my paws into the mud, I ran for the door.

CHAPTER 21

~ **Raine** ~

Plop. Plop. Plop. The steady drip of water was loud in my ears, and I slowly cracked my eyes open. Pain pulsed in my head and radiated throughout my whole body. *Goddess, did I get pummeled by an ogre?*

The darkness was dimly lit by torches lining the walls around me, and I blinked rapidly as my eyes adjusted to the blue light. An image of Kasey's gloating face formed in my mind, and it didn't take me long to figure out the bitch had knocked me out. *Where did she take me?*

Aside from the stone slab I was cuffed to in the middle of the room, the large space was bare, with smooth white walls and a single iron door opposite me. The musty air smelled of earth and mildew, and I gaped in horror at the single tube that protruded from my aching right wrist. The tube was colored red, and it took me a moment to realize I was actually seeing my blood leaving my body and going somewhere beyond my line of sight. From the continuous dripping, I guessed there was a steel bucket below the slab I was on, much like when I'd found Prince Azaren not too long ago in Warrick's lab. Nausea made me gag, and my head spun. *But…I'm not in Warrick's lab beneath the mountain. The room is the wrong shape, and none of his drawings or furniture are here. Was I taken to some secret location Locke and the others don't know about?* Panic shot through me at the thought. *So much for the hope of them finding me.*

My breathing became rapid as I tried yanking my hands upward, pulling against the cuffs and not caring when the metal rubbed painfully against my skin. I'm not really sure why I bothered trying. Like in the fae realm, the restraints held me fast, pinning me to the table like some sort of sick sacrifice.

What the fuck does he want with me? But it was a stupid question to even consider. Of course, the ancient vampire wanted me. Warrick had been studying the newbloods for years, and for the first time, he'd found himself an enigma. I shuddered when I remembered the curiosity that glinted in the vampire's eyes every time he stared at me. I needed to get the hell out of there.

Closing my eyes, I focused my mind and mentally tried to find the magic spark inside me. *If I could disintegrate the enchanted cuffs in the fae realm, these plain iron ones will be a piece of cake.*

Except…they weren't. In fact, I couldn't access my magic at all. I could feel the spark somewhere deep in the recesses of my mind, but it was as if my power had lessened. Every time I tried to reach for the magic, it would slip away from me, like some kind of skittish ghost. Gritting my teeth, I tried harder to mentally reach for it, but the power dulled with every passing moment like it was fading away. It wasn't like how the dazra had suppressed my magic, but more like…

"I wouldn't bother trying to use your power. You're beyond that now," said a silky masculine voice, and I jerked in surprise, snapping my eyes open.

Warrick stood just inside the doorway, and his cruel black eyes gleamed with delight as he stalked closer to me. Two outliers entered the room after him—four-legged beasts with crowns of spikes on their scaled heads and long snouts filled with rows of teeth. Their red eyes fixed hungrily on me, but following Warrick's command, they waited on either side of the door, their long forked tongues often darting from their open mouths to flick at the air.

I turned my attention from the outliers to the ancient vampire who had stopped at the foot of my stone slab. "Beyond that?" I asked. I wasn't sure what he meant, but dread filled my gut.

Before I could blink, Warrick was at my side and inspecting the tube that ran from my wrist. When his attention went back to my face, he gave me a cold, clinical smile. "I've long since known that our power is linked to our blood, and considering the amount of blood I've drained from you..." He trailed off as he became thoughtful. "I'd say the chances of you being able to access whatever magic you have is slim."

I glared at him and struggled against my restraints as he trailed a cold, clawed finger up the inside of my arm.

"For all you know, torturing me like this might be just what tips me over the edge. I could turn into a monster right now and kill you," I seethed, but despite my words, my chin wobbled, betraying my fear.

His lips curled upward with amusement as he stared at me like I was the most fascinating specimen he'd ever captured. "I highly doubt that, but in case you're right..."

I didn't see the dagger until the blade was buried deep in my thigh. Warrick's pale hand clasped the hilt of the weapon, and it wasn't until he wrenched the blade back out that pain exploded in my leg, and I cried out in agony.

"I don't imagine you'll last long now, but I figure it's worth trying a final time," Warrick said, speaking as casually as if he'd just offered me a glass of wine and we were sitting down for a meal rather than some sick torture session. "And even if you don't change, I'll have enough of your blood that I'll be able to test and work with it for some time."

I focused on breathing through the pain, but my whole body was weak, and even that task felt like it took what remained of my energy. I thought of the bond tying me to Kade and the others, and what Prince Azaren had said about it being a blessing intended to ensure my protection. Who put the magic on me, and would I be letting them down now by dying?

Goddess, I was so cold. When did it get so cold?

"Killing me won't change anything," I said weakly. "There are many in Katakin who don't want to be monsters. They'll find a way to break the curse." I didn't tell him about how the answers to breaking the curse were embedded in my memory. Without me, the secrets were lost unless Kade and the others went back to the fae realm and risked trying to obtain them again.

Warrick's face twisted with anger. "The monsters will do as they're told, and if they don't, my creatures will give them the mortal death they so desperately want." He drove the dagger into my leg again, this time in a spot just above my knee, and I bucked against the slab as agony made me want to scream. The urge to beg was on the tip of my tongue, but I clenched my jaw, tears leaking from the corners of my eyes.

Warrick cleared his throat, the anger disappearing from his face only to be replaced by an oddly calm expression. "No, they'll come around. From the state of you, I'm willing to wager that your little trip to the fae realm didn't end with you and my son making new friends, and when the fae attack this city, the monsters will understand I was right to create an army of beasts."

The fae, I knew, would be slaughtered, and so would many of the Katakin monsters. I already knew Kade and the others would go to the front lines to fight the fae, but what about Cara? Would she also be among the dead, yet another casualty of war?

At the thought of my sister, I growled, "What did you do to her?" I needed answers. At the very least, I needed to know if she was alive. If Cara was somewhere in the city, maybe she wouldn't fight in the war and there was a chance she would be spared. It was a risk bringing Warrick's attention to her, but I'd told Kade and the others about my sister, and I had to trust that if anything happened to me, they'd try to protect her from Warrick.

Confusion crossed Warrick's face, and I elaborated, "During a previous offering, a girl who wasn't of selection age was taken from my island. Tell me what you did to her."

Warrick continued to frown at me, but I saw the very moment understanding overcame him, his eyes becoming rounder. "So Jarin was telling the truth, then," he mused thoughtfully.

When I simply glowered back at him, Warrick sighed heavily. "I guess it doesn't hurt to tell you. You will, after all, be dead soon. I'd specifically instructed Jarin to bring me a younger specimen so I could test the difference in the way her blood reacted to the curse, but Jarin never was reliable. He came up with some excuse that he'd found a young girl and she'd gone through the portal with the group, but she never emerged on the other side." Disappointment crossed Warrick's features. "I never could trust that useless demon, and I'd assumed he was either lying or had his fun with her and had discarded her body before returning to Katakin. Imagine my surprise when I found him blurting the information to you when we both knew the council would not be happy to hear that I'd tried to get him to deviate from the agreed-upon ages for the newbloods. In any case, I won't have to worry about him divulging that information now." He paused. "Though if I'd known he was telling the truth about the girl, I would have kept him alive. I'd very much like to question him further. No matter."

I couldn't speak. Could hardly process what he was telling me. Cara had been taken into the portal, but she'd never arrived in Katakin. *She's not here.*

My mind couldn't make sense of it, and the world seemed to fall away from beneath me. If Cara hadn't come to Katakin, where had she gone? Bile crept up my throat as I realized my sister wasn't in the city. That she wasn't a newblood who was possibly happy somewhere with her new life. No, she was lost out there. Either lost or dead.

Magic. I needed my magic. It was the only way I was going to get out of this. The only way I could escape and try to find her. I tried to focus my mind, desperate to find that spark, but Warrick twisted the blade inside me, and I cried out again, unable to hold back my sobs.

I was so damn weak. My body tingled, and my vision began to tunnel as darkness started to take me. I forced myself to keep my eyes open, but as Warrick yanked out the dagger and buried it in my other leg, I smashed my eyes shut, not wanting to see the brutality. I wasn't sure how, but through the pain, I saw the irony in the situation. I'd always thought when the humans on my island were taken by the monsters, they were subjected to torture before being murdered, and now here I was, bleeding out at the hands of a vampire.

"You're a fucking monster," I snarled, wrenching my eyes open again, though the words didn't sound as venomous as I'd intended.

Warrick pulled the blade out and held it up, but his attention remained fixed on me. "Indeed, but I still haven't figured out why you're *not*. Perhaps I should have had my son and his friends tortured in front of you instead. The change has proven to be brought on by heightened emotions, and from what I gather, there's more going on among you five than you let on."

I tried not to show how his words affected me, but I must have failed, as his hysterical laughter filled the space. Goddess, the male needed serious mental help.

"If you've hurt them," I said through clenched teeth, and Warrick stopped laughing to stare down at me.

"You'll do what exactly? It's a wonder you're still alive, and if Locke and his friends try to attack this house, the wolves and my outliers will see to it that they're taken care of."

I blanched at his words. There was no way Locke and the others *wouldn't* come after me. Not when I was so close to death and the bond was probably making their chests feel like they might explode. The idea that the others were in danger had me fighting harder against the darkness that was trying to take me. My eyes began to close, my body resisting my mental commands to stay awake, but then I noticed it.

I could barely lift my head, but Warrick was still holding the dagger in the air. The dagger that had just been in *my* leg. My blood coated the blade, but the thick liquid that dripped from the weapon wasn't a vibrant crimson, the same color as a rich, red rose. No, it was darker, the color of purple grapes. My gaze dropped to the tube attached to my wrist. At the end closest to my hand, the color was changing, slowly becoming darker. My blood wasn't inky black like the monsters', nor was it blue like the fae's. *What?*

Warrick followed my line of sight to the tube, and a look of genuine surprise lit up his features. "It can't be..." he murmured.

If I'd thought I had been in pain before, it was nothing like the agony that ripped through me then. Molten lava raced through my veins, burning me from the inside out, and my back arched off the stone slab.

Warrick took a step back, the bloody dagger still in his hand, and for the first time, the male looked uncertain. "What's happening?" he demanded, but I didn't answer.

A cry that was definitely *not* human came from me as every bone in my body felt as though it shattered, but then my body was remolding, changing and shifting. My cuffs burst from my wrists and ankles, the metal flying across the room and crashing against the walls as my body became too large for the restraints. In a matter of seconds, my body grew so tall my head knocked against the ceiling, and I was no longer the same woman I used to be but a massive creature. In the recesses of my mind, I was vaguely aware of what had happened to me. That I *was* the creature, but it was as if my usual instincts had been overridden by those of the monster I'd become.

Power rumbled through me, magic igniting in every part of my body, and I'd never felt so alive. A vampire was before me, backing closer to the door, and I watched him through slitted eyes. Monsters were on either side of him, their tongues flicking into the air and their clawed feet pawing at the ground in agitation. In some part of my mind, I knew I recognized the male, but my thoughts were consumed with anger and the desire to make the world burn.

"The blood," the male rambled as he stared at me with round eyes, his expression a mixture of appreciation and curiosity. "How had I not suspected this? You must be part fae, and your mixed blood made you immune to the curse. But as the blood drained from you..."

He didn't finish. A roar expelled from my lungs, deafening as it echoed around the room and bounced off the walls. A hint of fear finally touched the vampire's features, and one of my massive, clawed paws lashed out, slamming him into the wall on one side of the room. I took a step forward, ready to crush him, but the two other monsters attacked, their claws scraping against my long snout and the side of my neck, making me bellow.

A monster jumped onto my back while the other bit at my face, and by the time they were both bleeding on the ground, trapped beneath my paws, the dark-haired vampire was gone. I still couldn't place who the male was, but fury went through me at the fact he had escaped.

Heat swelled in my belly, and when I roared in anger, searing blue flames rushed up my throat, engulfing the room in fire. The flames crackled and popped pleasantly against my scaled skin, and the iron door melted to the ground before me. I smashed through the narrow doorway and half the wall, my large paws taking me swiftly into the wide corridor and up a flight of stairs. My new animalistic desires took hold of me, and I didn't try to fight them. I gave in, letting the beast rule me.

More monsters were stationed higher in the house, but they burned just like the rest of the house did, nothing more than obstacles in my way. When I'd almost reached the ground floor, a familiar scent hit my nose, and a large wolf appeared before me, but I didn't stop turning the world to flame.

The wolf darted away, escaping the stream of fire spewing from my mouth, and I smashed through the house, breaking through the walls as if they were as thin as paper and emerging into the cool night air.

CHAPTER 22

Out in front of the mansion, it was carnage. The bodies of monsters were strewn across the muddy grass, and rain pelted down from above, washing away the blood. None of it bothered me.

The building burned at my back, smoke trailing into the air from the crackling blue flames, and I shook hot embers and bits of debris from my scales. My tail flicked, crashing through a wall and bringing down more of the house, and I lowered my head to the large puddle in front of me. A massive beast stared back, shimmering purple scales covering a wide body, each the size of a human hand. Four pointed red horns speared out of a large head, and round glittering gems trailed along a red chest. *My chest*, I realized. My long snout was filled with daggerlike teeth, and each of my four paws had razor-sharp talons that dug into the ground. I snorted, my nostrils flaring as my breath made the water ripple, marring the reflection, but a shout from nearby drew my attention away.

The large wolf with golden eyes watched me carefully, but I paid him no attention as I moved to where a silver-haired male and a large demon were fighting a monster. The monster was similar to the ones I'd encountered in the house, and somehow, I just knew it had to die. *Outlier.* The word popped into my head, and I knew it was what the monster was called, though I didn't know much else. Before the silver-haired male could deliver a killing blow, I snapped the outlier up in my teeth, crushing the creature's bones with my powerful jaw.

"Fuck, is that...Sharachi?" the demon shouted, but his words meant nothing to me.

"Her eyes," commented the silver-haired male, and his face hardened as he inhaled. "It appears Warrick got more than he bargained for when he took our dear Raine."

Ignoring the insignificant creatures, I pushed off from the ground and flapped my massive wings, launching into the air and flying above the house. Opening my jaw, I dropped the outlier's limp body onto the mansion and circled around, spewing fire onto what remained of the building. I doubted the dark-haired vampire was in there, but it was satisfying to see the mansion turn to ash, my fire still burning despite the rain.

But as I circled around again, my rage demanded more. The anger roiling inside me was like a living beast, and I set my sights on the rest of the city as I gave in to the turmoil.

My body sang with power, and I blew a stream of fire into the sky before swooping toward the closest houses. As I dropped low, something jumped onto my back, scampering up my left side. I stretched my neck, ready to snap the wolf up in my jaws, but two more pests leaped onto me, landing on my back and neck.

I swayed from side to side, twisting my head to snap behind me, and the wolf darted back, escaping my teeth.

"Whoa, there. We came here to rescue you, sweetheart," said a soothing male voice as thick arms wrapped around my neck.

"I'm quite sure she just rescued herself," pointed out another male, and I felt him lean forward and grip onto my scales.

Flying down the street, I smashed against the sides of buildings, trying to jostle them off while being careful not to let my wings suffer the impact.

"Damn, I knew she would turn into somethin' powerful, but did it have to be a dragon?" One of the males laughed.

When I twisted my head around again, the wolf had disappeared, and a human male was now perched on my back close to my tail. *Wolf shifter.*

"Fight against the instincts of your creature, Raine!" the wolf shifter shouted. "You *are* your creature. You need to take control!"

I responded by bucking and trying to throw all three of the males off, but they only held on tighter. Fire shot from my mouth, igniting the cobblestones beneath me, when a soulful tune sounded in my ears, cutting through the rush of the wind. Magic tugged at me, an unnatural desire making my mouth water, but I shook my head, breaking whatever spell was trying to take control of my mind.

"She's too strong!" one of the males shouted as the song abruptly ended. "I've never felt anything like it."

"We need to get her away from here before she burns down the city!" shouted a different voice, and I lifted my slitted gaze to the vampire who flew above me. His hair was dark, but it wasn't the same vampire from the mansion. Why wouldn't these pests leave me alone? I snarled, altering my course and heading straight for him.

The vampire pivoted and flew higher, and I followed, determined not to let him get away. After opening my mouth, I snapped my jaws closed, but the monster darted out of reach, coasting to the side, away from me. I snorted in frustration and flapped my wings harder, but it wasn't speed that was keeping the little vampire out of my maw. The monster spun, dived, and soared with a skill I didn't have, always keeping ahead of me. Soon I found myself flying higher until my head broke through a layer of silver clouds, the moonlight making them look like puffs of smoke.

A hand ran along the scales of my neck. "All right, sweetheart. You don't wanna eat our Locke there. He's a friend, remember?" There was a pause. "So maybe he's an ass sometimes, but he doesn't deserve to be eaten."

I ignored the male's pitiful words and snapped at the air where the vampire had just been a second before.

"Mahare, your beast is driven by your strongest emotions. You need to take control," repeated the wolf shifter.

Irritation went through me, and when I roared, fire shot from my maw, lighting up the night sky.

The vampire banked to the right, escaping the flames, and I turned sharply to follow him. A weight fell from my back as one of the males lost his grip on my slick scales. It was the one with the silver hair. Another of the males stretched out his hand, grabbing him before he fell out of reach, and I grunted in annoyance as he hoisted the silver-haired male back onto me.

The other male stroked my neck again. "Come on now, Sharachi. I know there's a part of you that has grown fond of us," he said soothingly.

"She's not thinking clearly right now," the wolf shifter growled.

The vampire stopped abruptly then, his wings shooting out wide. He spun toward me, hovering in the air. I opened my mouth, ready for a snack, but before I could snap him up, he curled his body, jumping onto my snout. He planted a flat hand on my forehead, and his tiny black eyes bored into mine. Heat swelled in my belly, and I was about to flick my nose up so I could toss him into the air and roast him when the tantalizing scents of cedarwood, ash, and spice filled my senses.

I kept my mouth shut and breathed in more deeply. Now that I wasn't solely focused on trying to eat the vampire and destroy the city, my other senses heightened. This time when I breathed in, I scented musk and leather, sandalwood and coffee, and sea salt and patchouli. They combined to make the most irresistible aroma that made my belly tighten and had one word forming in my mind. One word that overruled my anger.

Treasure.

I blinked my huge eyes at the vampire on my snout. No, not vampire, *Locke*. They were Locke, Asher, Kade, and Darian. My stomach plummeted as I realized what I'd almost done. I'd nearly killed them. Had nearly *eaten* them. But it wasn't them that hurt me; it was Warrick. And now my thoughts of burning the city were replaced with my desire to protect my treasures.

Because that was what these males were. They were my treasures, my *mates*, and I had to keep them safe.

Dipping my head, I speared down from the clouds with all four of my males on me. Down we flew until we were soaring through the mountains and over forests and valleys. I wouldn't go to the mountain of the monsters, the one where I'd spent my first few nights in Katakin, but another, smaller mountain jutted out of the earth not too far away, and I circled around it before I found what I was after.

A cave.

"Where is she takin' us?" Asher shouted.

"It doesn't matter. We're away from the city, so it'll have to do for now," Locke answered.

Dropping low, I flapped my wings, slowing our descent, then I tucked my wings in as we soared into the dark cave and my taloned feet scraped across the cool stone. Walking straight to the back of the cave, I checked to make sure it was empty before curving back around.

Locke, Darian, Kade, and Asher jumped from my back, the four of them facing me, their muscles tense as if they were ready to dart out of the way if I tried to turn them to ash.

Treasure. The word echoed in my mind again.

My treasure. Mine to keep. Mine to enjoy. I roared again, but this time, it wasn't a cry of anger. It was a roar of possession. A declaration to the world that these males belonged to me.

Stalking forward, I lowered my head, aiming for Locke. His dark eyes were wary, but he didn't move as I sniffed his legs and lifted my snout all the way up to his eyes. I breathed on his face, and his black hair ruffled from the gust of air.

"Well, at least she's no longer tryin' to eat or kill us," Asher said with a grin, and I turned my attention to him next, giving him the same treatment I'd given Locke. He chuckled as my snout lifted one of his arms into the air. Next was Darian, and my hot tongue darted out to taste the side of his face.

Sweet. Delicious.

"I'm not so sure she thinks we're off the menu," Darian commented with a smile, remaining deathly still while I continued to sniff him.

A growl came from Kade then, carnal and possessive, and desire flared low in my belly. It was the growl of an alpha challenging his mate, and my gaze shot to him with interest. "It's not eating she has in mind," Kade said. "She's a newblood. We've never had a dragon shifter before, but I imagine she has many of the same instincts as other shifters. She's going to want to test the limits of her power."

I eyed Kade curiously, wondering what he would do next. I knew I was Raine. Knew I wasn't just an animal, but my creature still ruled my body, and the need to assert my dominance rose inside me. Another growl rumbled in my throat, and Kade's eyes darkened as he answered my growl with another one of his own.

"Change back, Mahare. You have nothing to prove, and you already know we're yours," the wolf shifter said, not taking his golden eyes from me.

Asher cleared his throat. "What he said."

Power ran through me, and I flexed my muscles. I liked this. Enjoyed feeling invincible like there was nothing in this world that could stop me. But...my nostrils flared as I scented my males again. There was something I wanted more than power. I wanted *them. My treasures.*

"Focus on calming your mind, and picture yourself in your human form again. Push back that animalistic part of you," Kade coached, and this time, I tried to listen. I wanted them but not while I was a monster. What had the males called me? *A dragon.*

I snorted out more smoke and strained my mind, trying to suppress my creature. I pictured myself in my human form, with my smaller frame, fiery red hair, and amber eyes. *Not a monster. I'm not a fucking monster*, I chanted in my mind, but nothing happened, and I grunted in frustration.

Locke stepped closer to me, and there was something like sorrow in his eyes as he stared at me. Sorrow but also awe. "It's not about suppressing your monster; it's about accepting it."

Accepting it? I thought about his words and refocused my mind. This time, I coaxed my dragon to the back of my mind. I reminded my creature that she'd get another chance to come out and play soon. I was skeptical that it'd work, but to my relief, within a matter of moments, my body was shifting and shrinking.

Asher sighed heavily when I was completely back in my human form, his shoulders slumping with exhaustion. "You all right, sweetheart?"

I didn't stop for small talk. Desire coiled inside me, and I strode to Kade who was the closest, and smashed my lips against his. *My treasure.* Kade wound his arms around me and let me dominate his mouth like he knew just what I needed in that moment. My hands slid lower on his body, but he grunted in pain as my hands passed over his ribs.

Jerking back, I took a step away from him as my gaze fell to his chest. A large purple bruise marred his muddy skin, stretching across his chiseled torso, and my eyes grew wide. I wanted my treasures, but I didn't want to cause them pain.

"I'll be fine," Kade murmured, but scratches covered his body, and I winced as I wondered how many of them had come from riding my back while he was butt naked. The idea would have been humorous if the after-effects didn't look so damn painful. My gaze swiped from Kade to the others, and I swallowed hard. As a dragon, I hadn't realized how beaten and ragged they were.

Blood and gore covered Darian and Asher, the black smeared across their faces and matted in their hair, and

Locke's clothes were torn like something had tried to claw him to death.

The sight of them had memories of Warrick driving his blade into my leg rising to the surface, and my hand shot to my thigh. I pressed my fingers against the bare skin, but the wounds were no longer there.

Darian came forward with a look of concern, and he lifted my shaking hand as he scrutinized me. When he finished his inspection, his gaze settled on my face, and he pulled me close to him. "Thank the devils you're in one piece."

"Yes, but are all of you?" I asked, my throat tight. "You all look half-dead, and I just tried to eat you."

Darian's lips quirked up at the sides. "I can think of worse ways to die, lovely."

Asher grinned and brushed his blood-slick hair away from his face. "It's good to have you back, sweetheart."

When Darian pulled away, Locke was waiting for me. His hands slid down my arms as his dark eyes scoured my body, checking to make sure I was unharmed even though Darian had just inspected me. "What did Warrick do to you?" Locke asked, anger swirling in his eyes.

Letting out a long breath, I told them all that had happened. I explained about the change in my blood, the revelation that I was part fae, and the fact that Cara wasn't in Katakin.

When I was done, I found myself watching Kade carefully. I kept waiting for disgust to overcome his features now that he knew what I was. The wolf shifter hated the fae, so it made sense he would now hate me. But as my story unfolded, his eyes blazed with anger, yet it wasn't once directed at me. He stepped forward and threaded his hand with mine, squeezing my fingers. "We'll get that fucking vampire, and we'll find your sister. I promise you," he growled.

I stared at him, still waiting for disgust to cross his features, but he brushed his lips against mine before saying, "You are mine, Raine, and nothing could change that."

I blinked away the tears that glossed over my eyes.

Kade went on, "Besides, it seems the fae are no better or worse than the monsters in Katakin. It wasn't the fae that killed my family." He swallowed before continuing, "Zacal confessed to their murder right before I tore him apart."

My brows raised at this information, but I didn't comment. Though I'd pushed back my dragon instincts, I could still feel the creature inside me. I'd just turned my thoughts away from burning down the city, and asking more about Zacal would only reignite my anger.

Asher grinned stupidly at me, his expression so at odds with Kade's serious frown. "The Taratun council are going to be terrified when they see you," he said, and despite myself, a smile broke out on my face.

"You think so?" I asked.

"You're a dragon, darling," Darian said like the answer was obvious. "And a very fine one too."

"Pretty sure Ash shit himself when he first saw you, so those spineless council members stand no hope," Kade growled, and I wasn't sure whether to laugh at his comment or gape at the fact the wolf shifter had just made a joke.

"Says the wolf who nearly had his tail burned off when he fled from that house," Asher retorted.

I smiled at their banter, simply glad to have them around me. "So much for remaining human," I commented. "By the way, you might want to stay on my good side. For now, my dragon thinks you're her treasures, but she might go back to seeing you as pests."

Darian raised a brow at me. "And here I thought *I* was the one coveting treasure."

I thought then of what Darian had said a few nights ago: *You, my dear, are even more of a treasure than I thought you would be.* My smile grew. I knew perfectly well my dragon wasn't about to stop seeing them as treasure. Now that she'd scented them properly, she wanted to keep them, to hoard them from the world and guard them from harm. She didn't want to hurt them.

Locke had been silent since I'd told them what had happened with Warrick, and I turned to find him staring at the back of the cave, his face an unreadable mask.

"Locke?" I asked and placed a tentative hand on his shoulder.

When his gaze slid to mine, the fury that shone in his onyx eyes made me shiver. "I'll make him suffer, Raine. When I find him, I'll make him wish he'd never touched you."

I didn't need to ask to know he was talking about his father, Warrick. I also didn't need to ask to know he was going to make Warrick hurt for what he did to *me.*

I nodded my head. I wanted Warrick to suffer before he died. The ancient vampire didn't deserve mercy.

"We should head to Lyr's place," Kade said. "We need to get patched up and come up with a plan before we go after him again."

I turned to Kade. "Lyr's place?"

"It's a long story," Asher answered. "Let's just say we owe the tiger shifter *again*."

Kade seemed to hesitate before asking me, "Do you think you can shift again and fly us there? Otherwise, it'll take us half a night to make it back."

"Shift again?" I rolled my shoulders, releasing the tension. "All right, but no promises I won't eat you."

CHAPTER 23

~ Raine ~

Locke flew ahead of me, leading the way to a small clearing in the forest near Katakin City. When we landed on the soft grass, Kade, Asher, and Darian jumped from my back, and I shifted into my human form. Thankfully, the change was easier this time, but my emotions were still a mess. The protective instinct to snatch the males up and take them back to the cave where I could keep them safe made me jumpy and agitated, but I held myself together.

My monsters stood staring at my naked form, and I planted a hand on my hip, not at all fazed that they could see everything.

"We can't let her walk in like that," Locke commented. Taking off his cloak, he removed his shirt and handed it to me.

I pulled it over my head.

Kade didn't look concerned, seeming not to care that he was still completely naked. "She's a shifter now. Better get used to it."

"Great, we'll need to lug around clothin' for not one but two of you," Asher groaned.

Darian eyed me in the baggy shirt. "This will certainly be an adjustment."

"Then again, all we need to do is make Raine angry and she'll tear her clothes off," Asher added with a lopsided grin, clearly seeing the bright side.

"Yes, but I might also roast you," I pointed out, but the demon only shrugged like he thought the risk was worth it.

"Come on," Locke said, and we all turned to the small wooden cottage that stood in the middle of the clearing. The long planks of wood were thick with mold, and the angled roof looked as if it was close to caving in. I eyed the building skeptically. "Are you sure this is the place?"

"It's not how it appears," Darian answered cryptically, gliding toward the door.

"It's not a rickety old cottage in the woods?" I asked.

"Not like any you've seen," Asher replied with a grin, and the way he said it had me narrowing my eyes as I strode after him.

We entered through the wooden doorway and stepped into a humble space with a broken bed against one side, dead vines, and plant life covering the back wall, and a single chalk drawing framed and pinned to the wall opposite the bed. The picture was of a field of pink foxgloves, and while it wasn't the most skilled drawing, it was better than anything I could create.

"You were right, this *isn't* like any cottage I've seen," I mused.

"Perhaps they haven't made it back yet?" Darian suggested to the others as we peered around. The moment he said it, a ghostly figure materialized from the middle of the bed and came to stand before us. *What the hell?* I crouched, ready for a fight, but then I recognized the handsome face with a square jaw and pale-gray complexion. "Nic?" I asked, wrinkling my brow as I recalled the name. "You're one of Lyr's mates."

"And a wraith," Kade added.

Nic glared at us warily, his expression just as hostile as the last time I'd seen him. "Were you followed?"

"No," Locke replied bluntly. "Let us in."

Nic glowered at us for a moment longer, and his cold gaze lingered on me. The look wasn't anything close to sexual, but it still felt wrong to be scrutinized by a strange male while I was standing there in only a shirt. Locke stepped in front of me, shielding me from view.

"Don't look at her," he snarled possessively.

Nic leveled Locke's glare and turned, gesturing with his head toward the bed. "We've been waiting."

My gaze slid from the bed to Nic, then to my monsters. *Waiting?* "Uh, am I missing something?" I asked, but Nic pressed a button that was hidden by the dead vegetation on the back wall, and the bed moved to the side as a large hidden passage opened up in the floor.

Huh. Why didn't I suspect a hidden tunnel?

The wraith started down a flight of stone steps that led into darkness, and the rest of us followed closely behind. Asher grabbed hold of my arm like he was afraid I'd slip, but he needn't have worried. With my shifter abilities, the darkness was more of a pale green, and I could make out everything. *I knew becoming a monster would come with perks.* And even if I couldn't see, two carved railings lined the stairs.

When we reached the landing at the bottom, the space opened up into a wide area that was illuminated with blue fire torches along the walls and a huge chandelier hanging from the ceiling, and my breath caught in my throat. If I hadn't known we were deep underground, I would have thought we'd stepped into a mansion. Gleaming black tiles covered the floor, and massive pillars lined both sides of the cavernous space. The stone pillars were wrapped with thick vines that climbed all the way to the top, and the lush greenery spread across the ceiling that was dotted with glowing crystals. Large red roses sprouted around the green, the color matching the patterned red carpet that led between the pillars, and there were various places to sit and lounge. A series of doors lined the walls, and I wondered where each of them led.

Whoa. I recalled Kade and the others telling me that Lyr and her mates had blackmailed the council into letting them create a lower house of their own. *If this is a lower house, what are the higher houses like?*

"Do you like the flowers?" Lyr asked, appearing beside me as if she'd emerged from thin air. I jerked back in surprise, and her eyes sparkled with amusement as she flicked her white braid over her shoulder. "Dean likes to spice up the place every now and then. This time, it's roses."

Realizing she wasn't a threat or a random outlier trying to kill me, I relaxed. "Dean?"

As if he'd heard his name, a male with green skin and emerald eyes stepped out from a side room, and he smiled at us as he stopped next to Lyr. It was the same male I'd seen when I'd first met the tiger shifter and she'd given me the leather outfits to wear.

"Good to see you made it," Dean commented, and there was a kindness about him that made me believe his words were sincere.

"Come," Lyr said as she linked arms with me and led us all further into the space. "You look like you could all use a drink. I know I could."

Locke glared at Lyr's arm in mine. "We need more than a drink. Raine and Kade need some clothes, Kade needs to get patched up, and we need information."

Lyr waved a hand and kept tugging me along. "Then what are you waiting for?"

Locke looked as though he wanted to strangle Lyr, but he didn't say anything as the tiger shifter led us across the carpet to three ornate leather lounges surrounding a low oakwood table.

A male was sprawled on one of the couches, his long, feathery red wings splayed at his sides and a thick white bandage wrapped around his right bicep. He stood up at our arrival.

"Soren," Kade said in greeting, and the male dipped his head.

"Well, I feel better knowing you look even worse than I do," the male named Soren commented with a pained smile, and Kade grunted in response.

Lyr released my arm and moved to sit beside Soren, and Nic returned from one of the side rooms and passed me a bundle of clothing and a vial of glowing blue paste. I hadn't even noticed the wraith leave.

I changed quickly and passed Locke back his shirt while Darian helped Kade lather his chest and scratches with blue paste. When Kade was dressed, he settled next to the rest of us on the lounges. Dean handed us each a goblet of wine, but I placed mine on the small table before me, not in the mood for a drink.

When I peered across from me, Lyr was staring at me intently. Her hand flicked out from where it had been resting against her side near her blades, and I reacted without thinking. A stream of fire shot from my mouth, incinerating the red feather she'd tossed into the air. I'd thought it was a blade aimed at Kade, and it was clear now that that was her intention. The feather turned to ash, and I promptly clamped my lips shut.

Soren whistled. "Remind me not to get on your bad side."

Kade place a hand on my thigh as if to reassure me, and Asher outright grinned.

Lyr looked pleased as her intense stare remained on me, and I wasn't sure whether that was a good thing.

"So it's you," Nic said, his voice like gravel as he folded his arms in front of his chest and stood with his feet apart.

Darian took a sip from his goblet. "What is?"

"When we saw the dragon launch into the sky, we weren't sure if it was your Raine here or another of Locke's outliers, one that we hadn't seen before." Lyr leaned back and crossed her legs. "There will be other monsters in the city who saw you, and it won't take long before they figure out you weren't an outlier."

I remembered what Lyr had said when she'd helped me prepare for the Week of Orash. That by remaining human I could be a symbol of new hope for many of the monsters who wished to be human again. I couldn't help but wonder if I'd let her and those monsters down by changing. "Are you...disappointed that I turned?" I asked, my fingers fidgeting with my goblet.

Lyr shook her head and laughed. "The moment you used magic to save everyone in that ballroom during the Week of Orash, it was obvious you weren't entirely human, but I'll admit, I never expected you to become a dragon. In any case, you still lasted longer than any other human before turning into a monster, and right now, our biggest threat is Warrick and his outliers. You've fought against him twice now, and a dragon shifter might be just what we need."

Asher folded his arms above his head. "Yeah, I'm not so sure the vampire is our *biggest* threat."

Lyr stared quizzically at the demon, but Darian was the one to say, "Things went rather poorly in the fae kingdom of Zalei. War is on our horizon."

Nic, Dean, Soren, and Lyr all stiffened. "What do you mean, war?" Lyr asked.

"The fae think we assassinated their prince, and now they're coming here to eliminate us once and for all," Kade answered.

The tiger shifter tapped her long black nails on her leg, and she shared a look with Nic, Dean, and Soren before peering back at us. "Why *did* you go to the fae realm?"

she asked carefully. "There are some who are saying you've sided with the fae. That you rescued a fae prisoner."

My monsters tensed, but Darian answered, "We went to find a way to break the curse. And...we were hoping to defuse the risk of war between the monsters and the fae by returning Prince Azaren, who was tortured by Warrick. Unfortunately, things didn't play out as we'd hoped."

Lyr nodded slowly, and something like hope glinted in her eyes. "And did you find it? A way to break the curse?"

"No," Locke answered sharply before I could speak. "But we believe the fae still have the information we seek."

Disappointment flashed on Lyr's face, but she smoothed her expression. "This all started because of King Adrien's actions all those years ago," she said, hatred in her eyes as she spoke of the late king. "I've always believed we needed to find a way to mend the relationship between our kind, but if the fae have declared war, all we can do is defend ourselves."

Soren leaned forward, resting his elbows on his knees. "What if we gave them Warrick as a peace offering? We could say Warrick was the one who ordered you to try and assassinate Prince Azaren. You said Warrick was the one to torture the prince while he was here, so maybe that would appease his anger?"

Darian shook his head. "I doubt it. King Chalir's soldiers found us with the prince, and he's probably still seething that we escaped execution. The only other offering they'd possibly accept is King Adrien seeing as he murdered their late King Jazrec and betrayed Queen Izla. King Adrien was the one who started this whole mess, so he might have just been enough, but we all know he was slain all those years ago in the weeks after the curse was created. I heard the stories, as did everyone else. He was killed by some of his most trusted soldiers."

Lyr, Soren, Nic, and Dean all shared another look, and Lyr let out a long breath. "Well, not exactly."

"What do you mean?" Kade growled.

It was Dean who spoke up then, his green eyes focused on my males. "The king was never slain; he was entombed."

"Entombed?" Locke asked coldly.

Lyr clapped her hands together. "All you need to know is that King Adrien is somewhere safe and guarded, unable to do any harm. If we offer both King Adrien and Warrick up to King Chalir and the fae, do you think they'd be willing to form a truce? Especially if you all apologize profusely for whatever the hell happened back there."

Darian rubbed his chin thoughtfully. "We don't know if Prince Azaren survived the assassination attempt, but perhaps..."

"Capturin' Warrick is gonna be a little hard to do with Warrick's outliers guardin' the city. If the fae attack now, they'll be met with resistance, and once that blood is spilled on both sides, there might not be any way to come back from it. No matter the gifts we wield," Asher pointed out.

"Then we should join forces and move as quickly as possible," Lyr said with a smile. There was something about that smile and the way she focused her attention on me that made me pause.

"Wait, you don't just mean join forces, do you? You want us to join your house?" I asked in surprise.

She grinned. "If you mean staying here for a while, then yes. Warrick knows where you usually stay, and this place is about as safe as you can get while Warrick's outliers roam the city. But it's not really what I meant. Like I said, those who wish to become human again have rallied together. We've formed our own big...house of sorts, if you want to use the terms the council came up with all those years ago. Join us so we have a chance at surviving the war and Warrick's outliers. We're weak while we're divided, and Raine, your dragon is the most powerful monster we've seen in Katakin. Not to mention your magic would be a great asset. With you all on our side, we might stand a chance at defeating Warrick and his outliers before the fae make it here."

At first, none of us spoke. A part of me felt like it wasn't my fight. Now that I knew my sister wasn't in Katakin, I wanted to keep searching. But...this wasn't about my sister anymore. I thought of the four males around me, and my heart swelled as that intense desire to hoard them away and guard them from harm rushed through me. *My* males. My mates. The need to mark them as mine had my teeth elongating and sharpening, but I cleared my throat, pushing back the change. Cara wasn't in this world, but my monsters were, and the secrets of the curse were branded in my mind. And it wasn't just about the monsters. I thought of Prince Azaren and the fae. The fae hadn't been kind to us when they'd found out what we were, but they didn't deserve to be slaughtered by Warrick and his outliers.

You must be part fae, and your mixed blood made you immune to the curse. But as the blood drained from you... Warrick's words sounded in my head. Fae. I was part fae, and now part monster. Warrick mustn't have shared the news yet, as it was clear Lyr had no knowledge of it, and I could barely admit it to myself, but if it was true then it meant the fae were my kind too.

Lifting my chin, I peered over at Locke and the others. None of them looked too happy with the situation, but we couldn't hide from this. I went to voice my agreement when Nic cocked his head. "Intruders," he growled before he disappeared from sight.

Lyr and her mates jumped to their feet, and the rest of us did the same.

"I thought you said this place was secure," Locke said with a dark expression.

"It is," Lyr responded, her voice hard.

Nic appeared in the same spot where he'd been standing, and Lyr whipped her head toward him.

"Alpha Losak is here with a small portion of his shifters. Warrick learned of our alliance, and his outliers attacked Losak's house. There aren't many of them left." Nic delivered the news, his voice a gravelly whisper.

"Check if they were followed, and if not, then let them in," Lyr told Nic. "If Warrick has discovered the names of those allied to us, someone must have spoken. None of the others are safe."

Dean's face turned ashen. "Then we'd best prepare for more company."

Locke's eyes glossed over, becoming gray and sightless, and his body became deathly still. When his eyes cleared again a moment later, his jaw tightened.

"What is it?" Kade growled.

"That was Garan," Locke explained, and I knew he meant the gargoyle who could send mental messages to him. Locke's face was hard, and claws peeked from his fingers. "Outliers are attacking the watchtowers and killing the gargoyles."

BONUS SCENE

~ Cara ~

Ten years ago...

"Cara!" Raine's desperate cry sounded from across the clearing, but by the time I turned my head, I was already in the mouth of Procus—the cave on my island where the monsters always took the selected.

"Raine!" I tried to shout back, but the monster behind me shoved me forward, and my words came out as nothing more than an anguished cry. I stumbled in the darkness, my head banging into the woman in front of me. She cried out and jerked away, almost elbowing me in the eye, and I squeaked out an apology and righted myself.

"Quiet," one of the other monsters barked, and I pressed my trembling lips together.

Sixteen. I'm only sixteen. I wasn't even of selection age! I had to get back to Raine and my father. I should have had two more years before I would be forced to enter the lineup. Two more years of braiding my sister's hair and keeping her out of trouble. Two more years of hoping I'd turn out to be one of the lucky ones who weren't selected.

But as soon as the monster had spotted me in the forest, I'd known it was already over. No one escaped the monsters after they were selected, and no one ever returned to the island. Tears pricked at my eyes, and I drew in a long breath. I should have been angry at Raine. If she hadn't tried to spy on the monsters, I wouldn't have been in this mess, and we'd still be together. But Raine always had been too curious and outspoken for the lives we lived on that island. *An explorer*, she'd once said to me when I asked what job in the village she hoped to get when she grew up. I'd only laughed. No, I couldn't be angry at her, and I hoped she wouldn't blame herself for what happened to me.

Our group came to a halt, and I heard one of the women at the front of the line whisper that we'd reached a dead end. But the sound of stone scraping stone sounded in my ears, and one of the cloaked figures pushed aside a giant rock, blue light spilling out onto the walls.

The monsters led us deeper into the cave, and I stopped walking when a large circle of flames came into view.

"Keep moving, human," the monster behind me snarled, his huge body at my back, and I forced myself to continue forward. The first of the selected women entered the circle, and I watched in horror as they instantly disappeared from sight. I knew if I went into that ring, there was no returning to the island. To my family. To my life.

No. My throat tightened, and my heart pounded wildly as I neared the flames. The woman before me screamed, but the sound ended when one of the monsters tossed her into the ring and she vanished. I shook my head, still not believing this was my fate. *No. It's not my turn yet.*

I spun from the ring and darted to the left, hoping my thin frame would allow me to slip past the monster behind me, but my head smacked into a thick arm, and a warm hand gripped my neck tightly, forcing me to step back toward the circle. "Let go of me!" I shrieked, but the monster only cackled.

"I love it when they run," he said, leaning down to slide a long, hot tongue up the side of my face. The monster's foul breath made me gag, but he only smiled when I glared at him and tried to break free from his hold. "This one's going to fit right in," the monster jeered to the others, and he pushed me into the ring and let go.

. . . . ● . ● . ● . . . ●

The world fell away, and blue light engulfed me, the glaring color stinging my eyes like I was staring at a blue sun. I shut my eyes and gripped my arms, unable to tell what was up and what was down. And then I was falling. My eyes snapped open as my back impacted with hard earth and grass, and I glimpsed a night sky littered with stars before rolling over and throwing up.

When I'd emptied the contents of my stomach, I sat back on my knees and rubbed furiously at my face. All I could think about was the monster's wet tongue as it slid up my cheek and his words: *This one's going to fit right in*. What did he mean? Fit in where?

At the thought of the monsters, I waited for them to yank me to my feet. Waited for them to laugh, curse, and snarl at me to pull it together, but nothing happened as I sat there, and it remained silent around me save for the faint buzzing of insects.

Wiping my mouth with the back of my hand, I finally dared to look behind me. A ring of blue fire, just like the one I'd been pushed into, burned not far from where I was, but...there was no one else there. None of the selected from my island and *none* of the monsters. *Did I arrive before everyone else?* If that were the case, I could run and try to escape the monsters, but where would I go? I wasn't foolish enough to think I'd emerged somewhere back on my island. The forest lacked the smell of coconuts and ripened fruit, and even in the darkness, I could tell these weren't the trees I was used to.

No, the air smelled like burned honey and moss, and the tree trunks were a ghostly white in the moonlight. I jumped to my feet, my heart racing as I eyed the darkness between the trees and shrubs.

An uncomfortable feeling like I was being watched crept over me, and I took a small step backward. *It's only a forest. The plants can't hurt you*, I consoled myself, trying to calm my nerves. Rustling came from my right, and I jerked in that direction, my eyes wide. *Then again, if this is where the monsters live, maybe they can?*

The creature ran from the darkness, grunting and growling as its huge paws smacked on the dirt. It looked to be a cross between a bear and a stag, with thick green fur and glowing green eyes. Dropping its head toward the ground, it charged me, its massive, branch-like antlers aiming for my chest, and a horrified cry squeezed from my throat. Spinning around, I fled for the circle of fire. *If going through this thing brought me to this place, maybe it can send me back?*

One step. Two. I pitched forward, slipping on the grass and tumbling to the ground. Pain jarred up my chin as I landed flat, and I spat the dirt from my mouth. *The circle isn't far; you just need to get up!* As I scrambled to my feet, three cloaked figures emerged from the ring of fire, stepping into the forest.

"Well, that was a bore fest," a young male said with an exaggerated yawn, and I froze, not sure whether to keep fleeing toward the circle or to try to pivot in another direction.

"Watch out!" another of the cloaked figures shouted when he lifted his head and saw me. He ran in my direction, and his arms wrapped around my torso as he pulled me to the ground. We landed in a crumpled heap, the creature's antlers barely missing the figure's back as it charged past us.

"Stay there," the cloaked figure ordered me, and I was left gaping as he jumped to his feet.

As the creature rounded back, the three cloaked figures circled the animal, all of them with their arms held high. The creature reared up and pounded its front paws on the ground before letting out an agitated growl.

"Now this is more like it," commented the shortest figure.

The one who'd saved me jerked his head to the tallest cloaked figure. "Nathaniel, do you wanna help us out here?"

The cloaked figure, Nathaniel, only responded by starting to talk to the animal in whispering tones. Glowing orange light illuminated his fingertips as his soothing voice filtered between the trees, and I watched in disbelief as the bearlike creature slowly calmed, its head lifting and the angry glow of its eyes dulling.

Yellow flowers sprouted along the creature's green antlers, and Nathaniel stepped toward the animal, stroking his hands gently down its neck. The creature turned to him, rubbing its nose against Nathaniel's shoulder affectionately.

Nathaniel whispered one last thing into the animal's ear, and then the creature turned to the forest and ran into the dark, not sparing me another glance.

When the animal was gone, all three of the cloaked figures turned their attention to me, and I shuffled backward, keenly aware of the fact I probably should have run while they were busy.

"What's with her? You'd think she's never seen a Choram bear before," the shortest figure commented with a laugh.

I glared at them as I forced myself to my shaky feet. *Of course, they know I haven't seen one before. They're monsters... aren't they?* They clearly weren't the same monsters who were present at the selection, but who else could they be?

The moment I was standing, all three of them grew silent as they looked me over, taking in my tattered nightgown and cheeks streaked with tears. I waited for one of them to comment about me not being with the group of newly selected humans, but I was surprised when Nathaniel said, "What's she doing out here? We're too far from the city for her to be a runaway, and I haven't seen her in the camp." His deep voice was so smooth and calming that the muscles in my shoulders relaxed involuntarily, even though his words had questions racing through my mind.

What city is he talking about? And why is it that they don't know who I am?

The figure who had saved me pulled back the hood of his cloak, and I stood there gawking because he wasn't a monster like I'd expected. The man appeared to be only a couple of years older than me with shoulder-length black hair, piercing pale-blue eyes, and a warm smile that made my heart race.

A slight breeze picked up, the wind teasing my hair, and his smile fell as he frowned at me. It was only then that I noticed his ears. Unlike mine, his ended in pointed tips that peeked through his silky black locks. My heart pounded hard again as confusion made my mind whirl. I'd gone from thinking he was a monster, to hoping he was a man, to seeing he was...something else?

"What's wrong with her ears?" the shortest male commented, but no one answered.

The male with the black hair looked from me to the circle of blue fire and then swiftly back to me again.

"Wait, Xander, you can't think—?" Nathaniel began, but the dark-haired male, presumably Xander, was striding toward me. My body locked up, my brain not sure whether to tell me to flee or stay where I was, and he stopped in front of me. Holding out his hand, he smiled, showing a row of pearly white teeth, and there was something about that smile that drew me in. If he was a different kind of monster, at least he didn't have claws or fangs. "Welcome to Zalei," he said, his voice warm and inviting. "Realm of the fae."

I blinked dumbly back at him before managing, "Uh, thanks for saving my life. Realm of the what?"

RAINE'S STORY CONTINUES IN BOOK 4:
THE WARS OF MONSTERS
(WITH BONUS CHAPTERS FROM CARA'S POV)

WANT MORE?

Thank you so much for reading my story! I had such a fun time writing this book, and I really hope you enjoyed it! If you did, please consider leaving a review on Amazon or Goodreads. Reviews help readers discover my books, and I'm so grateful for each one!

Want more? Sign up for my newsletter via my website *www.miahartson.com* and you'll receive an exclusive, bonus scene written from Darian's POV (you can always unsubscribe after downloading the bonus scene).

Not a fan of email? You can also find me via my website *www.miahartson.com, Facebook page , Facebook group, Goodreads page or Bookbub.* I look forward to becoming friends!

HER CURSED PROTECTORS READING ORDER

Shadow Shifter (prequel)
The Blood of Monsters
The Cries of Monsters
The Curse of Monsters
The Wars of Monsters

ABOUT THE AUTHOR

Mia Hartson is an Australian fantasy and paranormal romance author who enjoys writing stories about badass heroines who have multiple partners. (Because the only thing better than one mate is four, right?)

Mia particularly enjoys writing stories with a heavy dose of fantasy, adventure, and spice that keeps you up at night. When she's not writing, Mia's going on adventures with her husband and two girls, singing her heart out, or devouring another book.

For more information about Mia Hartson, her books, and upcoming releases, visit her website www.miahartson.com, Facebook page, Goodreads page or Bookbub.